OPERATION TITAN

The line of Mosquitoes, flying nose to tail now, remained at zero-height. As they swung round the last river bend, their target appeared ahead. Shielded on either side by its screens of balloons and torpedo nets, straddling the broad river on its three huge piers, the bridge looked massive even at a range of four miles, and the men felt their hearts sink at the sight of it. Its flak defences added to the impression of impregnability, with tracer squirting up from both river banks and the sky pockmarked with bursting shells . . .

Moore's calm instruction, "Climb to 2,000 feet, now!" came as a relief, and as the Mosquitoes climbed heavenwards the men were able to turn their eyes, if only momentarily, from the awesome specter of death beneath them . . .

Bantam Books by Frederick E. Smith
Ask your bookseller for the books you have missed

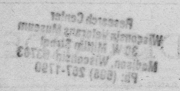

633
SQUADRON
OPERATION TITAN
BY FREDERICK E. SMITH

BANTAM BOOKS
TORONTO · NEW YORK · LONDON · SYDNEY

633 SQUADRON: OPERATION TITAN
A Bantam Book / March 1982

ISBN   0-553-20503-X

Published simultaneously in the United States and Canada

PRINTED IN THE UNITED STATES OF AMERICA

0 9 8 7 6 5 4 3 2 1

To
John and Kay

Acknowledgments

The author wishes to give credit to the following sources:

Bekker, *The Luftwaffe War Diaries* (Macdonald);
Constable and Tolivier, *Horrido!* (MacMillan);
Adolf Galland, *The First and the Last* (Methuen and Co.);
Richards and Saunders, *Royal Air Force 1939–1945* (H.M.S.O.);
Sir C. Webster and N. Frankland, *The Strategic Air Offensive
  Against Germany 1939–1945* (H.M.S.O.).

The Mosquitoes were peeling away and swooping down like kites in a high wind. Their target was a train of war supplies threading its way through a terrain of wooded hills. As the leading aircraft flattened out, two rockets speared from its wings and exploded in bright flashes alongside the track.

On the footplate of the train the fireman was urging on his driver. "Faster, man! Faster!" The driver, his unshaven face drenched in sweat, pushed his regulator to the limit of its quadrant. The locomotive's great pistons pounded faster and its iron lungs gasped out steam like a living creature fighting for survival.

A flak wagon at the rear of the train was already in action. Two LMGs were firing at the second Mosquito which was flattening from its dive and a 37mm pom-pom put its first burst of shells dead ahead of it. Startling its pilot at the very moment he released his two rockets, the missiles swerved off course and burst harmlessly among a clump of trees. As the cursing pilot swung away, the LMG gunners followed him and drilled a neat row of holes in the root of his starboard wing.

A second flak wagon, positioned in the middle of the train, began firing at the rest of the Mosquitoes circling above. As black puffs burst among them, an American voice let out a startled yell. "Goddam it, they've nearly shot my tail off."

An English voice, laconic and relaxed, answered the pilot. "Have you still got control, Millburn?"

There was humour in the reply. "I'll let you know before I crash, skipper. Yeah, I'm O.K."

"Stay out of range until we've finished. Number 3, down you go."

A third Mosquito peeled off and dived on the speeding train. All the gunners in the two flak wagons concentrated on it and a barrage of shells appeared in its path.

Recognizing the problem, the Squadron Commander changed his tactics. "Numbers 4 and 5 attack from opposite sides. Down you go!"

Obeying instantly, two Mosquitoes dived obliquely on both sides of the train, Number 5 slightly ahead to avoid collision. With the flak gunners forced to divide their fire-power, the crews were less harassed and were able to take more careful aim. But with steep hills protecting its flanks, the target was not easy and only one wagon was hit. The second pilot's yell of triumph turned into alarm as a shell struck his fuselage. Pulling out of his dive he tried to make height but a fuel tank suddenly exploded and the Mosquito cartwheeled into the hillside and burst into a hundred blazing fragments.

Someone muttered 'poor old Vic' over the R/T. That was all and yet the mood of 633 Squadron had perceptibly changed. Used to missions of high importance and high risk, they had tended to look upon trains as soft targets, particularly these days since the Luftwaffe appeared in strength only when a vital installation was threatened.

But it was never the German way to provide soft targets for anybody and the recent inclusion of flak wagons among their freight cars was a move to hit back. The pathetic pieces of burning wreckage below gave evidence it was an effective one.

Its very effectiveness, however, gave a sense of purpose to the Mosquito crews that had perhaps been lacking before. Vic Andrews and his navigator Charlie Warren had been popular colleagues, and in the illogical way men react when those they are attacking fight back, crews were now deter-mined to avenge them. Ignoring the intimidating flak, Num-bers 6 and 7 went after the speeding train like bull terriers after a felon.

They were just levelling out when the train crew, rounding a bend in the track, caught sight of the refuge for which they had been bursting the locomotive boilers. As the stoker yelled and pointed ahead, the driver slammed on his air brakes. With massive wheels screeching along the track and hurling out huge sparks, the entire assembly went sliding into a tunnel beneath a long hill ridge.

With their eyes fixed on the train, the Mosquito crews needed an urgent order from their Commander to alert them to their danger. Hauling back on their control columns, pilots saw the hills sweeping less than two hundred feet below them.

Inside the tunnel all was grinding metal and the thunder of steam as the train fought to stop before it broke out into the open again. Brilliant sparks lit up the black and grimy sides and the stench of steam and oil almost choked the occupants. Peering through the smoke, they saw the circle of light growing larger. Every man aboard let his breath out in relief as the locomotive halted less than twenty yards from the exit.

In the sky above there was less relief than frustration as the circling Mosquitoes waited in vain for the train to emerge. After a minute the Squadron Commander's calm voice broke the silence. "That's one that got away. Break it off and let's go home."

Reluctantly, and not a little vengefully, crews glanced back at the dark tunnel as they banked from their orbit and followed their leader northward.

The British crews were not returning to the island they had once known on that late April day in 1944. In many ways Britain now resembled a medieval walled city under siege. For over four years, protected only by its Royal Navy, its Air Force, and the strip of English Channel, the island had held out against the greatest army the world had ever seen while it had frantically mobilized its population and trained them in arms. Now its soldiers were waiting to sally forth in an attempt to break the enemy's stranglehold. Success would mean the liberation of Europe and a new dawn for mankind. Failure would mean the return of the Dark Ages.

By this time, however, Britain was not alone. In company with men from Europe who had escaped the yoke of Nazism and had trained to become soldiers of liberation, American soldiers were now pouring into Britain in ever

greater numbers. In January 1944 their number had been
750,000. By late April that number had swollen to 1,500,000
men. Side by side with the British and Canadians, the GIs
were to storm the western wall of Hitler's European fortress.

On a relatively small island, the problems of accommo-
dating such vast armies were enormous. Areas the size of cities
were needed for their billets, their training grounds, and for
the staggering amount of equipment that came with them. A
partial answer had been to allow the Americans to 'occupy'
the counties of Cornwall, Devon, and parts of Dorset. The
British and Canadian armies were based further along the
south coast in the counties of Hampshire and Sussex.

But the problem of space was only the tip of the iceberg.
To equip such great armies meant an even greater army of
workmen. All over Britain foundries blazed and poured out
rivers of steel. Aircraft came off production lines like automo-
biles. Ships of all shapes and sizes were made in shipyards,
along roads, and even prefabricated outside tiny workshops.
Thousands of factories and millions of workers produced everything from Bren gun carriers to bootlaces to make certain the
armies lacked nothing when the Day of Destiny arrived.

In addition ports worked day and night to unload the
queues of ships bringing in supplies for the American armies.
Roads became choked with military traffic, making civilian
movement almost impossible. Prohibited areas appeared everywhere, in forests, parks, farms, even in cities, as the enormous stockpile grew. The entire British populace was mobilized
and at times the very island itself seemed to be groaning
under the weight of its burden. There were men who feared
the country might never be the same again after such a
gigantic effort.

Yet all this sweat and sacrifice might be in vain if the
enemy were to discover which part of the French coast would
receive the Allied onslaught. To confuse him, the Allies had
begun launching heavy 'interdiction' air raids in early 1944 on
his transport and communication systems all over France
and Belgium. The purpose was twofold: to leave the enemy
uncertain where the invasion would take place and to hamper
his response when he was no longer in doubt. Even though
thousands of Allied fighters and ships patrolled the sky and
sea lanes to drive off his probing aircraft and U-boats, it was

manifestly impossible to conceal from him the massive build up of ships and troops on the centre and southwestern coast of Britain. So, highly subtle plans were already in motion to make him believe the concentration was a giant bluff and the real attack would come in the Pas de Calais area.

The invasion had originally been planned for May 1944 but a shortage of landing craft caused by the Italian campaign had compelled a month's delay. It was a delay that caused some consternation among the planners because the seventh of June was the absolute deadline. With a maximum of five weeks to go and acutely aware of the consequences of a wrong decision, men were still arguing about moon tables, tides, and whether a daylight or a night assault was preferable. An unpredictable factor was the weather, for all knew it could be decisive on the day.

But men could only plan against factors remotely under their control and the one that was giving Eisenhower and his staff the greatest concern was the problem of German reserves. Until the artificial harbours the Allies were to drag across the Channel were secured in position, the only armour they would be able to land on the beaches would be amphibious and thin-skinned. Would the Germans succeed in rushing up their heavy panzer divisions before the beachheads were widened and the Allies were able to match force with force? If they did, D-Day might turn into a disaster of unparalleled magnitude.

2

Adams made a note on the form, then glanced up. "Where was this, Ian?"

"About twenty miles from Saumur." The young Wing Commander held out his hand. "These are the coordinates."

Adams took the piece of paper. "And you think the train was carrying field artillery?"

"It looked that way. Everything was covered by tarpaulin, of course, but a couple of guns were blown off the wagon Machin hit. They ought to show on his cinéfilm."

The bespectacled Intelligence Officer nodded. He was seated at a large desk at the far end of a Nissen hut that was full of maps, posters, filing cabinets and scale models of German aircraft. Nicknamed 'The Confessional' by the aircrews, it served both as Adams' office and his debriefing centre. At the moment it was filled with young men in uniform sipping tea. Most were still wearing flying boots and a few were carrying their helmets and face masks. Like all intelligence officers, Frank Adams liked to catch the crews straight from a mission when their memories were still fresh.

Adams was in his mid-forties, a highly sensitive man who had never come to terms with his age or with the poor eyesight that had kept him out of aircrew. Blessed or cursed with a complex nature, he found war a monstrous obscenity while at the same time he envied these young fliers who brought hope to the enslaved people in Occupied Europe. Like a doctor too involved with his patients, Adams shared their joys and sorrows with an intensity that was physically ageing him. His shame at his safe job was never as acute as when he was discussing the death of young colleagues. His eyes were lowered as he asked the question that was almost routine at debriefings.

"Did you see Andrews hit, Ian?"

The Wing Commander nodded. "I think it was a 37mm shell in a fuel tank. He hit the hillside and blew up. There weren't any survivors."

Adams winced. "And you say the train stayed in the tunnel?"

"It did until we left. I was surprised we caught it in the open at all. That's why I think it must have been carrying an important consignment."

In full agreement with the young officer's reasoning, Adams nodded. "I think we can safely assume a field regiment is moving north. But I'd like to see your ciné and still films before I put in my report."

The officer he was interrogating was Ian Moore, the Squadron Commander. Medium in height and build, Moore was a fresh-complexioned man with wavy, fair hair. Like the rest of his crews, he was not wearing flying clothes. The April evening was mild and the Mosquito was a warm aircraft. Unlike his men, however, who mainly used their oldest uniforms for operations, Moore's uniform was beautifully tailored and pressed. His enemies—and they were few—would mutter that anyone with his wealthy background could afford the luxury, but they missed the point. Moore's uniform was an expression of his personality, the signature of a man who believed in keeping the wrappings of a package securely tied so that the contents did not spill out and disintegrate.

In many ways Ian Moore was a rarity among fighting men. Gifted with both intelligence and imagination, he was also aware of the positive handicaps both attributes could be in the mad butchery of war. Accordingly both were treated with caution and kept under tight rein. No one would blame himself more than Moore if any of his men lost their lives through a failure of detail on his part. But if that loss, however painful, was caused by circumstances outside his control, something that had happened often during his time of command, the iron control Moore kept over his emotions enabled him to withstand the blows better than most.

At the same time, no man is indestructable. Ever since Teddy Young's death a month ago for which, against all informed opinion, Moore blamed himself, there were some who believed they saw signs of strain in the young Squadron Commander.

The row of ribbons he wore beneath his RAF Wings included the DSO and Bar, the DFC and Bar, and the American Congressional Medal of Honor. In inclement weather he sometimes walked with a slight limp, the result of a serious leg wound received when giving cover to American troops during Operation Crucible the previous autumn. A puckered scar on his right cheek came from a flak shell that would have blown his face away had it burst a few inches closer.

The Squadron's two Flight Commanders were standing immediately behind Moore. One of them, Frank Harvey, was showing impatience at Adams' questions. Scowling, unable to contain himself any longer, he leaned forward. "If I were you, Ian, I'd give Greenwood a bollicking. If he'd let us carry a few 250-pounders we might have kicked that train up the arse even after it got into the tunnel."

Greenwood was the station's new armament officer, posted there after Lindsay's death in the German air attack on Sutton Craddock during Operation Cobra. A somewhat officious little man, he had dismissed with some impatience Harvey's pre-operational suggestion that light bombs should be carried.

The second Flight Commander, Tommy Millburn, gave a laugh of derision. "You kidding? You can't slide bombs along railroad tracks. Where've you been all these years?"

Harvey turned. He was a tall, raw-boned officer whose faded tunic was frayed at the cuffs and shiny from hundreds of hours in the air. A product of the depressed northern towns, with a face as craggy as his native Yorkshire fells, his scowl was said to give shingles to young recruits. It was in evidence now as he stared at Millburn.

"You ever heard of skip bombing, Millburn? Or were you still at school in those days?"

Millburn's eyes twinkled. At heart no one on the station had more respect for his fellow Flight Commander. Yet a puckish sense of humour would never let him miss an opportunity to provoke the prickly Yorkshireman.

An American, Millburn had been promoted to Flight

Commander after the death of Teddy Young. To the station Waafs he was God's gift to women with his good looks, unruly dark hair, and his readiness to play the field. To his fellow fliers, all veterans of many missions, he was a highly skillful and reliable colleague, and if in the past he had suffered from an excess of daring, this imbalance was now being rectified by his new responsibilities.

"Skip bombing against ships, maybe. But you can't skip 'em into railroad tunnels. They'd either bounce off the track or stick into the sleepers."

The knowledge he was right did nothing to improve Harvey's feelings over the loss of Andrews and Warren. "We still could have tried. Anything's better than letting the bastards make fools of us."

"What about that hill ridge over the tunnel?" Millburn asked. "If we'd gone arsing in any lower, we'd have pranged it for sure."

Conscious that the crews at the far end of the hut were now listening, Harvey lowered his voice. "Speak for your own lot, Millburn. I'll lay a quid or two my lads would have managed it." He turned back to Moore. "We ought to try something new, Ian, particularly as Jerry's now arming his trains. It's bloody frustrating to let him play hide and seek with us like this."

Adams' eyes were on the young Squadron Commander's face. Until only recently Moore's patience and tact were a byword on the station and knowing it took crews time to unwind after a mission, he would have treated the arguments between the Flight Commanders with patience and humour. Now, detecting irritation in his expression, Adams intervened hastily.

"It's true Jerry's using the tunnels very cleverly these days. But without dropping these new ten-ton bombs on them, it's difficult to see what else we can do."

Moore, facing the scowling Harvey and the grinning Millburn, clearly had no intention of joining the argument. "As we can't carry ten-tonners, there's not much point in you two niggling at one another, is there? Get your debriefing over and then make way for the men. If they're anything like me, they're ready for their dinner."

3

The small navigator with the Welsh accent pushed open the door of the billet and flung his helmet and face mask on his bed. "What the hell were you and Harvey arguing about in there? You forgotten the rest of us like to eat too?"

Millburn, newly changed into a fresh uniform, was checking his appearance in a cracked mirror that rested on the window ledge. He gave his disgruntled navigator a grin. "He thinks we ought to have flown right in after that train and stuck a bomb up its arse. I had to remind him it's kinda hairy inside tunnels."

The Welshman eyed him in disgust. "Is that what you were arguing about? Clobbering a train inside a hill?"

"That's right. Harvey thinks we ought to try skip bombing." For a moment Millburn's grin faded. "Mind you, seeing Andrews and Warren were in his flight, I guess he's got some cause to feel peeved."

The navigator was in no mood to show sympathy. "I'll bet the eggs'll be like doughnuts when they serve 'em. If you two want to talk crap to one another, why don't you do it in your own time?"

Millburn's grin returned. "You're in a hell of a mood for a guy who's soon going on a fortnight's leave, aren't you? Has Gwen called it off?"

He received a glare. "No, she hasn't. She's as keen as ever."

Millburn shook his head in wonder. "Two weeks with a little binder like you! Boyo, that dame's either a masochist or a heroine. Maybe that's what she is, a heroine. She's doing it for the war effort."

The reminder he was going on leave after one more

operation restored Gabby's temper. He gave the American a malicious grin. "Fourteen days, mush. A little cottage, a big bed, and no bloody orders from anybody. Isn't that something?"

"You want to watch that bed, buster. With your appetite you're likely to be going up with the window blinds before you get back."

The Welshman smirked lecherously. "Some men have what it takes, Millburn. Don't forget that."

"You think that's why they call you the Swansea Stallion? Kid, you've got it all wrong. They call you that because you're the easiest guy in the world to take for a ride. Any Waaf on the station knows that."

The navigator grinned and blew a raspberry. He was Johnnie Gabriel, known to all as Gabby or The Gremlin because of his small wiry frame and sharp features. He had been Millburn's navigator since the days the American had first flown with a Mitchell squadron. Although the two men could hardly have been more different in looks and in temperament, they were inseparable friends and notorious for their madcap pranks and tireless pursuit of women. In the past they had gone on leave together but this time it had not proved possible because of Millburn's recent promotion. Although either man would have died rather than admit it, both were feeling regret and, in the way of servicemen, were hiding their disappointment with banter and mockery.

Grinning, Millburn was checking his appearance in the mirror. Gabby, who was on duty that night, eyed him curiously. "What's all the shine for?"

Millburn made a final adjustment to his tie, then straightened. "I've got a date with that dame we met in Scarborough last week. The one who passed you over. I'm taking her out to dinner. Didn't I tell you?"

It was news that brought back all the Welshman's indignation. "So that's why you weren't in a hurry to eat. That's typical, Millburn. Bloody typical."

The grinning American slapped the navigator across the back with his cap as he walked past. "You want my advice, kiddo? Get all the sleep you can this week. Otherwise that wild Welsh woman's going to eat you up and spit out the pips."

*　　*　　*

A dog began barking excitedly as Harvey approached his
billet. As he opened the door a large black mongrel leapt up
at him and tried to lick his face. For a moment he responded,
cuffing its head. Then he pushed it impatiently aside. "Cut it
out, you silly old bugger."

The dog immediately ceased its gyrations. Sam, a one-
man dog if ever there was one, knew his master's moods
better than anyone on the station. Reducing his joy at his
master's return to a throaty whinny, he followed Harvey to
his bed on which the big Yorkshireman sank with a grunt.

Lighting a cigarette, Harvey stared at the floor. Casualties in his flight always upset him and he exhaled smoke as he
thought about the two letters he would have to write. The
Yorkshireman never left the harrowing task to the adjutant or
Moore, even though he had been known to spend an entire
evening on one letter. Words did not come easily to Harvey,
nor did the display of emotion, and yet his closest friends
would have been astonished had they known how many replies
he had received from bereaved parents and wives thanking
him for the warmth of his sympathy. Afraid these replies
might fall into the hands of his colleagues, Harvey always
made a point of burning them.

To the ground staff and the men in his flight, he was a
hard man. A mechanic had only to risk aircraft with shoddy
maintenance or a flier had only to disobey orders, and the
Yorkshireman was down on him like a ton of bricks. One-
hundred-percent thorough himself, Harvey did not reward
efficiency in others, he expected it. The cause reached back
to his childhood and his father, Arthur Harvey, a small grey
man partially crippled from World War I. Almost the first
words the infant Harvey had heard his father speak were:
"Never take on a job, lad, unless you do it properly."

For Harvey and millions like him it had been advice as
basic as the need to read and write. At that time in the north
of England, with queues of men waiting outside every factory
door, thoroughness was the only key to survival. But in truth
there was more to it than that. A man's work expressed his
character and there was shame in shoddy workmanship. The
prewar Northcountryman was poor in pocket but rich in
pride.

His background explained Harvey's attitude to the war.

During the struggle that had finally broken and killed his mother, Harvey had found all the war he needed in helping his family to survive, and if one could have drilled through his hard shell one would have found a deep and abiding hatred for those who added war to the list of life's miseries. Before that depth was reached, however, the drill would have uncovered Harvey's aversion to a society that had drained away the spirit and lifeblood of his parents. Today Arthur Harvey, now fifty-five, was working as a vanman for two pounds ten shillings a week. Harvey's mother had lain in an unmarked grave until Harvey had saved enough out of his service pay to buy her a headstone.

As always when thinking about his mother, Harvey found the memories too painful and forced his mind back to the present. Uncomplicated in his feelings for the enemy, Harvey always tried to avoid leading his men into tit for tat situations, believing that not even three enemy dead were worth one of his own. To lose a crew as he had that morning, without any real damage to the enemy, went against all his instincts and explained his present mood.

To make matters worse he had known young Andrews' wife. The couple had been married in Highgate only six weeks ago and Harvey had attended the wedding. Their obvious happiness had moved the Yorkshireman and he thanked God the girl was now back with her parents in Leicester. Had she remained in Highgate he would have felt obliged to break the news to her personally.

Inevitably his thoughts moved to Anna Reinhardt, the courageous German girl he had fallen in love with the previous year. Ten months had now passed since the SOE had sent her back into Occupied Europe: ten months that at times had seemed like ten years to Harvey. He wondered when the invasion of Europe would begin. Until a few months ago, when the first invasion rumours had started to circulate, it had seemed the war would go on forever. Now, if the invasion were a success, and that was by no means certain, the end would surely be in sight.

Yet everyone knew the enemy would fight even more fiercely the closer the Allies came to his Fatherland. And as the perimeters shrank, the density of the German armies and

aircraft would increase. The last months of the war could well
be more savage than any that had gone before.

Like many veterans, Harvey found that thought depressing. In the early days of the war, when the RAF had been
outnumbered on every front, he had decided he would not
live to see its end. It had not been a morbid decision. Along
with many realists, he had felt it wiser to accept the inevitable and then put it out of his mind. That way a man could
accept each new day as a gift and not as a threat.

But since he had met Anna Reinhardt, Harvey had felt a
change in him. He had fought against it, because in Harvey's
world a man seldom got what he desired and to hope was to
invite disaster. To some extent he had succeeded. With Anna
facing the monstrous Gestapo threat every day and with himself
a member of a squadron specializing in hazardous missions, the
scales were heavily loaded against their future together.

Recently, however, a vision had been returning to Harvey: a photograph in *Picture Post* a few months before the
outbreak of war, two small crosses intertwined in a First
World War cemetery, isolated from the great sea of graves
that seemed to stretch to the horizon, the graves of a British
and a German airman. Their date of death—eleven minutes
after eleven A.M. on November 11, 1918. Without the benefit of radio, the two men had fought to the death and crashed
together, unaware that on the shell-torn battlefield which
swallowed their young bodies, enemies had risen from their
trenches eleven minutes earlier to shake hands and hug one
another.

At the time Harvey had found it moving. Today the
picture was beginning to haunt him. And he knew it would
grow worse when the invasion came. Every passing day would
bring hope that he and Anna might survive and so every day
would bring its quota of fear.

Not that he would be alone. Millions of men on both
sides, numbed by the giant cataclysm around them, would
begin to reassess their chances of a future with their loved
ones. Brave men would begin to flinch at the mere scream of
a shell; volunteers would dry up.

Harvey was afraid it would happen to him. Recently he
had found himself hesitating before making an attack. Only

momentarily and certainly not long enough for his navigator
to notice, but Harvey had noticed it and wondered.

As always when the Yorkshireman turned introspective,
his dislike of excuses took over. Like most of the original
squadron, he had flown nearly three times as many operations as regulations demanded. Statistically he should have
been killed three times already. So what the hell was he
doing blaming Anna? His bloody nerves were starting to
crack, it was as simple as that.

If only he could see her again. He had no photographs of
her, and although sometimes her image was lifelike in his
mind, at other times he was unable to recall her face and
then he would feel a kind of panic.

At his feet Sam gave a solicitous whinny and laid a paw
on his foot. Staring down, Harvey cursed. If the lads had the
same insight as the dog, there'd be some ribald comments.
Cursing again, Harvey leaned across to his bedside cabinet
and drew out a bottle of whisky.

4

The evening wind, moaning over the pantiled roof of the
farmhouse, sounded subdued and apprehensive. Occasionally
it sent a warning draught into the attic below where three
men and a girl were waiting beside a portable radio. The girl,
dark-haired and attractive, was wearing a shapeless blouse
and a black skirt. The men wore French peasant dress of blue
serge and heavy boots.

The radio operator, weatherbeaten, wiry, and middle-
aged, had a cigarette dangling from his mouth and the phones
pressed to his ears. The other two men and the girl were
squatting on piles of straw behind him. One man was in his
late fifties, skinny, balding, and wearing a pair of rimless

spectacles. In spite of his peasant dress, his physical appearance and nervousness betrayed him as a man unaccustomed
to hardship and danger.

The same could not be said for his three colleagues who
worked for Allied Intelligence and Special Operations Executive. Jean Poix's task was to monitor radio messages from
London and to see they reached their destinations. His com-
rade, Henri Bonel, a dark nuggety man, had the task of
selecting suitable landing fields for clandestine night missions
and to send their descriptions and coordinates back to SOE.
The girl, Anna Reinhardt, being German, had a wider role
and it was her resourcefulness that had made possible both
the Rhine Maiden and Cobra missions.

Each time the moaning wind dropped, the BBC announc-
er's voice could be heard through the static. As the news
bulletin ended, the listeners drew closer to the radio operator. Lifting one earphone, he glanced at the girl. "The messages are beginning now, Lorenz."

She crouched at his elbow. The seemingly meaningless
French phrases that came every night could now be heard.
"The horse has six heads." "The car does not fit the garage."
The river flows uphill to the chateau." Two more messages
came and went and then Poix stiffened. Ten seconds later he
turned towards the girl excitedly. "It's on, Lorenz. Tonight."

The girl jumped to her feet and turned to the civilian.
"Did you hear that, Monsieur Boniface? They're fetching you
out tonight."

Before the nervous man could answer, Bonel gave a
grunt of protest. "They've picked a bad night, Lorenz. There've
been patrols in the area since the weekend. A wounded
English flier was found in a farmhouse. So they're combing
the district in case there are any more."

The girl frowned. "But I thought you said the area
around the field was clear."

"It is. But they still might be close enough to hear the
aircraft fly in."

"That's a chance we have to take. If the weather changes
we could lose the moon and our orders are to get Monsieur
Boniface to London as quickly as possible."

Although the girl's determination and courage were a
byword among his colleagues, Bonel felt he must put up a

fight. He cast a meaningful glance at the frightened Boniface. "Are you sure it's worth taking the risk?"

"Which is the bigger risk?" the girl demanded. "You know how important this is. So stop arguing and let's get started. You said it'll take us at least an hour to get to the field."

With a resigned grin at Poix, Bonel rose and doused his cigarette. Forty minutes later he was leading the girl, Boniface, and two newcomers down a country lane. All five were riding bicycles. Bonel's two extra men, a grocer and a butcher's assistant, were drawn from a local village. Riding alongside the French agent, the girl motioned back at them. "Where is the equipment they're going to need?"

"Everything's hidden near the field," Bonel told her. "It'll only take us a few minutes to be ready."

The moon was three-quarters full and the shadows of the trees that lined the lane looked impenetrable. As the cyclists approached a bend they heard the hum of an engine. Bonel shook his head at Boniface's nervous question. "No, monsieur. The Lysander isn't due until one o'clock." Turning, he ordered his party to dismount.

A few seconds later they saw a light flashing in the distance. Bonel gave a curse. "It's a German patrol. Get the bicycles off the road."

A stone hedge ran behind the trees. Heaving Boniface's bicycle unceremoniously over it, Bonel turned to help Anna but the lithe girl was having no difficulty with the climb. Further down the hedge, stones rattled as Bonel's two assistants also took cover.

The hum of the engine was louder now and a searchlight appeared, combing trees and sweeping across mist-covered fields. Bonel leaned towards Anna. "You should have done as I said. It's too dangerous tonight."

She shook her dark head. "No, we can't risk waiting. Too much is at stake."

The chilly night air rustled the leaves of a poplar. The vehicle was close now and German voices could be heard. Alongside the girl, Boniface was trembling with fright and she pressed his arm reassuringly.

Moss felt cold against her face as she peered through a crack in the stones. The vehicle was a flat-topped truck with a searchlight and a machine gun mounted behind the cab. Two soldiers were operating the searchlight and she could see the silhouettes of two more standing beside the machine gun as the beam traversed the field opposite. As it swung back, its brilliant light slitted through the gaps in the stone hedge and made her shrink back. Then the truck had passed and the hum of its engine began to fade, although its searchlight could still be seen playing on trees and hedges.

The small party reached the landing field ten minutes later. Flooded in moonlight, it was about 700 metres long and 200 metres wide with the grass close-cropped by cattle. Although it had a slight hollow filled with mist towards its eastern boundary, Bonel had judged it safe for an aircraft of a Lysander's capabilities.

The stone hedge ran along its southern boundary and Bonel fumbled beneath a pile of stones that cattle had pushed over. A moment later he drew out a large waterproof bag which contained three torches mounted on sharp sticks. Giving one to each of his assistants, he estimated the direction of the wind, then pointed towards the slight hollow. "Set your torches just beyond it, fifty metres apart. Don't switch them on until I give you the signal. If you catch sight of any Germans, get the hell out of it and we'll try again tomorrow night."

Hiding their bicycles in a thicket of brambles, the two men hurried off under cover of the stone hedge. Taking Anna's arm, Bonel led her and Boniface in the opposite direction until they reached the western end of the landing strip. A hawthorn hedge ran along this boundary and the trio kept in its shadow until they were halfway across the field. Here Bonel halted. "I'll wait here until they arrive. You two get to the far corner of the field and stay there until I call you."

The girl's protest was instinctive. "Why should we do that? We'll wait here with you."

Bonel shook his head. "No. I don't like the feel of it tonight. Over there you've a chance if anything goes wrong." Seeing she was about to protest again, Bonel silenced her with a warning glance at the frightened civilian. "Have you got your pistol with you?"

"Yes, of course I have."

"Then off you go. Wait until the aircraft has turned around for takeoff before you run out."

She had to pause twice to allow Boniface to regain his breath before they reached the far corner of the field where they settled down behind a bush. In the distance she heard the call of a fox. She wished the moonlight were less bright. Standing in it a man could be seen half a mile away and the shadows it was throwing were a perfect cover for enemy soldiers.

Six long minutes passed before she heard the distant drone of an engine. Rising from the bush she glanced around but could see no telltale searchlight and decided the Lysander was approaching. As the droning grew louder two faint lights down the field began to flicker. Bonel's two assistants had received their signal and were setting up their hooded torches.

She could see the Lysander now, a gull-like silhouette against the moon-washed sky. A hundred metres from her, Bonel had stepped from the cover of the hedge and was flashing his identification signal.

Above, the Lysander pilot could see the field clearly with its three landing lights. Along the route he had kept passing over large patches of fog, particularly along the Loire and the Saône, but to his relief the fog had cleared as he reached the higher ground. He was a young Australian who had been posted to Tempsford only four months ago and this was his deepest mission into France.

He banked the Lysander gently around the field until the three landing lights formed a giant inverted L. Below Bonel was still giving his identification signal. Replying with his own signal light, the Australian reduced his speed to 100 mph and wound back the tail trim. He then checked that his mixture control was normal and that his propeller was in fine pitch. Finding all in order, he throttled back and headed for the field.

With its high-wing configuration the Lysander looked like a giant night bird coming in to roost. Settling down on its immensely strong undercarriage it ran towards the second light and began braking. There it turned 90 degrees towards the third light, turned again, and began taxiing back towards Bonel.

The girl waited until the Lysander had made its last 180

degree turn in preparation for a fast takeoff before pushing
Boniface from the bushes and urging him towards it. In the
aircraft the young Australian was busy carrying out his cockpit drill. Drawing his pistol, his other hand on the throttle,
he waited for his reception committee to appear. When Bonel
ran beneath his starboard wingtip the Australian yelled 'good
luck' to the agent in the plane and slid his cabin roof back.
The agent, another Frenchman, threw his baggage to Bonel
and climbed down after it.

The girl arrived just as Bonel was hurrying the incoming
agent away from the aircraft. Although she exchanged smiles
with him, neither recognized the other. With the fearsome
Gestapo to consider, the British and French SOE agents did
their best to keep ignorant of each other's identities.

Bonel was just helping the girl and the breathless Boniface into the Lysander when it happened. There was a sudden rattle of automatic fire from the far end of the field. A
moment later a searchlight blazed on and caught the Lysander
in its beam. Linked by radio to a flight controller beacon, the
truck crew had been warned a Lysander was in the vicinity
and had crept back with extinguished searchlight in the hope
of catching the SOE agents red-handed.

The shocked pilot seemed momentarily frozen. Leaping
on the starboard undercarriage housing, Bonel banged his fist
on the fuselage. "Allez vite!" he yelled. "Get moving!"

The pilot awoke to his danger and pushed the throttle
forward. Grasping the incoming agent's arm, Bonel dragged
him towards the hawthorn hedge and pushed him through.
Across the field two soldiers were vaulting over the stone
hedge and running towards the Lysander, firing machine
carbines as they came. Unable to smash through the hedge,
the truck drove right up to it and opened fire with its fixed
machine gun.

Still spotlighted by the searchlight, the Lysander seemed
to pick up speed with agonizing slowness. As bullets rattled
against its wing and tore through its metal fuselage, the girl
motioned the terrified Boniface to curl himself up into a ball.
For a moment she believed the pilot was hit as the plane
gave a lurch. Then she heard the undercarriage thumping
and knew the aircraft was picking up speed again. A few

seconds later, with the searchlight still following it, it became airborne and banked steeply behind a line of poplars.

Like some great tentacle the searchlight hung on to the plane a moment longer before falling reluctantly away. As if to prove its presence had not been wasted, it lit up the shapes of two motionless bodies lying near the landing lights before sweeping back across the field where the German soldiers were hacking their way through the hedge in pursuit of Bonel and the new agent.

5

The camouflaged staff car rolled to a halt on the large forecourt. Before the Waaf driver had time to switch off the engine, its sole occupant, a small, wiry RAF Air Commodore, jumped out and paused by her window. "I might be some time, Hilary, so you'd better get yourself a cup of tea." He jabbed a finger at a couple of young provost lieutenants who were watching the car from a stone terrace above. "If you give those lads a smile, I'm sure they'll be happy to oblige."

The Waaf, a pretty, pert girl, thanked him and watched him hurry towards the steps that led up to the terrace. Air Commodore Arthur Davies, whose brisk and sprightly movements belied both his rank and age, was the founder of 633 Squadron. A mercurial and farsighted officer, he had conceived the need for a special operations unit back in 1942 when every front-line squadron in the RAF had been screaming out for more aircraft and it said much for Davies' perseverance that after nearly a year he had been allowed to carry out the experiment. The squadron's subsequent successes, in the Black Fjord in Norway, in the Rhine Maiden, Crucible, Valkyrie, and Cobra operations, had been complete vindications, to the point that Davies now had authorization

to approach the Mosquito manufacturer, de Haviland, and
request structural modifications to his aircraft whenever a
mission called for them. With the RAF no more free from
inter-unit rivalries than any other large military force, such a
privilege, not given even to the élite Pathfinder Force, provoked intense jealousies which meant that in spite of 633
Squadron's impressive record, Davies still had to fight hard
to keep its independence. Fortunately, being both aggressive
and resilient, he was ideally equipped for the task.

Henderson, the big Scottish CO of 633 Squadron, had
once called him a human bantamcock and those who had
experienced Davies' testiness thought the appellation an excellent one.

Some of that testiness became evident now as one of the
provost lieutenants stopped him and asked for his credentials.
"We've already been checked twice, lieutenant. Once at the
gate and once down the drive."

"I'm sorry about that, sir, but I have my orders."

"You're new here, aren't you?" Davies demanded.

"Yes, sir."

"Well, for Christ's sake take a good look at me so we
don't have to go through this nonsense every time I come."

The embarrassed young lieutenant led him down a corridor, tapped on a door, and opened it. "Air Commodore
Davies, sir," he announced.

The room Davies entered was a huge library with oak-
panelled walls. French windows at the far end gave a view of
the terrace, lawns, and a background of elm trees. A large
bush of red rhododendrons at the far side added a bright
splash of colour.

An elderly, slight man with a small military moustache
rose from the long table that ran down the centre of the room
and approached Davies with outstretched hand. Unfailing
courtesy was the hallmark of Brigadier Simms. "Thank you
for coming so promptly, Davies. We have everything ready
for you."

Davies shook the soldier's hand warmly. The elderly
Brigadier had come into his orbit during the first of 633
Squadron's special missions, in the Swartfjord in May 1943.
Since then the frail Brigadier, who in appearance and manner
seemed more suited to the courtroom than to the Special

Operations Executive, had been the link man when any new interservice mission was in the offing.

Standing to one side, the Brigadier nodded at a second man sitting at the far side of the table. "You'll see that in spite of his many commitments, General Staines has also managed to be here today."

Davies drew himself to attention and saluted as the man rose to his feet. In contrast to Simms, he could hardly have been more different in appearance. Weighing at least 220 pounds, with spiky hair and a leathery face, he looked like a heavyweight boxer past his prime. In fact Staines had once been a star on the American gridiron. Tough, humorous, with B-17 and Mustang squadrons under his command, he had first met Davies when 633 Squadron and a force of B-17s had launched a joint assault on the German Rhine Maiden establishments. The success of the mission, which had destroyed a massive threat to the 8th Air Force's offensive against Germany, had given Davies' ace squadron such prestige in Staines's eyes that since then he had always been willing to give help if help were needed.

He acknowledged Davies' salute with a grin and a large hand that reached across the table. His voice was gravelly, with a Texas accent. "Hi ya, Davies. How's tricks?"

Davies hid a wince at the powerful handshake. "Fine, thank you, sir. May I offer my congratulations?"

The American squinted down at the third star pinned to his tunic collar. "You know why I got this, don't you, Davies?"

"I think I've a good idea, sir."

"You've no idea at all," Staines grinned. "I got it because a few weeks ago I drank Carl Spaatz under the table. He couldn't have a two-star general doing that, so off went my recommendation. I'm working on it that if I do it twice more I'll be in charge of the whole goddam Air Force."

Davies noticed a half-filled glass of whisky standing on the table before the American. The Brigadier glanced at him. "Would you care for a drink, Davies?"

There had been a time when Davies felt that to refuse would have diminished himself in the tough American's eyes, although to his credit he had never given way. Now he knew their relationship was immune to such impressions. "Not for me, thanks. But I wouldn't mind a cup of tea if it's not too much trouble."

As the Brigadier picked up his telephone, Staines motioned Davies to sit opposite him. "Simms tells me you're about to stand down your squadron."

Davies nodded as he dropped into a chair. "Yes, sir. They'll need to put in some hard practice before they're ready for this job."

For a moment Staines' tone changed. "You sure make certain those guys earn their keep, don't you? But let's come to that in a minute. If your boys are going on stand-down, what about that party I promised 'em after the Cobra shindig? For Chrissake, they earned it."

Davies hesitated. "It's not going to be easy to fit it in once we've started training, sir."

"OK, but you haven't started yet. And this isn't one of those sooner-the-better missions. I think our crews should meet, Davies. Men fight for one another better when they've gotten pissed over the same bottle of bourbon."

Seeing Davies was only half-persuaded, Staines played his ace. "You can't say no, Davies. Not when it's a ding-dong to celebrate my promotion."

Davies gave a lopsided grin. "You're not playing it fair, sir."

"Why should I play it fair, goddam it? You promised the boys and so did I. We'll supply the booze and all the entertainment. All your boys have to do is fly down to South Wotten and fly back again."

Unused to the American way of doing things, Davies was looking shocked. "I can't authorize military aircraft for a party, sir."

Staines grinned. "I thought that might go against the grain. OK, I'll borrow a few Mitchells. Your boys can bunk up with us for the night and we'll fly 'em back the next morning. How does that hit you?"

Davies realized he had been outmanoeuvred and outflanked. "You make it difficult for me to refuse, sir."

"Then don't try to. We'll fix a date this afternoon and lay it on. It'll do us all good to let our hair down for one night." Seeing that the Brigadier was waiting for their conversation to cease, the Texan turned to him with a grin. "Sorry, but I always think it's a good idea to get the important things out of the way first. What about you coming too? All you need to do is contact Davies."

Simms looked apologetic. "I'd like nothing better, sir, but I'm afraid we're pretty stretched at the moment with the invasion imminent."

"We're all stretched," Staines grunted. "That's why a party is a damned good idea. Anyway, think about it and let Davies know if you change your mind."

As the Brigadier nodded, the telephone on the table rang. Answering it, the soldier listened a moment, then nodded. "Thank you, Taylor. Have they seen the films? Good. Very well; I'll tell them." Replacing the receiver, Simms turned to the two air force officers. "As you'll gather, gentlemen, the committee is ready to see us now."

As Staines heaved his great bulk out of his chair, the Brigadier walked to the far end of the library and opened a door. Through it Davies caught sight of a room filled with wall maps and communication equipment. A large table, illuminated by overhead lights, stood in the centre of the floor. Seven men, looking like gamblers playing cards, were sitting around it. Three were high-ranking staff officers, the other four were civilians. Photographs, files,. and sheets of paper covered with figures littered the table between them.

Two of the officers rose to salute Staines; the rest of the committee remained seated. One man, skinny, balding and bespectacled, was oblivious of the disturbance as he studied a batch of photographs. It was only when the Brigadier approached and spoke to him in French that he raised his head.

"Monsieur Boniface, allow me to introduce General Staines of the American 8th Air Force and Air Commodore Davies of the RAF. They are the officers you will be working with during the next few weeks." Turning his head, the Brigadier reverted to English. "Gentlemen, this is Monsieur Boniface, member of the Legion of Honour and a most distinguished French engineer."

Dusk had fallen and a bat could be seen flitting through the elms outside when the Brigadier and the two air force officers returned to the library. As Simms switched on the lights, Staines grinned wryly at Davies. "I have to hand it to you. You put up a good case. Did you work this scheme out on your own?"

Davies' modesty did him credit as he glanced at Simms. "No, I've needed too much SOE intelligence for that. I've also had to work hand in hand with the inventor of the weapon. So it's hardly a one-man effort."

Before the smiling Brigadier could protest, Staines went on: "All the same, you're going to need a weapon evaluation before that committee makes up its mind. Bureaucrats like traditional methods and your scheme is hardly that. As you can't do an evaluation without training, you do realize you might spend weeks putting your boys through their paces only for the committee to turn their thumbs down?"

Davies' somewhat brusque reply indicated the American had laid a finger on one of the weaknesses of his plan. "With so much at stake, it seems to me the risks are worth taking."

Staines grinned again. "In other words, go for broke. OK, count me in for all the help I can scrape up for you."

Davies rallied at the offer. "I would be grateful for it, sir. The job could take us some time and as there's certain to be a heavy demand for aircraft on D-Day, I can't expect to be given relays of fighter escorts, but your Mustangs with their extra range will be able to stay over the target as long as we can."

Staines nodded. "I've got the picture. Mind you, don't expect too much. There'll be just as many demands on my ships. But I'll do the best I can."

Satisfied, Davies turned to the Brigadier. "I'll make that phone call now, if I may."

Half a minute later a familiar voice sounded in the earpiece. "Hello, sir. Henderson here."

"Hello, Jock. Listen. I'm putting your boys on stand-down today. All right?"

Henderson sounded delighted. "That's good news, sir. The boys deserve it."

"How many of 'em are due for leave?"

"I can't say offhand. But two or three, I think."

"All leave's cancelled until further notice. Stick it on the notice boards right away."

Henderson's euphoria vanished like a puff of smoke.

"You're standing us down but cancelling all leave? What about evening passes?"

"Everything else stays the same. I don't want you drawing attention to yourselves."

"What's going on, sir?"

"Never mind that now. I'll be around in the morning. Tell Moore and Adams I want them in your office at 0930." As Henderson tried to ask a further question, Davies cut him off abruptly. "That's all for now, Jock. See you in the morning."

6

The door of Millburn's Flight Office burst open with a crash. Glancing up from his desk on which he was signing requisition forms, Millburn was about to shoot the offender down in flames when he saw it was Gabby bearing down on him. The Welshman was looking aghast. "Millburn! Have you seen these orders?"

The American gave a rueful grin. "You mean about all leave being cancelled? Yeah, it's tough. Real tough."

"That's all you've got to say? It's tough? Millburn, you've got to help me. Gwen's even got the cottage booked."

Millburn offered the distraught Welshman a cigarette. "Sorry, kid. The orders have come from Davies. So there's nothing any of us can do."

Gabby almost choked in his frustration. "It had to be that little sod, hadn't it? Who else would do a thing like this?"

Rising sharply, Millburn went to the door, glanced out, then closed it. "Cool it, kid, or you'll end up behind bars. You aren't the only one who's disappointed. Matthews was going on leave next week as well."

Gabby needed nothing more to turn his disappointment

on the American. "You don't give a damn, do you? You think it's funny."

Welcoming his navigator's change of mood, Millburn grinned. "It could be a blessing in disguise, boyo. I was a bit scared that after Gwen had finished with you she might bury you down a Welsh coal mine."

Gabby was breathing hard. "So you won't help?"

"Kiddo, I've already tried. I've spoken to both Moore and Pop Henderson. They're as sorry as I am but what can any of us do? There is one consolation. Since we're standing down, we can have all-night passes if we want them. So you can work off your frustration on the dames in Scarborough."

It was news that for the moment stopped Gabby in his tracks. "The bastard cancels our leave and then lets us have all-night passes? That doesn't make any kind of sense."

Millburn shrugged. "Since when do you expect things to make sense? We're at war, remember."

"So I've got to tell Gwen it's all off? Just like that?"

"I don't see what else you can do, kiddo. I'm sorry. I really am."

Breathing fire, Gabby marched to the door and turned. "I'd like to bloody kill Davies. You know that?"

"Sure you would, boyo," Millburn soothed. "Only before you do it, keep it to yourself. Otherwise he just might beat you to the punch."

Glaring at the American, muttering imprecations, Gabby walked out. A moment later the slam of the door made Millburn wince. Grinning ruefully, he picked up his pen and made a fresh assault on the requisition forms.

Unknown to Gabby, the object of his frustration was at that very moment drawing up in his staff car outside the Station Administration Block. With his usual briskness, Davies was out of the car almost before its wheels ceased rolling. After a few quick words with his driver, he hurried up the narrow path that led to the main entrance. Deceived by his agile movements, a young airman who was emerging from the Block carrying a dustpan and long-handled broom did not realize he was confronting an Air Commodore until the last moment. Flustered, the youngster snapped a salute and promptly dropped the broom right in Davies' path. With an

undignified yelp, the small Air Commodore caught it right
between his legs and collapsed into the flower bed alongside
the path. Rearing up, he glared at the horrified youth and
prepared to blast him with all four cannon. Realizing at the
last moment that nothing he could say would fit the occasion,
Davies snatched up his briefcase, threw a last glare at the
petrified youngster, then ran up the steps into the building.
In the camouflaged car outside, his pretty Waaf driver gave a
last hysterical sob and wiped her streaming eyes.

Three men were waiting for him in the CO's office:
Moore, Adams, and Henderson. The big Scot, a professional
airman, was a middle-aged, benign, broad-shouldered man
who was affectionately nicknamed Pop by his station personnel. As proud of his élite Squadron as Davies himself, Henderson viewed the Air Commodore with mixed feelings. On
the one hand, he admired his devotion to duty, his drive,
and his tenacity. On the other hand, he viewed Davies' use of
his squadron with caution, feeling that at times he committed
it to dangers beyond the call of duty. How much of this was
due to Davies' pride and confidence in his creation and how
much was due to personal ambition, Henderson had never
been able to decide.

All three men, who had seen the arrival of Davies' car
from the window, turned as he entered and stood at attention. Returning their salutes, Davies turned his scowl on
Henderson. "You don't specially train your sprogs to cripple
staff officers, do you?"

Henderson showed surprise. His voice had the faintest
trace of Highland brogue. "I don't follow you, sir."

"A grubby little bastard out there just threw a broom
right in front of me. I damn near broke my neck."

Henderson's sense of humour could not be contained.
"We don't train them to do it, sir. I think it just comes
naturally."

At the far side of the desk, Moore's mouth was twitch-
ing. Unable to decide whether to scowl or grin, Davies
contented himself with a gesture at the window. "How are
things coming along?"

Henderson knew the Air Commodore was talking about
the restoration of the airfield after the heavy German air raid
less than a month ago. "Pretty well, sir. We've got all the

essential services working again. The rest is more or less a cosmetic job."

"Good. Keep at it. The bastards aren't likely to try again, not after the flogging they got on the way home."

Henderson's nod was wry. "Let's hope not, sir. I never understood how they got through the last time."

Davies saw no reason why his respect for the Nazis should be anything else but grudging. "Bad weather was a big help. But they'd done a fair bit of planning. Our Intelligence boys say they'd built a dummy airfield to practice on."

Henderson whistled. "Then they must have known what we were up to."

"We can't be sure of that. More likely it was our attacks on Gestapo bases that scared them. They felt it would establish a precedent, which it has."

It was Henderson's chance to put the question all three men wanted to ask. "What's the score now, sir? Have we finished working for MacBride?"

"Oh, Christ, yes. You're back under my wing again." Davies, his good temper restored, grinned at the big Scot. "If that's any consolation to you."

Henderson's expression showed that whatever reservations he had about Davies' leadership, they were minute compared with his reservations about MacBride's. A Special Operations Executive officer, MacBride had been given temporary control of the squadron during which time he had ordered it to carry out the highly-unpopular Operation Cobra. Ruthless in his methods, MacBride was under suspicion of causing the unnecessary loss of three crews, among them the well-liked Flight Commander Teddy Young. With Moore blaming himself for having trusted the SOE officer, the repercussions of that unhappy episode were still evident on the station.

Henderson's sigh was pure relief. "I'm glad to hear that, sir."

Davies grinned. "Better watch it, Jock. I might be as unpopular as MacBride in a week or two."

The Scot exchanged a glance with Moore. Davies' visits to the station were more often than not a prelude to high endeavor and his orders the previous night had suggested this one was no exception. With the interdiction raids a vital part of the Allies' pre-invasion strategy, the withdrawal of a squadron of 633's calibre was evidence in itself something was in the wind. Although Henderson had the feeling he had little chance of learning the truth at this time and place, he felt it worth a try. "Have you got something special lined up for us, sir?"

Davies' frown and reply were intended to forestall further questions. In fact they only added piquancy to an already intriguing puzzle. "I might have, Jock. It all depends." Before the Scot could speak, he turned towards Moore. "What's the width of your aircraft, Ian? 57 feet?"

The young Squadron Commander was as surprised as anyone by the question. "Yes, sir. I think it is. Why?"

"Never mind why. Take the worst pilot in your squadron. What do you think his tolerance it?"

"Tolerance? I don't understand."

It took little to make Davies testy, particularly when he intended to give nothing away. "If you asked him to fly through a gap, how much tolerance would he need before he pranged a wingtip?"

As Adams gave Henderson a puzzled look, Moore gave the question thought. "It's hard to say. It depends on so many factors."

"What factors?"

"What other distractions he had. His speed, height, the weather conditions, the flak thrown at him. But under ideal conditions I'd say he needed at least ten feet on either side to be safe."

"Ten feet!" Davies looked shocked. "Christ, I could do better than that. You're playing it canny, Ian. Your boys are the best. Try again."

Handpicked by Davies to lead 633 Squadron after the loss of Roy Grenville in the Black Fjord, Moore was nevertheless always prepared to stand up to the testy Air Commodore when the occasion demanded it, possibly the reason Davies had such regard for him. "I can't give that kind of estimate off the cuff, sir. I first need to try it myself."

Davies' reply made all three men stare at him. "Maybe in a day or two you can. But first I want your boys to begin low-level flying exercises. Not 200 feet up but right down on the deck." The small Air Commodore glanced at Adams.

"This is where you come in, Frank. I want you to contact the Observer Corps and work out a number of routes. As this is going to be ultra low-level stuff, do your best to avoid populated areas or we'll get the usual bleats from MPs, mayors and the public. Use moors, rivers, railway tracks and that kind of thing. All right?"

As Adams nodded and moved towards the door, Davies checked him. "No; I'm going to want you today. Ring your assistant and tell her to get on with it. She's a capable lass."

Glancing at Henderson for permission, Adams picked up the telephone. Moore, who had been looking more and more quizzical during the last minute, interrupted Davies as he was opening his briefcase. "You do realize my boys are specialists at low-level flying, sir."

Davies' grin betrayed he had been expecting the rebuke. "I know they're the best, Ian. But I want 'em even better. This means everyone. All your replacements and reserve crews as well."

As Moore shrugged, Davies walked over to Henderson's desk and began pulling large photographs from his briefcase. "All right. Now I want you to take a look at these."

Henderson and Moore moved to his elbow. Adams, as curious as his colleagues and yet restricted by the telephone at his ear, screwed his head around in an attempt to see the photographs. Brow furrowed, Henderson picked up the first one for a closer look. It showed a large grassy field with two sets of white lines running across it. Although parallel, the lines were not straight, winding instead in serpent fashion from hedge to hedge. The Scot pointed at them. "What are these, sir?"

"Marker tapes," Davies told him. "About 200 feet apart."

Henderson pointed at two vehicles parked back to back at the far end of the tapes. "And these?"

Davies laid a second photograph on the table. It was an enlargement of the vehicles, showing them to be huge mobile cranes with their hoists lifted straight up. The men's eyes, however, were drawn to the curious structures the cranes were supporting. Dark in colour and opaque, they looked like enormous fans that had been raised vertically at one end while the other end lay flat on the transporters' decks. With the transporters standing back to back, the effect looked like two bookends standing on the grassy field.

Henderson's face was a study. "What on earth are those for, sir?"

Davies' voice was innocence itself. "They're going to be used for practice purposes, Jock."

The Scot's suspicions were acute now. "Who for, sir? Us?"

"That's right. Your boys are going to practice flying through those screens until they scrape their wingtips."

"You can't be serious, sir. What about the cranes? If they as much as touch one, it'll be curtains."

"The cranes are well back. There's at least a six foot fringe of cloth and flimsy woodwork on the vertical side. And it's specially made to break up on impact."

Henderson studied another photograph of the transporters. "How high are these screens, sir?"

"Fifty feet above the transporters."

"Fifty feet! Then they can't be that flimsy or they'd fold up in the wind or break up under their own weight. And at that height it won't take more than a jolt to spin the boys into the deck."

When Davies had doubts about an operation he was inclined to impatience, a weakness his listeners knew well. "For Christ's sake, Jock, the builders have assured me they're safe. That means they've put them through tests."

The canny Scot was not so easily placated when the safety of his crews was an issue. "All the same, sir, I'd like a closer look at those contraptions before I send any of my boys through them."

"You'll get a closer look," Davies snapped. "This evening." As the three men showed surprise, he went on: "I've arranged for a demonstration and I want the three of you to come with me." He handed Adams a file of notes. "These are the technical details. You'd better read through them before we leave. I want to be away by 1200 hours."

Adams was searching through the notes and coordinates provided with the photographs. "Where exactly is the field, sir?"

"Down in Herefordshire. That's why we need an early start. I can't take my Master because she's grounded for a

couple of days." As Adams nodded, Davies snapped his briefcase closed and turned back to Henderson. "Cheer up, Jock.
It's not all PT and cold showers. As the four of us are going to
be occupied today, you're at liberty to give your boys the day
off. In fact, as I've a party planned for 'em tomorrow night,
you can give 'em tomorrow off too, if you like."

Henderson stared. "A party, sir?"

"Yes. I thought it a good idea before they start their
training. General Staines is throwing it. He's sending Mitchells in to pick us up tomorrow afternoon and they'll bring us
back the next morning. The Mustang lads who escorted you
to Copenhagen will be there, so it should be quite a party."

Henderson's feelings were mixed. With Davies' special
missions usually frenetic affairs, there was something alarm-
ing in the measured way he was approaching this one. "A
couple of days off will do the boys good, sir. And the Yanks
always put on a good party."

"Then that's settled. You start training the day after
tomorrow." Davies nodded at Moore and Adams. "You two
can run along now. I'm sure you've plenty to do. Meet me
outside the Admin. Block at 1200 hours sharp."

As both men saluted and left the office, Davies turned to
Henderson. The Scot's look of anticipation faded as he shook
his head. "No, Jock, I can't say any more about the operation.
It's top secret plus. But if it comes off, it'll be one hell of a
thing for your squadron."

Sighing, Henderson nodded at Davies' briefcase. "There's
only one thing that low-level stuff can be for, sir. To fly into
Hitler's chancellery and put a bomb right up his backside."

Davies grinned. "Keep on thinking that, Jock, and you'll
fool everybody." He fished into his tunic pocket and pulled
out a sealed envelope. "That reminds me. Give this to Harvey, will you?"

In some surprise Henderson gazed down at the envelope
addressed to the Yorkshireman in Davies' handwriting. For a
member of his squadron to receive a personal letter from
Davies was unusual enough: to receive it at this moment
seemed significant. Reading his mind, Davies shook his head.
"No, it's nothing to do with this operation. Brigadier Simms
made the suggestion last night and after giving it careful
thought I decided to go along with him. But emphasize to

Harvey the urgent need to keep his mouth shut until he's obeyed my instructions. After that I don't think we've anything to worry about."

Henderson thought he was beginning to understand and eyed Davies with new respect. "I'll stress it, sir."

For the briefest of moments he imagined Davies was looking embarrassed. The Air Commodore's briskness dispelled the impression immediately. "All right, Jock, that's all until 1200 hours. Now how about joining me in the mess for coffee and a bite of chow? I had so much to do this morning I missed my breakfast."

7

Harvey drove slowly along the cliff road, searching the name of each hotel in turn. Prim and Victorian, they stood in a long row like elderly matrons awaiting royal presentation. At their feet the cliff of the North Bay shelved down to the sea. Halfway along the road, Harvey found his hotel and parked his old, bull-nosed Morris opposite. Seeing he was ten minutes early, he crossed the pavement and stared down.

The cliffs, enriched by gardens and tennis courts, were crisscrossed by paths that led down to the sea. With the tide high and a brisk easterly wind blowing, waves were sweeping across the bay like rampant cavalry. Here and there, on the paths and along the esplanade, RAF recruits, many of whom were billeted in the town, were taking in the sights and locals were walking their dogs. Few, if any, appeared to notice the grass growing through the tennis courts or the stragetically-placed barbed wire and pillboxes. On its North Bay at least, Scarborough, that most beautiful of seaside resorts, was carrying its wartime burdens with dignity.

Harvey's eyes moved to the castle on the high promon-

tory that stood above the old town. On its far side, the south
bay was another world with its tiny fishing harbour, its cockle
and winkle stalls, and its beach amusements. Yet its cheerful
vulgarity had its own special charm: the Northerner of that
day had a gift for enjoyment without malice.

Harvey glanced at his watch again. Davies' orders, which
he carried in his inner tunic pocket, were characteristically
terse. "Make no mention of this visit to anyone! Be at the
Ocean View Hotel in Scarborough at 3 p.m. prompt and ask
for Flight Officer Walton. She will explain everything."

Harvey knew no Waaf called Walton and in any case
could think of no reason why Henderson or Moore should be
kept ignorant of his meeting. The affair was a mystery, as
were the twinges of excitement he had felt before dismissing
them as fanciful and absurd.

Like most of its comrades, the hotel was showing signs of
wartime neglect. Brushing past a dusty palm, Harvey approached the hall porter's desk.

"I'm Squadron Leader Harvey. I've an appointment with
Flight Officer Walton. Give her a call, will you?"

The porter was an elderly man with thinning hair and a
stoop. Peering over his glasses, he walked to the back of his
office and picked up a phone. Half a minute later he gave a
nod. "Up you go, sir. The lift's over there. Room 34 on the
second floor."

The lift creaked asthmatically and stopped with a judder.
Heaving aside the safety door, Harvey stepped out into a
carpeted corridor. Two civilians passed him, deep in conversation. Commercial travellers was Harvey's guess. Reaching
an intersection he checked the room numbers and turned left.

Room 34 was the third down the corridor. Without knowing why, he hesitated outside it. His heart was beating fast
and his breathing was quicker than usual. Telling himself he
was behaving like a damned fool, he rapped hard on the
door.

There was no sound within the room. Puzzled, he knocked
again. This time the door opened.

He gave a violent start and his face drained of colour.
Too stunned to speak, he gazed in disbelief at the girl in the
doorway. Although pale herself, she managed a smile. "Hello,

Frank. I would have met you in the hall but they didn't think it wise. They are so security conscious."

Her voice, with its attractive accent, was a dream of the past. He made no attempt to kiss her: at that moment he had difficulty in speaking. "Anna. For God's sake. . . ."

She nodded, smiling. "It is me, Frank. But it has been a long time, hasn't it?"

His eyes were devouring her. She was wearing a green dress with a cameo brooch at her throat. Her black hair was longer than he remembered it and was lying loosely over her shoulders. Voices and footsteps sounded down the corridor but he noticed neither. Putting a hand on his arm she drew him inside and closed the door.

His heart was thudding hard. He watched her turn towards him, every graceful movement bringing back memories. She put a soft hand against his face. "Have you missed me a little, Frank?"

"Missed you?" His voice was thick with emotion. "When did you get here?"

She slipped her hand around his neck. "Never mind that now. I'm here. That's all that matters."

As in the past he suddenly felt gauche and clumsy beside her. Remembering, she gave a low laugh and kissed him full on the mouth. "You haven't changed, Frank. Put your arms around me."

He gazed at her. Although her grey eyes were glistening with tears they had the inner serenity that had always made him ashamed of his bloody-mindedness. Deep in his mind a sudden joyous voice was making its affirmation. This was his woman. This was the most beautiful woman on earth.

He felt her shapely body pressing against him and his arms went around her. For a minute they kissed like two parched travellers at an oasis. Her tears were wet and warm on his lips. Breathless, laughing and crying at the same time, she drew back from him at last. As he followed her, she put a slim hand over his mouth. "Give me a little time, Frank. I'm not used to this kind of happiness."

Harvey knew full well what she meant. Still trembling, he dropped into a chair. "When did you come?" he asked again.

"Two nights ago. By Lysander." She dried her eyes. "Would you like a drink? I have a bottle of whisky."

He nodded, watching her graceful figure cross over to a cabinet. "Why have they brought you back?"

She turned and smiled at him. "Do you want water in your whisky?"

"No. Is it a dangerous job like the last one?"

Avoiding his stare, she set the glass by his side. "No. At least not for me."

His voice turned eager. "Does that mean you're not going back?"

She put a hand over his mouth again. "So many questions. You know I am not allowed to answer them."

"But surely you can say if you're going back or not?"

"I do not know what plans they have for me. But I do know I will be here for some days. Perhaps even for a few weeks."

When he did not answer she knelt down beside him and put her head on his knee. "We must not be greedy, Frank. A few minutes ago you believed I was in France. Let us be grateful for the time we get together and enjoy every moment of it."

His face cleared. "Who arranged for you to see me? Brigadier Simms?"

Her answer surprised him. "He gave permission but it was Arthur Davies who made all the arrangements."

Harvey was thinking of the times he and the small Air Commodore had crossed swords. "So he has a heart after all."

"He has been very kind to me. So have they all."

Harvey, who had so often cursed Davies and the SOE for the hazardous missions they inflicted on the courageous German girl, was not letting them off as lightly as that. "So they should be, by God, after all you've done for them."

She ignored his flash of temper. Her eyes were searching his bony face. "You look thinner. Has your stomach wound healed properly?"

"Yes, it's fine." He gazed down at her oval face, full of beauty and intelligence. "God, you're beautiful," he muttered. "Even more beautiful than I remembered."

Her cheeks coloured slightly. "I told a small lie when you arrived. I could have met you downstairs but it would have meant my wearing the RAF uniform they gave me. I did not want to meet you in uniform. Also I preferred that we met in private."

He took another sip of whisky. "You did right. Sometimes it seems the whole world's wearing a uniform."

She could see there was still tension in him. Born and raised in poverty, Harvey had always found it difficult to believe this well-bred and intelligent girl could love him. Wisely she gave him time. "How is Sam?"

"He's fine. He'll be on cloud nine when he sees you."

"Where have you left him?"

"Back in camp. Adams will feed him tonight."

"Does that mean you have the rest of the day off?"

"Yes. I've a pass until noon tomorrow."

"But that's wonderful. How did you manage it?"

He shrugged. "Davies must have arranged it. I couldn't think why at the time."

"I told you. He has a good heart."

He drained his glass. "He wouldn't have given it if we hadn't been standing down."

"You are standing down? Do you know why?"

"No, but there's something in the wind. Davies took Moore and Henderson somewhere in his car today. He's almost certain to have another of his damned missions lined up. It's the only time he gives us any rest."

He did not notice how her eyes clouded at his words. She was silent awhile before she spoke again. "How is Ian?"

"Moore's all right. Why? Are you planning to see him?"

"No. I'm not allowed to."

"But if you can, you will?"

She remembered his jealousy of Moore and raised her face. "Are you and he still enemies?"

"No."

"Why is that?"

He shrugged. "Probably because he saved my life coming back from Bavaria. Didn't you know?"

She shook her head. "How could I know?"

With nearly a year and a hundred incidents since their last meeting he realized there were many things the other did not know. "Will you be able to stay here? In Scarborough?"

"Yes, I think so. At least until they brief me again. I

would rather have gone back to the Black Swan but Arthur thinks that is too risky."

The whisky was now doing its work, bringing him full realization of his good fortune. "That means we can meet every day!"

"Yes. That is if you can get away."

"That shouldn't be any problem." Harvey gave a wry grimace. "Are you sure I'm not dreaming this?"

Laughing, she rose to her knees and kissed him. "Does it feel like a dream?"

He grinned. "More than ever." Their eyes met and suddenly Harvey's inhibitions fell away. "God, Anna, I love you. I love you so much it hurts."

They lay on the bed together, resting after making love. Her hair was a black cascade on the pillow; her breasts were firm and full to his touch. Beside him he could feel the entire nakedness of her, her flat stomach, the smooth length of her thighs.

He gazed into her grey eyes and saw they were filled with tears. Lifting a calloused finger he tried to stroke them away. "You cried the last time I made love to you. Remember?"

"The last time?" she whispered. "We have only had the chance to make love once."

"You still cried."

"I told you why. I always cry when I am happy."

"No. You said it was because I had spoken to you about my mother. What is it this time?"

She was silent a moment, then smiled. "I was thinking about the letter you sent me. Just before Operation Cobra. It was so beautiful. Did you have to write it many times?"

He nodded ruefully. "So many times I lost count."

Her laugh was little more than a sob. "Thank you, Liebling. It made me so happy. Over there love means so much. No one can ever know how much."

He had never seen her like this before. Since they had made love her armour of self-discipline seemed to have fallen away and for the moment she was as vulnerable as any other woman. He thought about the loneliness of the agent, the ever-present threat of the Gestapo, and his face hardened.

"You're not going back to that hell. Do you hear me? Never again."

A faint line appeared on her smooth forehead. "Please. You must not talk like that."

"I mean it. I'm going to tell Davies and Simms. You've already done more than they've a right to ask."

Her gaze moved over his aggressive face. "Is this what love does to us, Frank? Makes life so precious that we do not want to lose it?"

"Isn't that how it should be? Isn't life precious?"

For a moment she pressed against him and her lips caressed him fiercely. "Oh, yes, Liebling. Life is wonderful. Life is a gift from God."

"Then don't take any more risks with yours," he pleaded. "Promise me."

Her quiet protest silenced him. "No more, Frank, please. For once we have tomorrow and the day after that. All I want tonight is to feel you beside me and to pretend the world is a million miles away."

8

Davies fidgeted and turned. "He's late, isn't he?"

The Signals Officer, a plump, balding soldier, made the mistake of prevaricating with the small Air Commodore. "Only a couple of minutes, sir."

"*Only* a couple of minutes! Christ, we aren't that late when we bomb Berlin. Get him on the blower and tell him to get his finger out!"

Giving Davies a glance, the Army major walked towards a Signals van that stood at one side of the large field. Davies turned resentfully towards Moore, Henderson and Adams who were chatting a few yards away. "If he isn't here soon,

the sun's going to be down behind those clouds and we might
have to call the whole thing off."

The clouds were heavy banks of nimbus lying over the
Welsh mountains to the west. Davies had spotted them on
his arrival and had been eyeing them uneasily ever since. His
camouflaged staff car, along with his Waaf driver, was parked
in a nearby lane behind a row of larches where a mixed
company of soldiers and Royal Engineers were patrolling the
perimeter of the field to keep any curious sightseers away.
The small party had left Sutton Craddock before lunch but
with many of the signposts still missing from the Pennine
roads, the driver had lost herself twice and they had arrived
sixty minutes late, forcing a postponement of the demonstration. The stout Army major, provided for the occasion by
Special Operations Executive, was thinking Davies had a
nerve to complain but guilt carries its own inequity as Davies'
expression showed. Seeing a twinkle in Moore's eyes, Davies
was about to compound his misdemeanor when better judgment prevailed and he turned his irritation back to its original
source.

"Bloody stupid, not putting those signposts back. They
don't still think Jerry's going to invade, do they? Anyway,
why did they have to pick a field this far away? There're fields
in Yorkshire, aren't there?"

Although no one said so, the unusual size of the grassy
field that stretched ahead was an answer in itself. With the
grass recently cut, parallel rows of white marking tapes could
be seen winding their curious way from distant hedge to
hedge. Two-thirds of the way along it and perhaps 200 yards
from the western end of the field, the transporters carrying
the high screens were already in place. Back to back, they
appeared to be about sixty feet apart.

But all the eyes of Davies' small party were fixed on a third
lorry parked halfway down the field and as yet well to the
side of the tapes. It was carrying an inflated barrage balloon
that was winched tightly down. With the evening breeze
tugging at the bag, it looked like some monstrous leech that
had just gorged itself. Squatting on the flat top of the transport beneath it, surrounded by gas cylinders, half a dozen
uniformed men were awaiting their instructions.

The distant hum of engines made all four men turn.

Squinting through his binoculars, Davies saw an aircraft sweeping over a hill range to the east. As he recognized the high tail fin and out-thrust engines of a Mosquito, he gave a grunt of relief and started towards the Signals van. "Let's get started before the light goes."

The three RAF officers followed him curiously. Alongside the van, with a microphone in his hand, the Signals Officer was giving the pilot instructions. As the Mosquito swept over the field and went into a climbing turn, Davies handed his binoculars to Moore. "Take a look at his wings."

Obeying, Moore could see both leading edges were reinforced by overlapping strips of metal from which clawlike levers protruded. "See the special cable cutters?" Davies asked.

Moore nodded. Henderson, as intensely curious as Adams alongside him, took the binoculars from Moore and focussed them. He gave a grunt of scorn. "Someone was drunk when he thought this lot up, sir. To start with, those wing reinforcements must take thirty knots from her speed."

"Fifteen knots," Davies told him. "Not that much when you think of the extra safety those cable cutters give her."

"If they work," the Scot grunted.

"They do work. They've been tested a dozen times. I've been assured of that."

Henderson remained sceptical. "For that poor devil's sake, I hope so, sir. Because the standard ones aren't that efficient."

The mechanism the two men were discussing was a device fixed in the leading edge of aircraft wings as a protection against barrage balloons. It consisted of a trip lever and anvil which protruded a few inches in front of the wing. Inside the wing was a cartridge and steel chisel. In theory, when a balloon cable struck a wing and slid along it towards the nearest propeller, it tripped the lever. In turn this exploded the cartridge and drove the chisel against the anvil, hopefully severing the cable en route.

Reports of the device's efficiency varied from crew to crew. Some swore its only success was registered against the fingers of unfortunate rookies who inserted them curiously into its mysterious slit. Hence, the wits declared, the universal expression of 'Get your finger out!'

"This cutter packs a much bigger punch," Davies said. "The trip lever is longer and the cartridge nearly twice the size."

Henderson looked far from reassured. "All the same, sir, it's a bloody dangerous business and I hope my boys aren't asked to try it."

Davies was keeping his patience well. "I've already told you; we're just playing the options at the moment. We'll decide what's possible and what isn't later."

Worried by the implications of all he was seeing, the Scot did not mince his words. "In my opinion, sir, the best way to handle balloons is to keep out of their way. But if they have to go, then why not shoot 'em down? It's a damn sight safer."

Davies' temper snapped at last. "Because they can be dangerous to shoot down. For Christ's sake, Jock, will you stop nattering and watch that Mossie?"

A couple of miles away the Mosquito was orbiting over the hill ridge as its pilot studied the layout of the field. Hearing a metallic voice in the Signal Officer's earphones, Davies turned towards him. "You finished yet, major?"

The man gave him a look of resignation. "What do you want, sir?"

"I want my Squadron Commander to be in direct touch with the pilot in case he has any questions to ask. And while you're about it, turn on the loudspeaker so the rest of us can hear."

Sighing, the major handed the microphone to Moore. "The pilot's call sign is Swallow, ours is Horsefly, and the target is Bookends."

Thanking him, Moore addressed the pilot. "Hello, Swallow. This is Horsefly. I'm Wing Commander Moore."

A breezy English voice answered him. "Hello, sir. Welcome to the Palladium."

Moore smiled. "Have you done this before?"

"Half a dozen times at Farnborough. But not here. So it might be an idea to keep your heads down."

For the moment Moore had lost sight of the Mosquito. "Where are you now?"

"At the far side of the hill. I'll be with you in thirty seconds."

"What approach speed do you use?"

"320 knots. Height, thirty feet." The breezy voice changed in tone. "Swallow called Bookends. What is your width?"

A new voice entered the channel. "Hello, Swallow. Our width is sixty-three feet. Ready when you are."

At the far end of the field Moore could see men jumping down from the two transporters and retiring a discreet distance away. The breezy voice returned. "You hear that, Wing Commander? That gives me three feet on either wingtip."

"Is that enough?"

"Yes, sir. I'll have no trouble at all."

"How does she handle with those reinforced wings?"

"She's a little bit sluggish, sir. But not bad considering."

The Mosquito was back in sight now and diving down the wooded slopes of the hill. Flattening out at low level, it approached the field at speed. Leaping like a giant cat over a distant line of trees, it flattened down between the parallel tapes. Dipping its wings from side to side as it followed their winding course, it swept past the watching men with a roar and headed straight for the transporters. With the screens looking solid and the gap impossibly narrow, men found themselves holding their breath. For a split second the Mosquito seemed to fill the entire gap but then, like a dog leaping through a hoop, it was through and going into a climbing turn. Before anyone could speak, the loudspeaker crackled again. "You see, sir. It's really a piece of cake. You could take another foot from either side and there'd still be no problem."

The Signals Officer was holding out his hand to Moore. "May I take over for a moment, Wing Commander?"

As Moore stood back, the loudspeaker sounded again. "Horsefly to Seaslug. It's your turn now. As quickly as you can."

A shout was heard and the engine of the transporter carrying the barrage balloon fired. A moment later, with the obscene bag struggling to break free, the huge combination moved forward. Halfway between the tapes it halted and as another order was shouted the great bag began to climb into the evening sky. With Davies in mind, Henderson made certain his whisper to Adams was a stage one. "I'm sorry for that laddie up there. It's the craziest stunt I've ever seen."

Although Davies' scowl checked Adams' reply, the
Intelligence Officer was in full agreement. With the balloon's
steel cable blocking the Mosquito's flight path, almost any
technical fault could result in the pilot's death.

The balloon was anchored at 500 feet, well below its
operational height but enough for the demonstration. As the
crew evacuated the transporter and retired à safe distance
away, the Signals major handed his microphone back to Moore.

"Hello, Swallow. Horsefly here again. What's your next
move?"

"Much the same as before, sir, except just before I reach
the cable. Then I swing to port a few degrees before I come
back on track and go through the Bookends."

"Then you're taking the cable on your starboard wing?"

"That's right, sir. I always make love on my right side.
But if anyone has another preference, the old girl isn't a bit
fussy."

Alongside Moore, Davies did not know whether to grin
or frown. "He's a fresh young devil. Tell him to get on with it
before the sun goes down."

Smiling, Moore switched on the microphone again. "How
soon can you see the cable, Swallow?"

"That depends on one's eyesight, sir. First you have to
make a judgment on the balloon's position in relation to the
transporter. That still leaves you a fair margin of error so you
have to move smartly when the cable comes into sight. I
suppose I've about four seconds to make the corrections."

Mouth dry, Adams glanced at Henderson. Before he
could speak, Moore's reply came over the loudspeaker. "All
right, Swallow. We're ready when you are. Good luck."

"Roger, sir. Here I come."

Diving down from the hills, the Mosquito came racing
towards the field again. As, rocking with speed, it flattened
down between the tapes, the watching men felt their muscles
tighten. From their vantage point the aircraft appeared to be
flying straight at the balloon cable but at the last moment it
skidded sharply to port. A split second later there was a
shower of sparks as the taut steel cable struck the reinforced
wing and slid towards the propeller. As the Mosquito momentarily flinched and Adams gave a gasp of fear, there was a dull
explosion and a loud twanging sound as the cable parted. The

upper half leapt after the balloon, the lower half fell to the ground where it whipped and coiled like an angry serpent. The Mosquito steadied, dived down a few feet, and flew cleanly between the two transporters.

There was a loud murmur of admiration from the relieved men. His voice hoarse, Henderson was unstinting in his praise. "That laddie deserves a medal. I never thought a Mossie's wing would take the strain."

Davies, his temper restored by the successful demonstration, gave him a grin. "What did I tell you, Jock? It works."

"It worked this time, sir. But what if the cable cutter's cartridge hadn't fired?"

"What if the kite's tail had fallen off?" Davies retorted impatiently. "Come on, Jock. Admit it isn't as dangerous as it looks."

Afraid of the consequences if he did, Henderson was doing no such thing. "One swallow doesn't make a summer, sir. That's a hellishly dangerous stunt."

About to argue, Davies gave a frown instead. "Forget about the balloon for the moment and concentrate on the bookends. You heard what that young pilot said and I doubt if he's half as experienced as most of your boys. Once they realize the screens can't hurt them, they'll sail through them without any trouble at all."

Although Henderson looked anything but reassured, he knew he had carried his protests to the limit. "When are they to start? After their low-level training?"

"They can fit in both at the same time. One flight can be out on low-level while the other practices on the bookends. They won't need to come down here. I'm arranging for the transporters to drive up to Sutton Craddock tonight, so you'll be practicing on your own cabbage patch."

All three men showed surprise. Moore's good-looking face wore a whimsical expression as he glanced at Adams. "That's going to start some wild rumours among the 'erks.' Are we to use tapes too?"

Davies nooded. "A gang of Royal Engineers will be coming along with the transporters. They'll set out a course as similar to this one as possible."

Gazing across the field, Henderson was no longer listen-

ing. The balloon, fitted with an exhaust valve that operated
when the cable was cut, was already deflating and sinking
down. On the field soldiers were unpegging and rolling up
the mysterious marker tapes. With the sun setting behind the
clouds and a grey mist beginning to rise, the Scot could not
shake off a sense of foreboding. Sighing, he turned towards
Davies. "Can't you give us some idea what all this is for,
sir?"

The briskness of Davies' tone was a refusal in itself. "Not
a chance, Jock. The stakes are too high. But I'll promise you
one thing. You'll be told everything in good time. Now let's
start moving." The small Air Commodore's wry glance towards
his staff car was intended to lighten the Scot's mood. "If that
girl of mine loses her way again, it could be a long hungry
night."

9

The door of Millburn's billet burst open with a crash,
letting in the morning sunlight. Still in bed, the American
opened one bloodshot eye. Framed in the bright doorway he
could see a small figure gesticulating excitedly. "Millburn!
Have you seen what's out on the field?"

Millburn let out a groan. "Go away."

Gabby advanced to his bedside. "Davies must have had
them sent. Something big's coming up."

Millburn squinted painfully up at him. "I said go away."

"But you must see these things. It's like Fred Carno's
circus. Everybody's out there."

Forgetting his condition Millburn sat up with a jerk,
only to let a gleeful demon drive a pickaxe into his head. "So
Fred Carno's circus is here. Who cares? If you don't get out
of here, you little sonofabitch, I'll tear your arms and legs

off." With his dire threat made, the American dropped back on his pillow again.

Gabby eyed him contemptuously. "What happened to you last night? You were so pissed I had to put you to bed. Wouldn't she give it to you?"

Millburn's eyes were already closed. Gabby prodded his arm maliciously. "You're a Flight Commander now. That means you're supposed to set an example, like getting up before the rest of us. And finding out what those transporters are for and why they've got those big screens fitted."

Millburn opened an eye again. "Transporters? Screens? What are you talking about?"

Gabby explained in more detail. By this time the American was fully awake. "Doesn't anyone know what they're for?"

"No one seems to."

"Did Davies come back with Moore and Henderson?"

"Yes. He was in the mess for breakfast. Something big's coming up, boyo. Everything points to it."

With a groan Millburn swung his legs out of bed. "All right, I'll come and take a look. Have a cup of coffee sent to me, will you? As black as it comes."

The American and the Welshman were not the only ones speculating on the purpose of the transporters. With airmen of all ranks celebrating the stand-down the previous evening, men had slept soundly when finally abed and it had been only the skeleton staff who had witnessed the massive vehicles edge through the station gates and trundle to the far end of the airfield. By this time, however, the word had gone round and dishevelled airmen, many suffering hangovers, were stumbling from their billets to gaze in astonishment at the freakish contraptions. With Davies present on the station, speculation was intense and to hide their concern, aircrews were venturing suggestions that ranged from the absurd to the ridiculous.

A number of them were congregated on the tarmac apron that separated the two hangars. Larkin, the stringy New Zealander, gave Van Breedenkamp a sardonic grin. "There's only one thing those screens can be for, sport. Phyllis Dixey's sending some of her girls to do a fan dance for us."

Gabby, who had run out again after waking up Millburn, overheard him. "If you're right, we're not going to see much. They're bloody big fans."

Larkin grinned at him. "They're bloody big girls. At least the ones I saw last week were."

A rich West Indian voice checked the laughter. "Stan" Baldwin, ex-Barbados lawyer and the only black man on the station, had a voice to match his big body and cheerful face. "You've got it all wrong, man. They're our secret weapon for the invasion. That's why we're practising low flying. They go ahead of us and nobody can see us coming."

"What are we going to attack?" someone shouted.

Baldwin's big grin spread. "Man, that's easy. First we hang Gabby's dirty socks and underpants on the Siegfried line. Then we drop the lot on Hitler's head. He yells for mercy and the war's over."

While all this banter and more serious speculation was in progress, Davies was having a last word with Moore in the CO's office. Behind him, Henderson was suppressing a yawn. It had been well after midnight before they had arrived back at the station and another hour had passed before Henderson had gotten to bed. To his dismay the irrepressible Davies had been up again at 0430 to supervise the positioning of the transporters.

"To recap, Ian, your men have the rest of the day off. Around 1600 hours the Yanks will be flying in transport for tonight's party. But tomorrow the serious training starts. You'll use your full complement and put 'em into two flights. You'll lead one, your senior Flight Commander the other. Give the boys plenty of latitude on their first run, fifteen feet on either side if you feel they need it. Then start closing the gap. As the transporter crews are linked to you with R/T, you shouldn't have any communication problems."

Moore nodded. "How long do you want the exercise to go on, sir?"

"You keep it up until your boys emulate the pilot down in Herefordshire," Davies told him.

Henderson gave a start. "That gap was only sixty-three feet, sir. Three feet from either wingtip."

"I know that, Jock. I can count too." As Henderson turned pink at the rebuff, Davies glanced back at Moore, whose good-looking face was expressionless. "With the experience your boys have, they should reach it quickly. Then we'll move on to the next phase of their training."

About to ask what new horrors lay ahead, Henderson caught Adams' warning glance and checked himself. "Are you going to the party tonight, sir?" he asked instead.

From his grunt it was clear Davies had been having second thoughts about the party. "I haven't much option. Staines feels we made him a promise and he's keeping me to it. But tell your boys to go steady on the drinks. I don't want half of them unserviceable tomorrow." He picked up his cap. "I'm off now to High Elms. I'll see you around 1530."

If any of the others had had the slightest doubt that something of importance was in the offing, the Air Commodore's remark would have killed it. When Davies visited the northern headquarters of Special Operations Executive, a special mission was guaranteed. As his spry footsteps echoed down the corridor, Henderson gave a groan. "63 feet. And more training to follow. What the hell has he got lined up for us?"

When no one answered, the Scot gazed resentfully at Adams. "You're our Intelligence Officer, Frank. Haven't you any ideas?"

Adams shook his head. "I was up half the night thinking about it. I suppose it must have something to do with the invasion but I can't think what."

Henderson scowled. "It can't be submarine pens or they'd be giving us prows to bash our way out of the other end." He moved irritably towards the door. "Let's go and take another look at those transporter screens. I'm still not satisfied they're safe."

If the personnel of 633 Squadron were puzzled about the role they were being asked to play, things were becoming clearer to the millions of British and American servicemen who were to take part in the invasion. With their preliminary training over, infantrymen were now going out in landing craft to 'invade' specially prepared beaches. Seasick, drenched in icy water, men were finding themselves trapped in coils of barbed wire while explosions hurled gravel over them and live ammunition screamed over their heads. With fatal acci-

dents a daily occurrence, the din and danger seemed realistic
enough but the battle-seasoned Commandos who devised the
exercises knew differently. The sound of war was present but
not its hellish slaughter.

The American and British navies were also in full training. One of their many roles on D-Day would be to ferry
across the English Channel the massive artificial harbours
known as Mulberries without which the entire operation
might fail. These complex structures, which had been under
construction for many months, were an enormous engineering feat. Basically they consisted of 146 huge caissons named
Phoenixes, ranging in size and weight from 1,672 tons to 60
giants of 6,044 tons. In all, 600,000 tons of concrete, 31,000
tons of steel, and 1,500 yards of steel shuttering had been
used in their construction. Built to float in rough seas but also
to sink in no less than 22 minutes, each Phoenix was provided
with a crew's quarters, two Bofors guns, and 20 tons of
ammunition. Built in huge excavations near the Thames,
their purpose had baffled every German reconnaissance aircraft lucky enough to penetrate the island's defences. When
dragged to preplanned positions off the Normandy coast, they
would be sunk and provide a base for elaborate causeways
which would facilitate the landing of trucks and tanks. To give
further protection from the sea, 70 old battleships were to be
sunk with them.

The Allied Air Forces were also at full stretch during
these preinvasion weeks, bombing V-1 rocket sites along the
French coast, attacking radar installations to 'blind' the Germans when the Allied ships sailed, and training to ferry over
to Normandy 20,000 airborne and glider troops who were to
be dropped behind the beachhead in the darkness before the
main assault began. Selected squadrons, using aluminum foil,
were also practicing highly complicated manoeuvres which
would be used on D-Day in an attempt to make the German
radar operators in the Pas de Calais area believe a massive
fleet of ships was advancing towards them.

To a keen observer, however, one thing was significant.
In spite of the many calls on them during those feverish days,
the Allied Air Forces were still hammering at the German
transport and communication systems. With all the staggering energy and ingenuity that was going into the invasion

effort, it remained clear that Eisenhower and his staff still
believed that its ultimate fate might rest on the success or
failure of the Germans to get their heavy Panzer divisions
first to the beachheads.

—————————— **10** ——————————

When Harvey arrived back at the station a few minutes
before noon the initial furore had died although speculation
was still rife. Catching sight of the transporters he changed
course and entered Adams' Nissen hut.

He could still smell cordite as he made his way towards
the Intelligence Officer's desk. With all its windows blown out
during the recent German air raid, the Confessional had
survived by a small miracle but most of its many maps, books
and pamphlets were still impregnated by smoke. Adams,
poring over the latest Intelligence reports, laid down his pipe
as the Yorkshireman approached. "Hello, Frank. What can I
do for you?"

Nodding at Adams' assistant, the slim and attractive Sue
Spencer, Harvey draped a leg over the desk. "What the hell's
going on? What are those contraptions down at the bottom of
the field?"

When Adams explained their purpose, Harvey stared at
him. "Fly between them. What for?"

"No one knows. But the exercises begin tomorrow. One
flight to work on the screens and the other to go out on
low-level practice." Adams made a wry face. "It's going to be
bedlam with kites flying fifty feet and less over the airfield."

A thought seemed to strike Harvey. Recovering, he put
a finger to his temple and screwed it around. "Maybe Davies
is losing his marbles. The keen type usually do sooner or
later."

Adams smiled. "I doubt that. He seemed pretty sharp last night."

"What happened last night?"

Uncertain whether he should talk about it, Adams played safe. "I'm sure Ian will tell you everything at the briefing. In the meantime it might be a good idea to talk to your reserve crews. Davies wants everyone to take part in these exercises."

As Harvey studied him, Adams expected one of his sarcastic comments. Instead the Yorkshireman shrugged. "I get it. Another of Davies' hush-hush jobs. I hope he doesn't intend to throw my rookies in at the deep end. He has a nasty habit of doing that."

Adams thought it wise to change the subject. "Intelligence has just sent me a revised list of enemy flak posts. Can I see you about them some time?"

"Why not now? I'm free until lunch."

Adams hesitated. "Give me fifteen minutes and I'll be ready for you. If you like, I'll bring the list to your office."

"Fine." Harvey paused. "Are you going to the party tonight?"

"I think so. We don't want to upset Staines. You'll be coming, won't you?"

"Me? I've better things to do than drink with a bunch of crazy kids. What time do the exercises begin tomorrow?"

"0900 hours."

Harvey grinned. "0900 hours? The lads won't get their eyes pried open before lunchtime. Not if the Yanks push the boat out as they usually do."

Adams smiled back. "I thought it was a bit ambitious myself."

"I'm telling you: Davies is losing his way. Still, I suppose flying through hoops is better than flying through Hunland." The Yorkshireman turned his grin on Sue Spencer. "Remind me to bounce my wheels on your roof when I come over."

As he strode out, the couple could hear him whistling. Adams turned to the girl in astonishment. "What's happened to him?"

She laughed. "It's very simple. He's met a girl."

Adams gave a grimace of disgust. "Trust a woman to think that. No; he's got it too bad for Anna Reinhardt. He's not the sort who'd fall for anyone else while she's in danger over there."

He could see she was not convinced. "Something's changed him. It stands out a mile."

Adams returned to his study of the enemy flak posts. "I know one thing. No one deserves it more."

Adams was about to enter Harvey's Flight Office when he saw the Yorkshireman was talking to two young fliers. Harvey waved him forward as he hesitated. "Come and sit down, Frank. I won't be long."

Adams dropped into a chair beside the Yorkshireman's desk. The two young men standing before it looked no older than sixth-form schoolboys. The pilot, who still had a trace of acne, had brushed-back hair and a somewhat pinched face. His navigator was more sturdily built with a complexion a girl would have envied. Neither could hide his excitement as Harvey turned back to them.

"Remember, you two. Go steady on the drink tonight. If you're coming out with me tomorrow, you're going to need your wits about you. Understand?"

Sugden, the pilot, nodded eagerly. Like his navigator, MacAllister, he had a regional accent. "Yes, sir. What are the screens for, sir? Can you tell us?"

Although the Yorkshireman gave his famous scowl, the watching Adams felt it was from habit rather than intent. "Don't ask questions and you'll get no lies, Sugden. Just do as you're told and everything will sort itself out."

The young men's eyes were bright with excitement as they glanced at one another. "Does it mean we might be going into action, sir?" MacAllister asked.

Adams was thinking of two teenagers just hearing they had been picked for the school's first team as Harvey gave a reluctant nod. "I'm not sure. But it's just possible."

There was a chorus of delight. "Thank you, sir."

This time Adams knew the Yorkshireman's scowl was genuine. "Don't thank me. If I had my way you'd still be doing circuits and bumps. Now remember—watch the drinking and skylarking tonight. Off you go."

The youngsters saluted, then almost ran out of the office. The door had barely closed before their shouts of excitement could be heard. Adams sighed. "They still think it's a game of cricket, don't they?"

Harvey was lighting a cigarette. His voice was full of distaste. "I liked it better in the old days."

Adams knew what he meant. Until recently, replacements had been volunteers from front-line squadrons who had been attracted by either the fame of the unit or its special service role. Not all of these had been accepted by Moore: the obvious glamour seekers had been shown the back door. But those he had retained had been battle-seasoned men, some with an entire tour of thirty operations to their name.

In early 1944 this supply had begun to dry up. Frontline squadron commanders, resentful at losing their best men, had started to rebel and put up barriers. Also, as 633 Squadron's fame had spread, so had the statistics of its casualties and it was now widely believed to be a suicide unit. A third reason was the massive ground attacks the Air Forces were mounting on France and Germany. At low level an experienced man was as vulnerable to ground fire as a recruit and so casualties were thinning out replacements.

As a consequence 633 Squadron was having more and more to train its crews straight from the Operation Training Units, a situation none of the flight commanders liked because statistics showed that only one in two novice crews survived their first operational flight. After that their survival chances improved but only agonizingly slowly.

Adams suddenly noticed Harvey's eyes were on him. "What do you think of those two kids?"

Taken by surprise, Adams hesitated. "They both seem good types. Why?"

Harvey made a gesture of disgust. "They've seen too many films. You know what young Sugden asked me on his first day here? Did we stop firing at Jerry if his guns jammed? That's how they see war. Chivalry, uniforms, and girls. Nice glamorous wounds in the arms and legs. No 20mm shells up the arse. No guts sliding out or fire burning a man's face off."

Adams was not deceived. It was always Harvey's way to disguise his feelings and although the Yorkshireman was a faithful guardian to all his men, Adams had a strong suspicion that Sugden and MacAllister had a special place in his heart. The answer was not difficult to find. Like Harvey, both men were products of the Depression. Both had dragged themselves up by their bootlaces to reach a standard of education that had allowed them to receive aircrew training.

At the same time Adams was careful not to let Harvey know his suspicions. "I'm sure you're right. Films like *Hell's Angels* and *Dawn Patrol* must have affected all our thinking. They certainly did mine. I'm not sure they still don't when I hear engines starting up at dawn."

He saw Harvey staring at him. Realizing how he was giving himself away, Adams went on hastily: "They're making more of those films than ever. Bands playing when the troops go off to war and girls kissing them when they come back. I suppose it's necessary for propaganda but it must make it hell for men when they come up against the real thing."

Harvey's grunt expressed his disgust. "Death to soft music! It's a bloody crime. They should have told the truth straight after the last war but I suppose there wasn't any money in it."

Adams was a man always ready for philosophical discussion. "When you come to think of it, it's an interesting theme. It makes you wonder how much the rest of our thinking is conditioned by the films we've seen. Happy endings and that kind of thing. After all, films are mass entertainment and most of us used to go a couple of times a week, particularly as children."

Harvey was about to say that if anyone could afford to go twice a week to the cinema, he deserved to have his thinking conditioned. Instead he motioned to the map and literature Adams was carrying. "Let's take a look at those new flak posts. I'll see my other two rookies this afternoon."

11

The young glassy-eyed pilot stumbled into Moore. Recognizing him, his flushed face brightened. "Hello, skipper. How're y' doing?"

"I'm doing fine, Sugden. How are you doing?"

"Great, skipper. Just great." The youngster gave a belch. "These Yanks throw a hell of a party, don't they, skipper?"

Moore smiled at the stocky Air Force major standing beside him at the bar. "They do, Sugden. What are you looking for? A drink?"

"In a minute, skipper. Gotta have a leak first. You know where to go?"

The American major took the pilot by the shoulders and gently steered him around. "You see that door over there? That'll take you straight to the john."

Sugden peered through the fog of cigarette smoke and packed airmen. "Which door, sir?"

Dent winked at Moore. "Try the one in the middle and you'll be OK."

Muttering his thanks, the young pilot began weaving his way through the ranks of chattering airmen. Moore shook his head ruefully. "It's going to be fun and games getting them all back. They'll be paralytic by the morning."

"Don't let that worry you," Dent told him. "We're keeping three Mitchell crews on ice. And we've plenty of labour to pack your stiffs in. You'll be OK."

Alan Dent was a New Yorker, a brown-haired man with a good sense of humour. A couple of years older than most of the pilots he commanded, he had provided escort to 633 Squadron when they had broken up Hitler's birthday celebrations in Copenhagen the previous month. He and his men had also saved Moore's life when the Englishman's crippled Mosquito had been attacked by Focke-Wulfs during the events leading up to the Operation Cobra affair. It was because the British and American crews had never met in person that Staines had leaned on Davies to agree to a party.

It had commenced just after 1600 hours when five Mitchells had landed at Sutton Craddock to pick up all 633 Squadron's aircrews and any senior officer who could be spared. From there the Mitchells had flown to Staines' main base in Suffolk where the big Texan and his executive officers had been waiting to welcome their guests. From that moment on it was a night no one was likely to forget.

First had come a dinner of a lavishness that the British, used to meagre rations, had found mind-boggling. With wine flowing freely, the loyal toasts to the President and the Queen had been followed by Staines congratulating the Mosquito squadron on its successful Cobra mission and Davies thanking the wing of Mustangs for its support. With the formal duties completed, festivities had begun in earnest.

First the crews had been entertained by a comedian and three of Phyllis Dixey's striptease girls, brought up specially from the Windmill Theatre that afternoon. Then, after the howls, cheers, and wolf whistles had died away, the serious business of the night had begun. In the huge mess, British and American crews intermingled while sweating waiters hurried back and forth with drinks.

Not all had been sweet harmony at first. With aircrews trained to be aggressive, with chauvinistic rivalry between military units almost a part of wartime life, and with alcohol washing away restraint, fierce arguments had broken out here and there. One of Millburn's pilots, a quarrelsome man named Eric Miller, had almost come to blows with a Mustang pilot and had to be forcibly restrained. Paddy Machin, Baldwin's pilot, had had a fracas with a B-17 navigator over who should buy one of Phyllis Dixey's girls a drink, although the girl had defused the situation by marching off with a handsome B-17 captain, to the chagrin of both men. On a less serious level, a grinning Millburn had found Gabby needing help when the Welshman, an inebriated gnome, had begun lecturing three American pilots on the inadequacy of the B-17's bomb load, oblivious of the fact they were all B-17 crewmen.

At the same time, it had not taken the crews long to realize that beneath their different uniforms they shared the same hopes and fears and by the time Sugden was making his uncertain way towards the toilet, fraternization was in full swing and the din was assaulting the senses. In one corner of the hall a mixed party of airmen and a few local girls were clustered around a piano singing the latest popular songs. Henderson, Adams, and Sue Spencer were among them. The big Scot, with whisky available at the nod of the head, was clearly enjoying himself and Adams, usually a light drinker but now pink-cheeked, was singing his head off. In the centre of the floor four Mustang pilots were doing a barbershop rendering of 'The Whiffenpoof Song' with Mosquito crews cheering every maudlin line. At the long bar a swarm of airmen were crowded around the Windmill girls and at the far end of the room fraternization had reached its apogee: a team of Britons was taking on a team of Americans at their own version of football. Presiding over all this mayhem and bedlam was the massive figure of Staines. Surrounded by half a dozen of his executive officers, beaming and expansive, he was clearly revelling in the mad antics going on around him.

Davies was a member of this group. Catching sight of him and knowing Dent had been warned that a major operation was in the offing, Moore turned towards the American. "Look at Davies' expression. He's trying to work out how Staines talked him into having this party at a time like this."

Dent grinned. "Yeah. Old Scratchy can be very persuasive."

"Is that what you call him—Old Scratchy?"

"That or Thunderass. It depends on the circumstances. He can put the boot in hard when he feels like it." Glancing around him, Dent realized the very bedlam was security in itself. "What's going on, Ian? Have you any idea?"

Moore shook his head. "No. I can't even make an educated guess. But if you've been tipped off about it, it must be another joint operation."

"Yeah, that's about the only certain thing. Old Scratchy's playing it so close to his chest he's rubbing the pips off." Dent's voice turned whimsical as he nodded at the revelry around him. "Let's just hope this isn't the dinner they give condemned men before they lead them to the rope."

Across the room Millburn had just pulled Gabby away from another argument with a massive American navigator. "What's the matter with you tonight, you little slob?" he hissed. "These guys are buying our drinks, remember?"

A fire-eater when in his cups, Gabby glared at the American navigator who was standing facing him with arms akimbo. "He called me a limey. Didn't you hear him?"

Millburn grinned at the American. "So what? You are a limey."

Gabby struggled to break free. "Let me go, Millburn. I can take him."

"Take him?" A sarcastic Cockney voice sounded above the din. "You couldn't take your own grandmother. You're as pissed as a fart."

Forgetting the American, Gabby swung around on the grinning Hopkinson. "Who's pissed, you Cockney pillock?"

"You are. You couldn't walk across the Forth Bridge without falling off."

With Gabby proud of his equilibrium, no statement could have been more provocative, as Hopkinson well knew. "What about that church tower near Cromer? I walked that in a Force Seven wind, didn't I? And what about the gun butt wall? Did I walk it or didn't I?"

"No, you fell off it,' Hopkinson told him. "Arse over tip."

Provoked, Gabby scowled. "You want a bet, Hopkinson."

"What on? You making the pisshouse without falling over?"

Men were grinning and crowded closer as Gabby glared at the Cockney. Then a triumphant smile lit up his face. "What about those cross members in the B-17 hangar?"

Even Hopkinson gave a start at this. Shortly after their arrival the Mosquito crews had paid a visit to one of the hangars in which the B-17s were serviced and had been impressed by their height and size. "Don't talk sludge. Those girders are fifty feet high. Maybe more."

"So what. The Cromer tower was a hundred." Aware he now held the initiative, Gabby gave a malicious smile. "You're all wind and water, Hopkinson. Put your money down and I'll walk from one side to the other."

About to reach into his pocket, Hopkinson saw Millburn

shake his head and withdrew his hand. "You're drunk. Go and put your head in a fire bucket."

Before Gabby could jeer at the Cockney, Miller pushed in front of him. Eyes suffused with drink, the pilot waved a note in his face. "I'll take you on. Five quid to say you can't."

As cheers and shouts came from the onlookers, the big American B-17 navigator drew out a fistful of notes. "I say you're all talk too, limey. Here's my dough to prove it."

Gabby could have had no greater incentive. Gazing around, he located Henderson near the piano and Davies talking to one of Staines' officers at the far end of the bar. "Go out one by one," he told his audience. "Or they'll twig there's something on."

The huge American grinned at a colleague. "This I gotta see. Let's go."

Gabby was making for a nearby door when Millburn grabbed his arm. "Hold it! You're my navigator, remember? That means you don't break your neck until I say so."

Catcalls and shouts rose from the onlookers. Gabby's scowl was withering. "What's come over you, mush? Has that promotion gone to your head?"

Aware he had once been one of the Welshman's worst provocateurs, Millburn hesitated. It proved fatal as the jeers grew around him. "All right. But only on one condition. I want a parachute for the stupid sonofabitch to fall into."

One of the Americans nodded and pushed away. Miller, with a look of anticipation on his flushed face, followed him. The rest of the grinning men left the mess one by one and regrouped in the first of the hangars. A B-17 with two stripped-down engines stood inside it. Mechanics, working with portable electric lamps, gazed in astonishment at the laughing, jostling crowd of British and American aircrews.

Although the main hangar lights were switched on, the roof was a shadowy tangle of steel girders. As men peered upward, someone gave a whistle. "For Chrissake, how's the guy going to get up there?"

Gabby had already solved that problem, obtaining a rope from one of the mechanics. With the big American lending a hand, it was finally thrown over a cross member and anchored to a stationary tractor. As mechanics left the B-17 to join the excited onlookers, Gabby seized the rope and grinned at Millburn. "All right, mush?"

Millburn, who had sobered up on seeing the height of the roof, was bitterly regretting his decision. "Wait, you crazy little bastard. I want that parachute first."

Miller and an American pilot pushed through the crowd, the latter carrying a parachute pack. Taking it from him, Miller jerked on the ripcord, releasing the canopy. Shouting and laughing, men grabbed its scalloped edges and stretched it out until it made a huge safety net. About to warn Gabby to take care, Millburn heard a cheer and saw that the Welshman was already halfway up the rope. A dismayed American voice brought a roar of laughter. "This isn't no fair bet. The guy's a goddamned monkey."

With Gabby already past the nearest roof light, dazzled men were having difficulty following his progress. A mechanic switched off the light and two portable lamps were focussed on the Welshman. By this time he had reached the transverse girder and was sitting straddle-legged across it. His voice echoed down. "Ok. I'm ready."

Millburn cast an anxious glance at the circle of men gripping the safety net. "Watch it, you guys. Keep right beneath him."

A hush fell as Gabby rose slowly to his feet. Arms outstretched he began to edge forward. As the ring of breathless men stared upwards, someone cursed. "You hear that, you guys? He's singing."

Hopkinson turned on the man with a grin. "Of course he's singing. He's Welsh, isn't he?"

It was no surprise to any of the Mosquito crews. With his need for excitement always stimulated by alcohol, Gabby seldom failed to sing during his madcap stunts. His chant, slightly off-key, echoed eerily down. "This is my story, this is my song. I've been in this Air Force too flaming long. . . ."

The chant broke as the small figure swayed precariously. Gritting his teeth, Millburn waited until the moment of danger was past, then gave a yell of frustration. "Shut up, you little moron, and watch what you're doing."

Ignoring him, Gabby began singing again. "So roll out the Nelson, the Rodney, Renown. They can't sink the Hood 'cos the bastard's gone down. . . ."

By this time the Welshman was approaching the centre of the huge hangar. Spotlighted by the two lamps, he looked like a fly trying to crawl across a shadowy web of steel. Urging the men carrying the safety net to keep beneath him, Millburn gave a start. Until now neither he nor the rest of the crews had noticed that the nose of the B17 extended beneath the girder the Welshman was traversing. Glancing up, Millburn gave an urgent shout. "Gabby, go back! We can't give you cover all the way."

Instead of sobering the Welshman, the excitement was increasing his recklessness. Ignoring Millburn, he kept edging forward until he was almost directly above the B-17. Below, Millburn was frantically pushing and shoving the laughing men towards the far side of the B-17 but they came to a halt as the canopy and its ropes snagged on the aircraft's port wheel. Calling for help from the rest of the onlookers, the sweating Millburn struggled to free the silk.

In the meanwhile Gabby had met his first obstacle, two diagonal cross-members bolted to the main transverse beam. Hoisting one leg over them and then the other, he paused a moment and grinned down at the B-17 and Millburn's struggling team. "Stop panicking, Millburn. This is a piece of cake."

Ignoring the curse that floated up to him, he started forward again, the B-17's fuselage some twenty feet below. But as he straightened, his luck ran out as his head struck one of the cross members. For a couple of seconds his arms waved wildly as he fought for balance. Then, with a yelp of dismay, he toppled down.

Below, Millburn had managed to free the canopy and was pushing his crew under the nose of the B-17 and beneath its starboard wing. Hearing Gabby's yell he glanced up just in time to see the Welshman falling. Yelling a warning, he heard a metallic thud above that made him wince. It was followed by a second thud a moment later as Gabby bounced from the nacelle of the B-17 on to its starboard wing. From there he slid down and fell in a heap into the hastily tightened safety net.

Hurling men aside in his anxiety, Millburn bent over the Welshman's limp body. "How is it, kid? Is it bad?"

There was no answer. Seeing the Welshman's eyes were

closed, Millburn glanced up at the hushed onlookers. "Don't just stand there! Someone get a doctor."

Before anyone could move, Gabby's eyes opened. "What happened?"

"Are you in pain?" Millburn demanded.

"I'm not sure."

"What do you mean, you're not sure?" Seeing the Welshman was able to move his limbs, Millburn's concern turned into fury. "You crazy little moron. I ought to slap you straight in front of a court martial."

Grinning shamefacedly, Gabby tried to sit up. As he let out a howl of anguish, the American gave a start of suspicion. "Wait a minute. You haven't pulled this stunt to get yourself leave, have you?"

He received a glare of indignation. "What are you talking about, Millburn? I think I've broken my leg."

Millburn bent down suspiciously. "Which one?"

"The left one." Gabby let out another howl of pain as the American tried to straighten it. "What're you trying to do? I tell you it's broken."

Breathing hard, Millburn straightened. "This time you've really done it, haven't you? You know what it means if Henderson or Moore finds out. You'll go straight into the can."

Gabby frowned up at him. "You're not going to tell them, are you?"

"I ought to," Millburn said grimly. "By the Lord Harry I ought." He glanced round the ring of muttering men. "I hope you guys have got the picture. If our CO or any of our executive officers find out about this, we're all for the high drop. So your story is he was inspecting the B-17 when he slipped and fell out of the entry door. OK?"

As men nodded, Millburn turned to the huge American navigator. "Get me a doctor now, will you, buddy? He'll have to have that leg set."

12

Davies' face was a study. "Five?"

Having played no part in the decision to attend Staines' bacchanal, Henderson felt his nod of apology was something of a concession. "I'm afraid so, sir. Matthews, Larkin, Machin, Miller and Gabriel. Mind you, only one's serious. Gabriel fractured a leg falling out of a B-17."

"Pissed, of course."

"I can't say that for certain, sir."

"Of course he was pissed," Davies snapped. "Five bloody casualties. And the rest of 'em with heads like turnips. Christ, we've had fewer casualties after a ding-dong with the Jerries. How long's it going to be before they're airworthy?"

"The MO says they should all have recovered by the morning. Except Gabriel, of course."

Davies scowled. "If the MO's put 'em off duty today, I suppose there's nothing we can do. But I want the rest of them in the air this afternoon, hangover or not."

"Moore knows that, sir. They'll be airborne in time."

Davies was studying the Scot's face. "How are you feeling yourself?"

"I'm all right, sir."

"You don't look it. You look like a dog's dinner."

Henderson stiffened. "With respect, sir, you're a bit pale yourself this morning."

Davies frowned. "I am?"

"Yes, sir. Decidedly pale."

The small Air Commodore's frown suddenly turned into a shamefaced grin. "It was quite a party, wasn't it, Jock?"

Henderson relaxed. "Yes, sir. A hell of a party. To be honest, I'm feeling like death warmed over."

Davies dropped thankfully into a chair. "Then for God's sake send that girl of yours for some black coffee and aspirins. We can't face those young bastards looking worse than they do."

The afternoon that followed was one that Sutton Craddock's neighbours were long to remember, although it began uneventfully enough with Harvey's depleted flight taking off just after 1430 hours and heading north. With the Yorkshireman operating with two new crews, Moore had felt it was preferable to give them one day's low-level practice before confronting them with the transporters. The next day the flight order would be reversed.

This left Millburn's flight to tackle the forbidding-looking screens. Here Moore had resisted Davies' original plan to build a duplicate course to the one down in Herefordshire, demanding instead that on the first run the transporters should be a full ninety feet apart and that a single straight tape should guide aircraft through them. At first, Davies had resisted.

"That's killing the point, Ian. They must learn to fly through the gap without any assistance."

"I know that, sir. And they will later. But although you say those screens can't harm us, they look as if they can and that's what might cause problems and accidents. I want my boys to get their run up and height correct before they have to worry about collisions."

Davies had grumbled but finally agreed. "All right. Do it your way. Only for Christ's sake don't take all day about it."

The new preparations had not taken long. With the transporters already stationed at the southwest corner of the airfield to save the Mosquitoes from having to fly over the administration buildings and billets, Moore had a white marker tape laid from them to the water tower in the northeastern corner. He had then ordered the transporters to give him a gap of seventy feet. Although it was twenty feet less than he intended his crews to face, he felt they would face ninety feet with more confidence when they followed him. Telling Millburn and his men to stand by, he then took off and headed towards the water tower.

Coming in low with the water tower on his right side, he

settled down to thirty feet. Beside him the usually imperturbable Hopkinson was looking anxious. "You're sure those screens are safe, skipper?"

"You saw them yesterday, Hoppy. They're just lathes and canvas."

"Maybe they are. But at this speed couldn't they still swing us into the deck?"

Moore was too occupied to answer. Seeing the tape was running beneath his starboard engine he applied gentle rudder until it was dead in line with his bulletproof windshield. Because of A-Apple's high ground speed, the cropped summer grass looked flat and textureless beneath its racing propellers. For a second the north-south runway blurred past. Then the grass was back and the two transporters were filling the windshield.

With their huge canvas screens looking solid in the afternoon sunlight, Moore felt his muscles tighten. Seventy feet between them looked impossibly narrow. Fighting an impulse to draw back on the control column, he held the Mosquito steady and the screens flashed past on either side. Letting out his breath, he went into a climbing turn. Beside him Hopkinson was also showing his relief. "Not bad, skipper. Mind you, we weren't far off that right-hand screen."

Moore gave him a smile. "I'll try to do better next time, Hoppy." He lifted his face mask. "Squadron Commander to Bookends. You can make your gap ninety feet now."

As the transporters moved further apart, Millburn and two of his crews joined Moore orbiting over the airfield. Moore's instructions were deliberately casual. "All right, Tommy. Down you go. Keep the tape in your windshield and you'll have no problems."

As aware as Moore that the exercise was causing a certain nervousness among the crews, Millburn's reply was in the same vein. "It's a piece of cake, skipper. It's wide enough now to take a drunken Lancaster." Turning, the American grinned at his navigator. "I'd better not cock it up after that or I'll never hear the end of it."

It was a remark intended to break down barriers as much as reassure. With Gabby brought up from Suffolk by ambulance and now residing in the Highgate General Hospital, Millburn had been given a new navigator that morning, a

New Zealander named Dalton whose pilot had been taken sick a week ago. Although he had plenty of combat experience, Dalton was a shy young man who spent little time in the mess and appeared to have few close friends.

Diving down towards the water tower, Millburn latched on to the tape and sank down to a height of thirty feet. Ahead, the screens looked like solid towers destined to tear the wings off any aircraft that touched them. Concentrating hard, Millburn held the Mosquito steady and watched the screens flash past. As he began climbing, he glanced at Dalton again. Although the young man's face was slightly pale, he gave the American a smile. Millburn's nod was approving. "That wasn't too bad for a guy with a hangover, was it, kid?"

"No, sir. It was very good."

Millburn's tone changed. "O.K., Van Breedenkamp. Down you come."

With both the South African and Machin completing the course without incident, Millburn called up his next three crews. Wall had no trouble but Smith hit the right-hand screen and came climbing back into orbit with a six foot strip of canvas flapping from his outer rocket launcher. It meant a ten minute delay while the transporter crew repaired the damage but, with the men given evidence that a near miss did not mean disaster, it proved a blessing in disguise. Nerves immediately slackened and the rest of the crews completed the course without further incident. Nevertheless, to consolidate their confidence, Moore sent every man up for one more run before moving on to the next step in the exercise.

As so often happened when events of high importance were taking place at RAF Sutton Craddock, the occupants of The Black Swan, the old pub that stood beside the road near the main gates, had the best view of all. Used to the sound of aircraft, neither Joe Kearns, the owner, nor his barmaid Maisie had taken much account of Harvey's flight taking off. The thunder of aircraft diving down at speed only to climb away again was another matter, reminiscent of the German air attack a few weeks ago that had nearly destroyed the airfield and put the inn itself at risk. Hurrying into the front bedroom that gave a view over the perimeter fence, the couple were able to see the transporters through a gap in the hangars. Maisie, a big handsome girl with bold features and black hair, turned to Kearns, her eyes wide. "What the hell are those things? An' why are they flyin' through them?"

Kearns shook his head. In his middle fifties, he was a stoutly-built man with thinning white hair and a country-man's ruddy face. "It must be some kind of practice, lass."

The noise was rattling every loose window in the inn. As the couple stood watching, another Mosquito dived down. For a moment it disappeared behind the control tower and a hangar, only to appear again as it swept diagonally across the field. As it flashed between the screens, Kearns drew in his breath. "That's a dangerous stunt, isn't it?"

Maisie, whose attachment to the squadron had become a legend over the years, was showing alarm. "You know what it means, don't you? They've a low-level job comin' up. And those're the most dangerous of all."

The din of diving engines ceased for a while when Moore ordered the tape to be removed and the transporters to close in another ten feet. When flying resumed, collisions began to occur as pilots lost their aiming point, forcing Moore to order one further round before narrowing the gap any further.

With the experienced pilots quick to correct their mistakes, this round was completed without mishap. Encouraged, and with the sun still high in the sky, Moore was about to extend the exercise when one of the transporter crews reported a shortage of repair material. With no other option, Moore notified Davies and then cancelled the training until the following morning. At the same time, knowing Harvey's aircraft would be running short of fuel and also that his new crews would be feeling the strain of low-level flying, he recalled the Yorkshireman to the station. Secretly delighted, Harvey wasted no time in complying and after giving Moore an account of the day's happenings, he was soon accelerating his bull-nosed Morris past The Black Swan on his way to Scarborough.

In the meantime Davies, who had spent most of the afternoon watching the exercises from the control tower, had made his way to Henderson's office where the Scot was struggling to catch up with his paperwork.

"It's gone well, Jock. Better than I hoped."

Unused to praise from the small Air Commodore, Henderson accepted it cautiously. "I'm glad you're happy about it, sir."

"Yes. So far so good. But your Flight Commanders will have to take charge of the training tomorrow. I want you and Moore to come down to Weybridge with me."

Henderson cocked up his ears. "Weybridge?"

"Yes. We're going to meet a very interesting man and to see some films." Before Henderson could question him, Davies went on: "There's one other thing. Before this exercise with the transporters is completed, I'm having a refinement added."

"What kind of refinement, sir?" When Davies explained, the Scot looked shocked. "You didn't have this on that demonstration in Herefordshire the other night."

"That's true," Davies admitted. "We rushed things a bit and this new idea has just come up. But there's nothing to get worked up about. The idea is to make things safer for your boys on the day, not more dangerous."

"We haven't got the screens down to 63 feet yet," Henderson pointed out. "So you can hardly introduce anything new for a couple of days."

Davies waved a hand. "That's all right. We've got the time. I want your boys one-hundred-percent ready for this one."

Henderson felt unease rather than relief. To be given so much time for a special mission by Davies had an ominous ring about it. "It would help if we'd some idea what it was all about, sir."

Davies took this further probing well. "See it as a conundrum, Jock. Put together all the pieces I've given you so far, and then take an educated guess. Maybe the picture will look clearer when you've met this chap at Weybridge." The grin Davies gave the puzzled Scot was full of malice. "Be fair to me, Jock. You can't say I'm not giving you plenty of clues."

Harvey halted the Morris and turned to the girl at his side. "Feel like a little walk?"

She smiled. "I was just going to suggest it."

Leaving the car at the roadside, they followed a narrow path that led to a shallow hill. Clumps of gorse lay around them. The dipping sun had momentarily slid behind a cloud and great shafts of light were radiating across the sky.

The air was still. A curlew dipped down curiously, then gave its lonely cry and flew away. He felt her hand press on his arm but she did not speak.

They reached the hilltop fifteen minutes later. The sun was now a huge ember on the edge of the sky. The moors ran towards it, fold after fold as far as the eye could see. As she took a deep breath, he turned to her. "You like it here, don't you?"

"I love it here," she said quietly. "I have never stopped thinking of that day last summer when you first brought me."

Sitting on an outcrop of rock, they watched the approach of the night. The ember on the horizon glowed, sank, and was gone. The cloud above it caught fire and lit up the sky. It turned from scarlet to gold, from gold to magenta purple. To the east a single star appeared. Rivulets of silver mist widened in the dark folds of the hills. Here and there, ignoring the regulations, the warm lights of isolated farmhouses began to glimmer. In the silence they could hear their own heartbeats. Harvey was afraid to move. If he lived a thousand years he knew he would never be happier than at this moment.

A far off drone broke the spell. It grew louder, making the still air tremble, and Harvey knew it was a dozen or more heavy bombers flying to join the mainstream that would be heading towards Europe. The girl glanced up. "Heaven here, hell over there. How can men bear to do this every night? I could not."

He shook his head. "No. We're the lucky ones. Once we're back, we're out of danger." Before she could reply, he went on: "Look at us now. Pulled out of action to do circus stunts. I'd hardly call that the hard life, would you?"

She glanced at him. "Circus stunts?"

He had no qualms at telling her what the squadron was doing. If she could not be trusted, the world could blow itself apart as far as Harvey was concerned. "No one has any idea what it's all about. The boys are beginning to think Davies has gone crazy."

"No," she said quietly. "Davies has a reason for everything he does."

She did not see how closely he was studying her face. "It

can't be anything that serious or urgent," he said, "or he wouldn't allow us all out of camp every night, would he?"

About to reply, she checked herself and gave a cry of protest. "Please, Frank. Let us try to forget the war for a few days."

The heavy drone had receded into the distance. Far away a dog barked and an echo answered it from the sleeping hills. To the east the moon was a silver bubble and its light lay all around them, on the gorse and the distant, shining sea. As their lips drew closer and met, it seemed to Harvey that neither men nor fate could rend apart a love as perfect as this.

13

Davies opened the railway carriage door, stared down the corridor, then closed it again. Apart from himself, Moore, and Henderson, the compartment was empty, a wartime luxury granted him by the needs of security. Settling back in his seat, he motioned the two men closer.

"The man you're going to meet at Weybridge is a Dr. Barnes Wallis, a scientist and inventor. He's the boffin who invented the geodetic construction of the Wellington bomber, the forerunner of the Lancaster. He also designed the bomb that Guy Gibson and his boys dropped on the Ruhr dams."

There was a stir of interest from his listeners as Davies went on: "I'm told he comes up with ideas all the time. Some appear a bit cranky at first, yet everything he's been allowed to build seems to have been a success. On the surface he appears a gentle soul, but underneath he's as resilient as old boots. It took him a hell of a time to persuade Beaverbrook to let him build Guy Gibson's bomb and even when he got permission there were hundreds of snags before the thing worked. But he won in the end and you both know the result. Not that it made him happy. The Brigadier says Wallis was shocked when he saw 617's casualty list. As he had come up with the idea, he felt guilty for all the deaths."

Henderson's grunt was approving. "At least he doesn't sound like a cold-blooded boffin."

"He's not. You'll find him as keen as mustard on the one hand, and yet fretful at the casualties he might cause on the other."

Henderson decided the mystery was growing worse by the moment. "Does this mean we're going to be working with him like 617 did, sir?"

Davies waited while the train rushed over a set of points. When the sound died away, his caution had returned. "I don't want to say too much here, Jock. Wait for the rest until we get to Weybridge."

The Mosquito with the odd bulge beneath its bomb bay was flying no more than fifty feet above the sea. Ahead was a warship, a formidable hulk of steel lying broadside to the line of attack. At about a half mile range a spherical object fell from the Mosquito's bomb bay. Striking the sea with a heavy splash, it reappeared and began to skip across the waves like a giant stone, striking the ship just above its waterline. Sparks flew from the impact but there was no explosion. As the object sank, the Mosquito circled to attack the ship again. A second spherical object fell, leapt across the waves and again brought a shower of sparks from the steel hulk before sinking.

A caption ended the film: *Most Secret Trial Number 5*. Then the room lights came on, momentarily blinding its occupants. Davies addressed Henderson and Moore who were sitting alongside him.

"First, notice that caption. You can't get anything more secret than that, so don't even talk in your sleep. Now for the general facts. The code name for the weapon is *Highball*. The kite was a Mosquito BIV, specially modified by Vickers Armstrong to take the bomb." Davies glanced at the white-haired, mild-faced civilian wearing spectacles who was seated at the far side of Henderson. "I don't think Dr. Barnes Wallis will mind my saying this weapon system has caused him problems over the last few months but, as you see, they've all been ironed out and now the system works."

The sight of the ship had dismayed Henderson. Anti-shipping strikes were always costly and in the back of every bomber squadron CO's mind at that time of the war was the murderous *Tirpitz* lying behind her torpedo nets in Norway. "This is an anti-ship weapon, is it, sir?"

Davies knew full well what was behind the question. "I'm going to let Dr. Wallis give you details about the bomb, Jock." His voice betrayed his respect for the scientist as he addressed him directly. "I understand this is more or less a smaller version of the bomb dropped by 617 Squadron, sir. Is that right?"

The inventor's voice was as mild as his appearance. "That's quite correct, Davies. The main difference is the weight and shape. You'll remember *Upkeep* was more like an oil drum while this weapon is spherical."

Moore leaned forward. "Am I right in thinking it had a back spin when it was falling?"

"You're quite right, Wing Commander. We achieve that by a small air turbine that works from an air scoop on the port side of the bomb bay. The bomb itself is mounted between two triangular frames that are connected by a belt and pulley to the turbine motor. All we do is activate the turbine and the weapon begins spinning between its mountings. We can produce any speed between 100 and 1000 revolutions per minute. The fusing and release are achieved electrically, as with other bombs."

"What's the point of the back spin?" Henderson asked.

"That's what makes it skip over the water. In doing that it evades boom and torpedo defences. It also makes it cling to and run down the side of a ship before exploding."

Henderson defied Davies's frown. "So it is essentially an anti-shipping bomb?"

"That was my first intention. But since then we have realized it can be used against other targets. For example, it can be bounced into tunnels or shafts."

Henderson glanced at Moore. "Tunnels and shafts?"

"Yes. Targets that would otherwise be inaccessible against bombs falling from a vertical plane."

"Can I ask its weight?"

"Its explosive charge is 600 lbs of Torpex. Its diameter is 32 inches. As you saw from the film, a modified BIV Mosquito can carry two."

"What height should it be dropped from?" Moore asked.

"That depends on the target. But it can be dropped from fifty feet. Even lower if necessary."

Davies intervened before any more questions could be asked. "All right, you've seen the bomb. We're here because Dr. Wallis has obtained permission to use it in battle conditions."

"Then it hasn't been tried yet, sir?" Moore asked.

"No," Wallis told him. "Our Service Chiefs are too afraid it might fall into enemy hands." Taking off his glasses, the scientist wiped them with his handkerchief, a curiously disarming gesture. "You see the problem is that we have far more shipping than the enemy and therefore if he developed the bomb he could do more damage to us than we could do to him. It's difficult to argue against this and goodness knows how long they would have kept it in wraps if we hadn't pointed out to them that it has other uses and it might well be the answer to. . . ."

At this point Davies, who had been making frantic signals of warning to the scientist, broke in hastily. "They don't know the target yet, sir. I'm under the strictest orders to keep it secret for the moment."

The look he received was mildly reprehensible. "The military mind does make things very difficult, Davies."

"Not really, sir." Davies turned towards his rapt listeners. "Dr. Wallis has persuaded the Chiefs of Staff his bomb might be the answer to a major problem we have but they are demanding two things from him before they make a final decision. First, the evaluation target must be one that gives the enemy the least chance of guessing the weapon's secret, and second, the target must be one that proves its effectiveness."

"What sort of target can that be?" Henderson asked.

Wallis answered the question. "We feel a railway tunnel is the answer. We can choose one well away from military observers and still strike a blow that will silence our critics. I am told the German supply trains are finding tunnels useful hiding places during our daylight attacks. *Highball* should be able to flush them out."

Moore, who had been silent for the last couple of minutes, was looking puzzled. "In the trials we just saw, the bomb had a back spin. I understand that helps it to skip over obstacles and to cling to the side of the ship when it strikes. But if we attack a tunnel, won't the back spin cause it to snag on the sleepers whereas we want the bomb to bound forward?"

The scientist gave Moore a look of respect. "You're quite right, Wing Commander. That is why the turbine in the bomb bay is designed to rotate in either direction. For tunnels or shafts, you give the bomb a forward rotation and in most cases a lower revving speed. Does that answer your question?"

Moore smiled. "Very well, sir."

Henderson was trying to put it all together as he turned to Davies. "So, on the one hand, you want us to go on practicing at low level and using the screens and, on the other hand, you want us to take part in Dr. Wallis's battle evaluation."

"That's right. But one thing at a time. At first we're only going to use three crews for the tunnel job. They'll have to start training with the bomb in the next day or two. Later on, all your boys will learn how to use it. But we must wait for that until the top brass give us the green light."

"So all these activities are bound together?" Henderson said.

Davies' curt answer made him regret the somewhat unnecessary remark. "I'd have thought that fairly obvious." Before the Scot could answer, Davies turned to Moore. "You understand now why you're staying here overnight, Ian. Dr. Wallis has promised to take you into the testing bay and give you the nuts and bolts of how the bomb works. Afterwards one of Vickers's pilots will take you on a test run. But I'd like you back at Sutton Craddock by 1800 hours tomorrow. You'll be flown back."

Moore nodded. "Who are you thinking of using for the evaluation attack, sir?"

Davies frowned. "I don't know yet. I want to think about it. They'll have to be crews who can keep their mouths shut."

"Then why not use Harvey, Millburn, and myself?" Moore glanced at Henderson. "I'm sure Harvey would like a crack at a tunnel. He feels a bit personal towards those German trains since they shot Andrew down."

"I'm not sure I want to risk all three of you," Davies muttered. "In any case, it would mean you doing a couple of days training on the bomb first."

"That's no problem. Harvey's flight will have completed the first exercise today and both flights should get through the second phase tomorrow."

"You're a bit optimistic, aren't you?"

Moore shook his head. "They're quick to pick it up. Anyway, we can put Van Breedenkamp and Larkin in charge of any further training. They're both reliable men."

Davies nodded reluctantly. "All right. I'll think about it and let you know when you get back tomorrow."

With Barnes Wallis present, Henderson was wondering if Davies might be more forthcoming on a question that had nagged him ever since the spectacular trial down in Herefordshire. "Where does that wirecutting stunt come into all this, sir? Is that something my boys will have to do eventually?"

Davies' refusal to be drawn out disappointed the Scot. "I've told you, Jock—one thing at a time. Your boys will be kept busy enough learning to drop this new bomb if the trial comes off and we get the green light."

Henderson had to be content. "What about modified BIVs? Are there going to be enough to go around?"

"No. We'll have to borrow them from 618 Squadron who've been training to use the bomb against shipping. At one time there was talk of using them for this job but as your squadron has had so much more specialist experience, you were chosen."

"So we'll have to borrow all their Mosquitoes if the big job is sanctioned?" Henderson asked.

Davies gave one of his sudden impish grins. "That's right. You can imagine how happy they'll be. We'll have to go in strength to collect 'em or we could get ourselves lynched."

14

The sky was overcast and there was a chill in the early morning breeze when Harvey walked to the edge of the tarmac apron. Lifting a pair of binoculars he stared at the two distant transporters. Their position was the same as the previous day with one significant change. The screens had been heightened a few feet and the tops were joined by orange crossbeams. At that distance it was difficult to judge their height but Harvey guessed it at between sixty and seventy feet. Scowling, the Yorkshireman walked back to his flight office and put a call through to Henderson.

The Scot was still shaving when his telephone rang. Cursing, he wiped his lathered face and pushed into his office. "Hello. Who's that?"

The gruff blunt voice could belong to only one man. "Harvey here, sir. Have you taken a look at those crossbeams yet?"

"No. They only went up during the night. What's the problem?"

"The problem is they look as solid as steel girders. And they're a full three feet thick."

"Well, they're not girders," Henderson grunted. "They're just strips of wood and canvas like the screens. So what's all the fuss about?"

From the sound of his breathing, Harvey was holding back his temper with an effort. "The fuss is what they look like, sir, not what they are. Both Millburn and myself are worried in case the lads give them too much clearance and hit the deck. And anyway I'm not so sure they're as harmless as you make out. They could be dangerous if they struck a propeller."

79

The usually phlegmatic Scot needed nothing more than the mention of Millburn to make him match Harvey's mood. Enjoying low-level flying, Millburn tended to carry it to extremes. Ever since Henderson had returned from Weybridge, he had been swamped by irate phone calls about the behaviour of the American's flight during its exercise the previous day. The calls had come from all quarters and had ranged from the serious to the absurd. A local MP had announced he was putting a question to the House about the high-handed irresponsibility of RAF Station Commanders. A large grocery firm had complained that one of their drivers had panicked on seeing a line of Mosquitoes heading towards him and had driven his vehicle into a ditch. A local farmer had fulminated that the same Mosquitoes had stampeded his cows and caused two abortions on the spot. A pigeon fancier had wailed that the fearful din had scattered his birds to the four winds and none had yet returned. With a vision of litigation stretching forward to the crack of doom, the harassed Henderson had barely slept and this onslaught of Harvey's was proving too much.

"If you've got complaints, Harvey, give them to Air Commodore Davies, not to me. In the meantime, I suggest you get on with it and brief the lads. Davies is coming back today and I don't want you all sitting on your backsides when he arrives."

Harvey's scowl was still evident when he climbed on the platform of the Operations Room half an hour later. "There'll be no low-level flying today. Both flights are to practice on the screens. Like the previous two days, we'll go up three at a time. My flight will have the first session; Squadron Leader Millburn's flight will have the second." He glanced at the American who was sharing the platform with him. "So if your lot wants to play darts in your flight office for the first two hours, that's up to you."

Millburn, who like Harvey had sensed the crews' apprehension, decided it was an occasion for humour. "No; we'll stick around and watch. It's not every day Barnum and Bailey come to town."

Only two laughs sounded. Giving Millburn a look, Harvey turned back to the intent crews. "For our first run, we'll have the tape down across the field. Then we'll take it away.

Keep your height lower this time. If you remember all you've learned so far, you shouldn't have any problems."

The eager young face of Sugden could be seen among the ranks of the muttering men. A pilot alongside him put up a hand. "How solid is that bar they've put across, sir?"

"According to Air Commodore Davies, it's not solid at all. Just a stiffened piece of canvas."

Mutters of scepticism broke out. The name of Davies did not connote a long and safe life. "Then if we hit it, we should be all right, skipper?" The question came from a slim young pilot.

Harvey's humour was nothing if not mordant. "You'll be on cloud nine, Purcell. Laughing your head off while the rest of us struggle on." As a few dubious laughs sounded, the Yorkshireman grinned. "For Chrissake, no one's trying to get rid of us. At least not in this way. The beam's just wind and piss like the screens most of you have hit already."

From the looks and whispers it was clear few men were convinced. Noticing it, Harvey tried contempt. "What's the matter with you all? It's a damn sight better than clobbering the Ruhr, isn't it?"

A deep whisper came from the back of the assembly. "We'll let you know later, skipper."

Harvey scowled. "The trouble with you lot is you don't know how you're born. Just ignore the bloody crossbar and you'll have no problems. Any more questions?"

When none were forthcoming, Harvey ended the short briefing. Watching the men as they filed out, he caught sight of Hanson, his navigator, and called him back. "I shan't be wanting you right away. You can sit this one out and have a cup of tea."

Hanson, a stocky young man, looked puzzled. "Aren't we flying with the others, skipper?"

Harvey was already halfway up the Operation Room steps. "Wait for me in the flight office."

Hanson learned the reason ten minutes later when walking away with the rest of the crews from the locker room. The thunder of D-Danny warming up was echoing across the airfield. Puzzled, he pushed past half a dozen colleagues. "Why the hell is he going up without me?" he complained.

D-Danny was already moving towards the north-south runway. Taxiing to the far end of the field, it turned and began gathering speed, spray flying from its wheels. Thundering over the watching crews, it did a quick circuit of the field and then came in low over the corner fence. Skimming over the recently laid tape, it seemed about to make a perfect pass between the transporters and overhead beam when at the last moment its nose jerked up to strike the beam head on. For a moment the breathless onlookers flinched, only to see the crossbar fly apart and fall in two halves. At the far side of the transporters D-Danny began climbing into the grey morning sky.

A buzz broke out among the crews. A loud laugh interrupted it. Richardson, the Equipment Officer who was walking across the tarmac with the men, had once fallen foul of Harvey over a matter of engine spares and the burly, ginger-headed Richardson did not forgive easily. "That was a bit flashy, wasn't it? Being put in charge must have gone to his head."

Richardson's rank prevented his receiving more than resentful glances from the men. Millburn had no such inhibitions. Pushing forward to Richardson's side, he gave a growl of dislike. "That guy wouldn't know how to be flashy, you sonofabitch. He's got more guts in his little finger than you've got up your arsehole. So belt up."

The hot-tempered Richardson spun round. For a long moment the two men's eyes clashed. Then Richardson cursed and walked away. Ignoring the grins of appreciation from the men nearby, Millburn started forward. "All right, you guys. You've seen for yourselves that bar's no more dangerous than a stick of candy. Now sort yourselves out and be ready to go when it's repaired."

At the far end of the field D-Danny was settling down to land. As its tyres squealed on the runway, crews began making their way to their flight offices. Their conversation and jokes suggested the ghost of the crossbar had been laid to rest and the exercise reduced to more manageable proportions.

Moore was flown into Sutton Craddock just after 1800 hours that evening. A jeep was waiting for him and drove him straight to the CO's office where Davies was closeted with

Henderson. Curious and eager, the Air Commodore wasted no time on courtesies. "Well, how did you get on? Do you know everything about *Highball* now?"

Moore smiled. "I hope so, sir. They were very thorough."

"Did you get a test flight in?"

"Yes. We went down to Reculvers and dropped two bombs."

"What's your verdict? Is it easy to use or difficult?"

Moore hesitated. "I found the sight rather cumbersome— at least it will be for a narrow target like a tunnel. Quite honestly, I think we'd get better results if the pilots could use their own judgment and drop the bomb themselves."

"Like in skip bombing?" Davies asked.

"Yes, sir."

Davies gave a noncommittal grunt. "Well, you'll soon have the chance to find out. I've been told I'm only allowed to let your senior officers have full details of the bomb at this time. So you, Harvey, and Millburn will leave in the morning for 618's base at Skitten."

"Yes, sir." Before Davies could say more, Moore glanced at Henderson. "Why did Harvey end the exercise? I told him to carry on until the light went."

"He stopped it to save fuel," Henderson told him. "The boys had it off pat by the middle of the afternoon." Seeing Moore's surprise, the Scot went on to explain Harvey's action that morning. "Once he'd proven the crossbar couldn't do any harm, they found it easy."

Moore smiled ruefully. "And I was going to bollick him for disobeying orders!" He turned to Davies. "Have you told Harvey and Millburn yet?"

"All they need to know, yes. I've told them to be ready to move off with you at 0800 hours tomorrow."

At that moment the telephone rang. Henderson offered the receiver to Moore. "Harvey would like a word with you."

"Hello, Frank. You did a good job today. What can I do for you?"

"I was wondering if you needed me again tonight, Ian?"

Moore showed surprise. "I'd like a chat about the day's exercise, yes." He glanced up at Davies. "I take it you'll want the exercises to go on while we're away, sir?"

"Oh, Christ, yes. We're nowhere near our clearance

limits yet. If the boys are that good, pull in the screens again
and lower the crossbar another ten feet."

Moore turned back to the telephone. "The exercises are
to go on, Frank, so we'll need to talk to your Deputy Commanders." When Harvey did not reply, he went on: "What's
your problem? Have you something on?"

There was a pause, then Harvey's voice turned brusque.
"No, it doesn't matter. Forget it."

Moore stood staring at the telephone as the line went
dead. His surprise grew at Davies' question. "Are you sure
you need him tonight, Ian? Couldn't you and Millburn talk to
the Deputy Commanders? And you can tell Harvey about the
bomb on your way up to Skitten."

Puzzled that Davies should show such consideration
towards a man who had often been a thorn in his side, Moore
was also nettled that Davies would interfere in a matter that
was entirely a Squadron Commander's concern. At such times
the young Englishman's cultured voice could chill with dis-
pleasure. "With respect, sir, I feel these are far more important issues than a night out in town."

It was a reprimand that brought two red spots high up
on Davies' cheeks. Expecting the thunder of cannon fire to
follow, Henderson heard only a sharp rifle shot. "Damn it,
Moore, you don't think I'd interfere without good reason, do
you? The truth is Anna Reinhardt's back in England. And I
think she's done enough for us to deserve seeing Harvey for
a few nights, don't you?" Furious the admission had been
forced from him, Davies took it out on the unfortunate Harvey.
"Although whether that bloody-minded Yorkshireman deserves
it is another matter."

Moore had given a violent start at the news. Although
he recovered immediately, Henderson was reminded of what
he and Adams had long suspected—that Harvey was not the
only man on the station in love with the courageous German
girl. He listened to Moore's question. "Is she staying locally,
sir?"

"No," Davies grunted. "At least not that locally. She's in
a hotel in Scarborough. We're keeping her presence quiet for
safety's sake. Simms thinks she might be sent back to Europe
once the invasion starts. So neither of you breathe a word

about this. But as Harvey's going off to Skitten with you tomorrow, I feel she ought to see him tonight."

Without another word Moore turned and picked up the telephone. "Get hold of Squadron Leader Harvey for me, will you? Tell him to phone me back right away."

15

Davies flew back into Sutton Craddock three days later. Meeting Henderson on the airfield, he wasted no time in preliminaries. "Have you heard from Moore and the Brigadier yet?"

"Yes, sir. Moore expects to be here around 1100 hours. The Brigadier is already on his way."

"You've warned all personnel to keep their mouths shut?"

"Yes, sir. Everyone's been told."

"And you've got the Operations Room ready?"

Henderson nodded patiently. "Yes. The maps are up and it's under security guard."

"Then let's go straight there. We can have coffee sent in. It'll give me the chance to have a chat with the Brigadier when he arrives."

Adams, who had earlier received a message from Henderson that he might be needed that morning, was not the only man on the station who watched the jeep with curiosity and apprehension as it went speeding towards the Operations Room. The previous night a second warning had gone up on the notice boards. Under the pain of court-martial, nothing seen or heard on the airfield could be discussed outside the station. As many lives might be at stake, the punishment for any infringement would be severe. To make certain the warning reached every man and woman, officers and NCOs were ordered to pass it on by word of mouth. After the extraordi-

nary antics of the last few days, this order, extreme even by
security standards, suggested to the most phlegmatical airman
that matters were moving towards a climax.

The arrival of four Mosquitoes that morning seemed
the final endorsement. All were BIVs but with a difference.
One, flown in by a pilot from Benson, was a photoreconnaissance version with a transparent nose with three vertical
cameras and one oblique camera. However, it was the other
Mosquitoes, flown in by Moore and his two Flight Commanders, that drew the attention of all the aircrews and
half the ground staff as well. Carrying no armament all were
fitted with multiple ejector exhaust stubs to obtain extra
speed but it was their bomb bays that attracted the attention.
Although Special Police threw a cordon around all three
aircraft the moment they came to a halt, even at a distance
men could see their unusual shape. Bulging down below the
fuselage, the bomb doors appeared to be half cut away, expos-
ing a mysterious mechanism within the bomb bay itself.
Larkin, who had procured a pair of binoculars from the locker
room, swore he could see winches and pulleys and his binoculars were in high demand before the SPs politely but firmly
took them away and widened the cordon. Interest then centred
on the four crews who had flown the Mosquitoes in, and it
took a curt word from Moore before the curious pilots and
navigators fell back and allowed the eight men to enter the
Operations Room.

Adams and Simms were present in the bunker when
Moore led his crews down the steps. Davies was standing
beside Marsden, the Signals Officer. Marsden, with phones
held against one ear, was clearly having difficulty in listening
to incoming traffic and Davies at the same time, and showed
relief when the Air Commodore turned his attention to Moore.

"Everything gone all right, Ian?"

"Yes, sir. When are you expecting the bombs?"

"They're coming by special escort. They should be here
before noon." Davies glanced at Henderson. "Don't forget—
no one must go near them."

The Scot, who was finding all this security onerous,
suppressed a sigh. "Someone has to load them into the kites,
sir."

"That's all taken care of," Davies said. "Special armourers

are coming with them." Then, seeing the Scot's expression, he became irritable. "Damn it, Jock, it's not my fault they're treating this weapon like the Holy Grail. I'm only obeying orders myself."

"I appreciate that, sir. It's not the bomb I'm thinking of; it's the operation itself. I don't see how any enemy could guess from the stunts we're performing what it's going to be—not when we can't guess ourselves. But if there is a danger, then why don't we confine everyone to camp until it's over?"

Davies' restlessness betrayed his inner conflict. "Because Jerry knows all about us, Jock. That raid on us last month proved it. If we cut communications and isolate ourselves, it's certain to draw his attention."

"But what if some erk gets drunk and blathers?"

"You've put out a severe enough warning. And your censoring officers have sharpened their blue pencils. If a leak should occur, then we've just got to hope Jerry finds it as puzzling as you do. I think he probably will."

The Scot's expression hinted nothing was more likely as Davies turned to the waiting crews. "As I think you already know, we're sending you out to clobber a tunnel. We can't tell you which one yet because that depends on Jerry's traffic movements." Here Davies nodded at Marsden listening at his radio. "Certain agents in France have informed us that three trains carrying guns, ammunition and strategic supplies passed through Besancon early this morning. As the freight is urgent Jerry's likely to make a daylight dash and so we've sent long-range Typhoons out looking for them. When the Tiffies make contact, they'll attack but since we understand the trains are being routed through the Massif Central, the chances are high one or more will find shelter in a tunnel for the rest of the day. If this happens, the Tiffies will send us the coordinates while they ensure the train doesn't leapfrog into the next tunnel. This will mean a quick scramble, so your navigators will have to map read. I'd also go out at low level if I were you, although that must be your Squadron Commander's decision. Any questions so far?"

"What happens if the Tiffies clobber all three trains, sir?" Millburn asked.

"Then we wait for another tip-off. Our French agents

know the importance of stopping Jerry's supplies, so they're watching everything that moves."

"You do know these BIVs are unarmed, sir?" The blunt question came from Harvey. "What escort are we getting?"

Not for the first time, Davies wondered how it was the Yorkshireman's questions always nettled him. "Your Wing Commander thinks you're fast enough not to need an escort on the way out, particularly since Jerry is saving his strength these days. But I've arranged for a flight of Typhoons to give you cover while you're over the target. You're also taking a photoreconnaissance Mosquito with you." Davies' eyes moved to the tall young man sporting an enormous moustache who was standing alongside Moore. "You probably recognize Flight Lieutenant Simpson. He took the photographs of the Ruhpolding valley for us during the Rhine Maiden affair. His photographs will enable the bomb's effectiveness to be assessed, so take care of him."

As the pilot grinned and bowed, Harvey put up his hand again. "If this trial's a success, do we take it the rest of the lads will be receiving the same weapon training we've just had?"

With Simpson present, it was not a question Davies wanted and he answered it with a scowl. "You people can't take one thing at a time, can you? Let's get this job done first, then we'll talk about the next step. The truth is there won't be a next step if this operation isn't a success, and that could have some nasty repercussions."

Pausing to let his listeners make what they could out of his remark, Davies went on: "So do your very best. Also remember, neither the bomb nor its mechanism must fall into enemy hands. Make certain the bombs are fused before you drop them and, if you should crash, your first duty is to blow up the contents of the bomb bay before you try to escape. All right, that's all for now. We'll be in touch as soon as the right message comes through."

16

The six Typhoons were circling like hawks over the stretch of wooded hills. "Hello, Catfish one. The dogs are here. Nine o'clock."

A second Typhoon dipped a port wing. Below, in a fingers-four formation, four Mosquitoes were racing in from the northwest. "I've got 'em, skipper." Both voices were aggressively Australian. "What the hell makes 'em think they've sharper teeth than us?"

In A-Apple, flying at point, the comments could be heard clearly. With 633 Squadron considered by many to be the darlings of the RAF and the Typhoon pilots priding themselves as specialists in ground strafing and train busting, the situation was ripe for sardonic comment, particularly from Australians. Catching Hopkinson's expression, Moore smiled as he addressed his mike. "Hello, Catfish Leader. Sorry to take over the hunt but the master-of-hounds insists we have some exercise too. Where's the fox hiding?"

The first Australian voice became reluctantly professional. "Hello, Foxhound Leader. Our guys bagged the first two a few miles back but this one went to ground around 1400 hours and hasn't put a nose out since. She's under that second range of hills."

Below, the steel track contoured its way along the steep gorges and wooded hills of the Massif. Ordering his Mosquitoes into a line-astern formation, Moore led them into a climbing turn. Before he levelled out, the lynx eyes of Hoppy had picked out the tunnel. "There, skipper. At two o'clock. And you know something? It's going to be a bastard to clobber."

Moore saw the reason a moment later. The tunnel, perhaps eight hundred yards long, ran beneath a wooded escarpment. The terrain to the southeast was relatively flat but to the northwest, it was broken in a series of narrow, steepsided valleys. As it emerged from the tunnel, the track could be seen winding along the valleys before breaking out into the plains beyond. Hoppy was gazing down. "Couldn't we clobber the eastern end?"

Moore was busy weighing the pros and cons. His orders were clear enough. French agents had reported that it was the practice of drivers to steam to the far end of tunnels before halting their trains and so Davies had ordered the attack to be made from the northwest. Before Moore had left the Operations Room, Davies had drawn him aside. "I can't stress enough how important it is this operation's a success, Ian. There could be all kinds of problems for the invasion if it isn't." Realizing what he had said, Davies had given a sheepish grin. "You aren't a fool, Ian. You must have guessed there's a connection."

"We'll do our best, sir, of course."

"Good man. I know you will. We must prove this bomb works. And there is a secondary consideration." At this point Davies' eyes had shone with the professional eagerness that occasionally disturbed those who worked with him. "It'll be a hell of a feather in our caps if we're given the chance to pull off the big one."

Moore's problem was his ignorance of the bomb's ultimate target. If its effectiveness against tunnels was the main consideration, then an attack from the eastern end with a straight track and no distracting hillsides was a far better option. If, on the other hand, the contents of the tunnel were its objective, then with the tunnel a half mile long there would be every chance the train could steam out unharmed even if the eastern end were demolished. And that could be used by critics as proof the new weapon was a failure.

It was typical of Moore that when he made his decision it was incisive. "Foxhound Leader here. We're going in from the northwest. Keep clear until my first bomb bursts. Then attack as ordered. Catfish Leader, please give us cover."

Dropping a wing, A-Apple sliced down. The hills below turned from folds of rough cloth into spiky trees and rocky outcrops. For a moment the thin steel track disappeared as

Moore banked around. Then it swung into view again, reaching out down a steep-sided valley.

Latching on to it, Moore sank lower. Flying at a safer height on his starboard beam, the photoreconnaissance Mosquito followed him. The thin thread of steel became a double track of rails and sleepers. As A-Apple raced along it, the sides of the valley closed in, trapping the noise of its engines and turning it into thunder. A crow, squatting on a telegraph pole, gave a squawk of fright and flapped frantically away. As Hoppy yelled a question, Moore nodded and a few seconds later a curious tremor ran through the Mosquito. Inside its bomb bay the first of the two *Highballs* was beginning to rotate as the rush of air from the scoop outside began to activate its turbine rotor.

The tremor increased as A-Apple followed the bends in the valley. Ahead the track looked as if it were on a giant conveyor belt, moving slowly at first and then streaming beneath in a blur of speed. As Moore banked, then straightened, a road bridge appeared ahead. Hoppy gave a yell and Moore heaved hard on the control column. Leaping up like a Salmon, the Mosquito cleared the bridge by only a few feet. Moore could feel the sweat on his hands as he allowed A-Apple to sink down again.

From the vibration in the bomb bay and the counter in front of Hoppy, Moore knew that the first bomb was now spinning at 500 rpm. At his signal the Cockney switched on both the master and selector switches and then peered through the bombsight. Unlike the standard sight that gazed through the floor of the fuselage, the *Highball* sight bore more resemblance to a gunsight, as it was positioned in front of the windshield with range bars to allow for the size of the target. Checking that the circuit indicator light was on, Hoppy waited for the target to appear.

It came as A-Apple swept round a shallow bend and entered a straight length of track. Beside Moore, Hoppy voiced his apprehension, a rare occasion for the veteran navigator. "I don't like the look of that hill, skipper. Don't leave it too long or we'll never get out."

Moore also found the sight intimidating. The tunnel appeared as a tiny dark hole at the foot of a high hill that swept round to join the northern flank of valley down which

A-Apple was racing. At a quick estimate Moore judged the hill to be a mile and a half away and knew the limits of success and failure were going to be narrow.

With his altimeter virtually useless at that height he had to gauge his height visually. Too great a height meant the bomb's angle of fall might be too severe, destroying its ability to skim over the ground. Too low a height might send it bouncing back into the aircraft, with disastrous results. Seeing from the corner of his eye that Hoppy was attempting to use the bombsight, Moore shook his head. "Forget it. Leave the release to me."

The hillside was now leaping at them as if bent on their destruction. The tunnel was growing from a dark speck to a wide reinforced ellipsoid from which wisps of steam were emerging. Watching it intently, Moore was about to release his first bomb when two lines of glowing shells broke out from the trees and came swirling towards them. Hoppy's yell was spontaneous. "Christ, skipper! Look out!"

His shout had not died away before another fork of tracer stabbed out from the hillside that joined the approach valley. In both cases the fire was accurately aimed. The Mosquito flinched as a shell struck her wing.

With the opportunity to release the bomb gone, Moore was now having to fight for survival. Ramming both throttles forward, he heaved back on the control column and gave the Mosquito right rudder. With her wings groaning under the stress, A-Apple strove to avoid the hill that was now filling the windshield. Helpless in his seat Hoppy could do nothing but close his eyes and pray. For a moment A-Apple seemed to hang vertically on her propellers. Then, with a scream of engines that was more agony than triumph, she broke free and came climbing out of the valley.

Hoppy's cry was heartfelt. "For God's sake, skipper. Don't ever do that to me again."

Breathless with shock, Moore did not try to reply. As he checked A-Apple for damage, he heard Harvey's startled voice. "You all right, Ian?"

Moore's reply was curt. "Yes. I'll try again in a minute."

As both Mosquito pilots protested it was their turn next, another startled voice broke in. "Sorry, Foxhound Leader.

We didn't know about those flak posts. They didn't open up earlier. We're coming down now to take care of 'em."

Ordering Harvey and Millburn into orbit, Moore watched the six Typhoons peel away and plummet down. Splitting into two sections, they went at the flak posts like wolves.

The post above the tunnel was quickly put out of action. The one further up the hillside proved more intractable. Armed only to give the Mosquitoes protection against air attack, the Typhoons were not carrying their standard 60 lb rockets, and with the steep hill giving the post protection, the pilots were finding it difficult to get within effective 20mm range. One Typhoon was hit and veered away with a smoking engine. As a second pilot misjudged his distance and almost flew into the hill, Moore hastily intervened. "Let's try it another way, Catfish Leader. Fly with me as I go in."

"O.K., Foxhound Leader. We'll keep the bastards busy while you do your stuff."

Moore had a quick word with Harvey and Millburn as he went down. "Keep well out of range until your turn comes."

Obeying, the two Mosquitoes climbed to four thousand feet. Moore, knowing the terrain better this time, entered the steep valley nearer to its final stretch of track. Six hundred feet above him on his port beam, ready to open fire at the flak post when it came into range, the five remaining Typhoons were flying in line abreast. The PR Mosquito was back in station on his starboard beam. Millburn and Harvey, now fully alerted to the dangers of the mission, were watching Moore's progress intently from above.

It was an ideal situation for the lone Focke-Wulf hiding among the cumulus two thousand feet above the Mosquitoes. Captain Dieter Sommer was there by pure accident. Although his squadron was withdrawn from action until the Allies invaded, Sommer, whose new A3 had been suffering teething troubles, had been given permission to carry out high altitude tests that afternoon. Orbiting at 26,000 feet, he had suddenly received a call from his flight controller. "BIV Mosquitoes in Gustav-Quelle. Hanni - zero. Escort, six Typhoons. Have you enough fuel to take a look?"

Sommer had barely glanced at his fuel gauge before giving his answer. "I've enough fuel, Flight Control. I'm on my way."

Sommer was a young Westphalian who had never lost his appetite for combat. Born of poor parents, he had won a scholarship to an Adolf Hitler School where he had gained his senior matriculation. Knowing this could lead him to a commission, Sommer had applied for service in the Luftwaffe in 1939 and early the next year had been sent to No. II Flying Training Regiment near Berlin for his initial training. From there he had been transferred to Kriegschule, the Military Academy where he had learned to fly in old Focke-Wulf 44s. After soloing and becoming a corporal, he had gone on to the No. I Fighter School at Werneuchen where he had been accepted as a Flight Cadet. In December 1940 he had joined three thousand other future officers of the Army, Navy, Air Force and Waffen S.S. in the Berlin Sportpalast where he had been addressed by the Führer himself.

It had been the day of days in young Sommer's life. Three thousand arms extended stiffly in salute as the Führer marched through the massed ranks to the podium. The hushed silence, then the voice, vibrant with energy and will power. The great field of idealistic young faces rapt with adoration. Another hush, and then the Oath. Three thousand voices pledging life and devotion to the Führer and to the Fatherland. The ecstasy Sommer had known that day had remained with him ever since.

In the three and a half years that followed, Sommer had never broken his oath. He had fought the British over the Channel and in North Africa, the Russians over the Steppes, and the Americans in their attacks on the Fatherland. Now a Squadron Commander, he had been shot down twice, destroyed forty-five enemy aircraft, and had been awarded the Iron Cross First and Second Class. His worn uniform bore the bronze, silver, and gold wings of a pilot who had flown over two hundred missions.

In other words Sommer had become a deadly fighter pilot and he was showing all his experience now as he slid from cloud to cloud. With the Typhoons present, his task was not to attack but to see what the Mosquitoes were doing. At the same time, with their great speed and manoeuvrability, Mosquitoes were considered a prize for any fighter pilot, and to date Sommer had not bagged one. Knowing the BIVs were unarmed, his thirst grew and when the Typhoons went down into the valley to help Moore, he knew his chance had come. Creeping forward until he was almost above D-Danny, Sommer suddenly went down like a gannet.

Only Millburn's yell saved Harvey. "Hawk, Red One! Behind you!"

On pure reflex Harvey threw D-Danny into a violent turn. At the same moment a massive blast of cannon and MG fire tore a rectangle in the sky alongside him. Heart in his mouth, Harvey stared back and saw the blurred shape of Sommer's Focke-Wulf latching on to his tail. Yelling a warning to his navigator, Harvey swung violently to starboard as another blizzard of tracer sought to destroy him.

Below, the Typhoons were alerted and were climbing desperately to give aid. Moore, anxious for Harvey's safety, had already broken off his attack. The only pilot near enough to give help was Millburn, and although unarmed himself the American made one desperate attempt to divert the Focke Wulf but the enemy pilot's speed carried him away.

In D-Danny, Harvey knew that if he allowed himself to be driven away from the area he was a dead man. His only chance was to play for time. With the BIV too sluggish to match the Focke-Wulf in aerobatics, he threw her into a tight circle, hoping he could overstretch the Focke-Wulf's curve of pursuit. Wings vertical, the aircraft spun dizzily round one another like two cycles on a wall of death.

In the seconds that followed, Harvey was fully aware what his gamble entailed. If he tried to break from the circle he would run straight into the Focke-Wulf's guns. But if help did not come quickly, the lighter aircraft would close the circle with the same fatal result.

The tail assembly of D-Danny was already creeping into the range bar of Sommer's reflector sight when Millburn arrived. Ignoring all personal danger he went at Sommer like a bull at a gate. Forced to break away to avoid collision, Sommer tried to take his revenge on the American, only for Harvey to repeat Millburn's performance and divert the German's fire.

Although the two Mosquito pilots were highly skilled, it was an unequal battle that could have had only one outcome had the frantic Typhoons not been closing within range. Knowing they were the one Allied fighter that could match his aircraft's speed, Sommer was too experienced a pilot to throw good money after bad. Firing a last vengeful burst at Millburn, he dived for cover among the hills and disappeared.

Moore's voice sounded above the shouts of the Typhoon pilots. "Good work, you two. Have you any damage, Frank?"

Harvey was sweating and trembling from his efforts. His gruff voice tried to hide it. "I don't think so. Shall I go down?"

"No. First make sure your kite's OK. I'm going to have another try myself. Then it's Tommy's turn. Catfish Leader, leave three of your boys up aloft this time, will you?"

The twangy Australian voice sounded contrite. "Roger, Foxhound Leader."

With only two Typhoons on his port side, Moore entered the valley again. With the tunnel flak post out of action, he was able to give his full attention to the release of the bomb although the menace of the approaching hillside was a distraction in itself. Aiming A-Apple's nose as best he could, he released the bomb and immediately swung the Mosquito into a climbing turn. Behind him the two escorting Typhoons, spitting shells from their cannon, broke away to port. Protected by trees and a screen of rocks, the German flak gunners immediately turned their attention on A-Apple. As fiery shells swirled past a wingtip, Moore glanced back and saw a cloud of smoke rising thirty yards from the tunnel entrance. "What happened, Hoppy?"

"I think the bomb must have bounced sideways off a sleeper, skipper."

Nodding, Moore called Millburn down. "See if you can do any better. Only give yourself plenty of time to fly out. That hillside's lethal."

Joining Harvey above, Moore watched the American make his attack. At present the flak post was silent as its crew waited for the Mosquito and its escort to appear. Inside T-Tommy, Millburn grinned at his new navigator. "What do you say, kid? Shall we give 'em a bullseye the first time?"

If the young New Zealander was shaken after the encounter with the Focke-Wulf, he was hiding it well. "I don't see why not, sir."

Millburn eyed him with respect. Although the navigator's temperament could hardly have been more different from

the capricious and fun-loving Gabby, he had shown himself
so far to be quick to learn and dependable. Now it appeared
he was equally reliable under fire. "What's the *Highball*
revving at, kid?"

"500, skipper. She's ready."

The last bend in the track was approaching. Sweeping
round it, Millburn took a deep breath. "OK. Switches on."

"Switches on, sir. Master switch and number one."

Millburn's eyes fixed on the towering hill ahead. The flak
post had opened fire and shells were swirling towards the
Typhoons on his port side. As one aircraft suddenly swerved,
the American's attention was diverted. Only for a second but
at the high speed the Mosquito was travelling, the vectors
had changed when Millburn glanced back at the hill. Suddenly instinct, experience, every faculty honed from years of
combat screamed at him that he had waited too long and he
had only a split second to act.

Without warning Dalton was hurled back into his seat as
T-Tommy fought for height. The reeling terrain went grey
before the men's eyes as g forces drove blood down into their
bellies and legs. Screaming its protest the Mosquito seemed
about to break up as spars cracked under the tremendous
strain of the climb. For a moment it faltered as a wingtip
brushed the top branches of a fir. Then it staggered clear and
dived away to escape the shells that were now following it.

Millburn turned his sweating face towards Dalton. "Sorry,
kid. I made a balls of that, didn't I?"

Although white-faced, the New Zealander managed a
smile. "You couldn't help it, sir. It's a tight fit down there."

In A-Apple above Hoppy dropped back in his seat. "It's
a bloody death trap, skipper. We should have tackled it from
the other end."

Moore ignored him. "What's the situation, Tommy?"

"I'm not sure, skipper. I'll need to check her."

"Give me a report as soon as you can. Are you ready,
Frank?"

In D-Danny Harvey braced himself. Although still suffering from shock, the grim-faced Yorkshireman felt if he as
much as hesitated his confidence might be irreparably damaged. He put his Mosquito into a dive before Moore finished
speaking: "Get everything ready in good time. You've got

only seconds to do your work, once you enter that last stretch of track."

Harvey glanced at his shaken navigator. "You hear that?"

Hanson swallowed and nodded. "Yes, skipper."

Darting like a swift through the narrow valley, D-Danny leapt over the bridge, then settled down on the track again. Beneath him Harvey could feel the Mosquito trembling under the rotation of the bomb. As he swept round the bend, he lowered D-Danny until its slipstream hurled cinders into the flanking bushes. His shout silenced Hanson who was reading numbers from the bombsight. "Never mind all that shit! I'll drop the thing. Are all the switches on?"

"Yes, skipper. Everything's ready."

The flak post had already opened fire. Having learned by this time which aircraft represented a threat to the tunnel, the gunners concentrated their fire on D-Danny from the onset. Moving lazily at first, shells came swirling viciously towards the windshield. Cursing as his mouth turned dry, Harvey tried to ignore them as he lined up the Mosquito's nose with the dark entrance of the tunnel.

With D-Danny flying at over five miles a minute there were only seconds to aim and release the bomb. In his mind Harvey was counting . . . one . . . two . . . three . . . At four he pressed the release button and heaved back on the control column in almost the same movement. As D-Danny soared upwards the rotating bomb fell away, to land almost in the dead centre of the track. Bounding forward like a wheel coming off a speeding car it held its line and made for the tunnel entrance. As it disappeared inside, D-Danny cleared the hill and began climbing towards the aircraft above.

Tense crews were staring down. Long seconds passed and then yells of triumph were heard as a great plug of smoke, full of debris, shot out of the tunnel. A moment later, in a huge cloud of dust, the entire entrance collapsed on itself, followed by a landslide of soil, rock and trees that buried the track for thirty yards.

Although grimly satisfied—he had not forgotten Andrews and Warren—Harvey was feeling reaction as he and the PR Mosquito slid into station behind Moore. As always Moore was generous with his praise. "Great work, Frank. Davies will be over the moon when he gets the news."

Harvey ignored the comment. "What about our spare stores? Are you sure we can't jettison 'em?"

Harvey was referring to Davies' highly unpopular order that, owing to their scarcity, all unused *Highballs* should be brought back. Aware that too much had been said already with German monitors certain to be picking up every word, Moore was careful with his reply. "You heard the orders, Frank. Just make certain your fusing switches are off. You too, Tommy."

Millburn gave his navigator a wry grin. "You guys should worry. I've still got two of the goddamned things left."

Hoppy leaned across to Moore's microphone. "After the way you play the field, Yank, you're lucky."

Millburn grinned. "Jealousy'll get you nowhere, Cockney boy."

With Moore aware of his crews' need to release tension, his reprimand had a tolerant edge. "Save it for the mess tonight, all of you. Catfish Leader, we're going home."

There was respect now in the voice that answered him. "That was some job, Foxhound Leader. We'll keep a watch for you."

With the Mosquitoes back in their fingers-four formation and the remaining Typhoons giving them top cover, the aircraft headed back for the French coast and England.

17

Davies gave a start. "Guns? How can we put guns in 'em?"

"We must have them, sir." Murmurs of agreement came from the two Flight Commanders as Moore went on: "We could have been wiped out today without dropping a single bomb."

"That was an accident. It won't happen on the day."

"How can you be sure? From all this training we're obviously going to carry out a low level attack of some kind. We're sitting ducks at that height without armament."

Davies scowled. "You'll be getting an escort."

"We had one today, sir, and look what happened. There's another factor. If we'd had guns, they would have been a distraction to those flak posts. As it was they made it difficult for us to fly straight and level."

"But, dammit Moore, it's not possible. They'll never get cannon in, not even the short-barreled kind. The bomb bays are too full."

Moore was not giving an inch. "Even Brownings will be better than nothing. We must have some armament, sir."

With his scowl deepening, Davies turned towards the white-haired civilian alongside him. Barnes Wallis had flown into Sutton Craddock shortly after Moore and his men had taken off and had spent the next two hours anxiously waiting for news. His anxiety had seemed equally shared between concern for the crews' safety and the success or failure of his invention. Adams, that observer of human nature, had found this mental conflict fascinating. There was no doubt that because of his inventions Wallis had probably caused more enemy casualties than the most bloodthirsty Allied general, and there had been a time when Adams would have argued that it was this inability of scientists to reconcile their better natures to their inventions that posed one of the greatest threats to mankind. Now Adams was more tolerant, accepting that scientists were also human beings who had to work within the framework other human beings had created. From the few words he had passed with Wallis, Adams was now satisfied he was a kindly man who, convinced his country was threatened by one of the worst tyrannies the world had known, felt it was his duty to defend England with every means his inventive ability could bring it.

"What do you think, sir?" Davies asked. "Is it possible?"

"There might be one or two problems, Davies. But I can't really see why not."

Davies turned back to Moore who, along with his two flight Commanders and the PR pilot, had come into the Operations Room immediately after landing. "All right, I'll have a talk with de Haviland. If it can be done, we'll see if the Ministry will order a crash programme, although with everyone already working flat out I can't promise anything. Now, do you mind if we talk about the operation itself? What exactly happened?"

Moore gave a resume of the four attacks the Mosquitoes had made. When he had finished, Davies glanced at the PR pilot. "Had you a good view of all this?"

The tall pilot, with his enormous moustache, had the accent and self-assurance of a West End playboy. "Top hole, sir. Better than a front seat at the Windmill."

Davies gave him a look. "Where are the photographs now?"

"Half a dozen of your Waafs swooped on us when we landed. They promised to have them ready in an hour's time."

Giving him another look, Davies moved aside for Wallis. "Have you any questions to ask, sir?"

The scientist, who had already congratulated the crews on their success, turned to Moore. "What were your main problems, Wing Commander?"

"They weren't really connected with the weapon, sir. We were just unlucky finding a tunnel with flak protection. But in my opinion the bomb did everything you hoped for."

Millburn agreed as Wallis glanced at him. "The bomb's OK but we were cramped for air space. And your bombsight's too complicated for small targets. It's better to leave it to the pilot's judgment."

When Harvey contented himself with a nod, Wallis gave a sigh of relief. "Thank you, gentlemen. You've given us a strong case to put before the Committee."

At this point Davies broke in. "Surely they'll have to agree now, won't they?"

Wallis's shrug was wry. "I've learned never to be too optimistic about military committees, Davies. But I agree it's difficult to see how they can turn us down now, although I suppose they might ask for one more trial."

Davies brightened. "If they do, that's no problem." He turned towards the weary pilots. "All right, you can go and change now. And get yourselves a meal. I shan't be needing you again today."

As the men saluted and left, Davies turned with a grumble to Henderson who, like Adams, had been a silent witness at the debriefing. "Those guns are a damned nuisance. I thought we had plenty of time. Now we might be pushed."

"All the same, you can see Moore's point," Henderson argued. "And there's a factor he didn't mention. The lads are used to hitting back. If they don't have guns it might affect them psychologically."

Davies turned to Wallis. "Do you really think it's possible to put guns in them, sir?"

When it came to engineering problems, Wallis was always an optimist. "I need to look into the fuselage but I'm fairly sure it can be done one way or the other. Perhaps not with four Brownings but certainly with two or three."

With Davies excited by the day's events, it was enough to bring back his sense of well-being as he picked up his cap and glanced at Henderson. "The committee is meeting late tonight to hear the result of the trial, so Dr. Wallis and I are going there immediately. I want the photographs and ciné films flown down as soon as they're developed. I'll be back in the morning to let you know the outcome and to see the Brigadier." When the Scot nodded, Davies gave him a gnome-like grin of expectation. "It's looking good, Jock. I can't see how they can turn us down now—they can't afford to. So fasten your seat belt. The next few days could be exciting."

That evening Millburn paid Gabby a visit in the hospital. He found him, with his broken leg in splints, chatting with a pretty young nurse. Grinning, the American tossed a packet of cigarettes on his bed. "So you're at it again, boyo?" He turned to the girl. "You want to watch him, honey. They don't call him the Swansea Stallion for nothing."

Gabby scowled. "You always pick the wrong time to arrive, don't you?"

Millburn winked at the blushing probationer. "Keep him on bromide, honey, or he might do you a mischief."

Giggling, the girl withdrew to the far end of the ward where another two nurses had their eyes on the good-looking American with his row of decorations. "What did you want to say a thing like that for?" Gabby complained. "You've probably put her off me."

Millburn sat on the edge of the bed. "By letting her think you're a randy little bastard? When the word gets around, they'll be queuing up for your signature."

The scowling Gabby found another complaint. "You've been a long time coming to see me."

"Sure. All I have to do is come and see you. There isn't a war going on, you know. That's just a dirty Nazi rumour. How long do you expect to be in here anyway?"

Gabby eyed the three giggling girls. "I'm in no hurry. I think I'll let Davies finish that operation first."

Millburn scowled. "That's where I made my mistake. I should have had you slapped in the can for self-inflicted injuries." A thought struck the American as he glanced at the nurses. "What have you told those kids about your leg?"

Gabby gave a slight start, then innocence spread over his face. "What could I tell them? It's all in the medical report."

"I know it's in the medical report. But you've played the old soldier before. You've probably spun them a line that the report's just a cover up and you really got wounded on a secret mission. That'd be just your style."

"Don't talk a lot of cock, Millburn."

Grinning, Millburn turned. "Let's have a word with one of them and find out."

Gabby grabbed his arm. "What's the matter with you, Millburn? You've shot a line or two in your time, haven't you?"

The American's grin spread. "You little phoney! You stay in here one day more than necessary and I'll have every nurse in the place chasing you with doses of castor oil."

Henderson's red telephone rang just after 0130 hours the following morning. Half-asleep, the Scot stumbled into his office, stubbed his toe, and roundly swore. "Hello. Who is it?"

"It's Air Commodore Davies, sir."

Henderson's tone moderated. "Put him on, then."

Davies sounded jubilant. "We've pulled it off, Jock. We've got the job."

The Scot's attempt to sound pleased was a failure. "Congratulations, sir. What happens now?"

"We start training in earnest. But I don't want any

suspicions aroused; the boys can still go out in the evenings, although it's more important than ever they watch their tongues. I'll give you all details in the morning. Put a security guard around Adams's office and tell Moore to meet us there."

"What time will this be, sir?"

"Make it 0900 hours sharp. I'll be leaving here early, so keep a bite of breakfast warm for me."

Henderson felt he ought to say something. "Dr. Wallis must be pleased."

"He's arse over tip," Davies declared. "But then we all are." Even at that distance Davies' excitement was manifest. "It was touch and go at times but finally we managed to persuade them. Now it's up to us. It's a hell of a responsibility, as you'll soon find out, but I know we can pull it off." .

"Will you be letting General Staines know?"

"Of course. He's been waiting for their decision like the rest of us and in any case we're going to need his help. That's it then, Jock. See you in a few hours' time."

18

Henderson had been fearing this news ever since his trip down to Herefordshire. "You realize how dangerous this exercise is, sir, don't you?"

"I do fly a bit myself, Jock," Davies snapped. "And you saw how easily that youngster from Boscome Down coped."

"But if the operation calls for balloons to be taken out, why can't we shoot them down? Surely that would be safer than trying to cut their cables."

"That's where you're wrong. On the kind of target we're going to face, Jerry's likely to have guns zeroed on the balloons. On top of that I've heard his balloons are bastards to shoot down even when incendiaries are used."

Davies glanced at Moore for confirmation. The Squadron Commander, helping himself to coffee that a Waaf had brought in five minutes earlier, lowered his cup. "I've never tried it myself but I've heard rumours it is difficult. Did you say you wanted me to ask for volunteers, sir?"

The three men, along with Adams, were closeted in the Intelligence Officer's Nissen hut. Davies nodded. "I thought you'd prefer it that way. But if you want to detail four crews, I've no objections."

"I'll need to do that in any case, sir. If you remember, it's a squadron tradition for all crews to step forward when volunteers are called for."

Davies looked slightly ruffled by his failure to remember. "All right, then. Select four crews. Pick men with the best eyesight. Four reinforced Mossies will be flown in later this morning. The two transporters carrying the balloons should also arrive in an hour or two."

The men stared at him. Henderson looked horrified. "You're not thinking of having the exercise here?"

Davies looked defiant. "Why not? It's the most sensible place if you think about it. It saves time flying down to Herefordshire and more important, we've got all the backup services right on the job."

His listeners knew he was referring to crash wagons and ambulances. "I don't like this, sir," Henderson muttered. "It'll have a bad effect on the lads if we have a crash right in the middle of the field."

Not for the first time Davies' irritation betrayed him. "Nobody's going to crash, Jock. We'll practise first with thin ropes and pilot balloons. We won't move on to the real thing until everything is mastered."

The Scot was clearly not happy. "What about our squadron training to use Dr. Wallis's bomb?"

"We shall begin that tomorrow once this cable cutting stunt is over."

Moore broke in here. "As this job is dangerous, I feel my Flight Commanders and myself should be the ones to tackle it, sir."

Davies shook his head. "No. We've got a special job for you three. You'll learn all about it later."

"I'm talking about today's exercise, sir, not about the operation itself."

Davies frowned. "I don't see your problem. You know the cutters work. You saw the demonstration down in Herefordshire."

"I saw it but my men didn't. I don't think it's fair to give them the job without giving them proof."

"Damn it, Moore, why must you always argue with me?" Even as he snapped the words, Davies knew he was being unjust. The only time he had ever known Moore to show dissent was when the young Englishman was ordered not to share the same dangers as his men.

"With respect, sir, you're not being fair to me either. My duty is to lead my men, not to follow them. If something were to go wrong with this exercise I should feel responsible. I don't think you have the right to ask that of me."

Moore's talk of responsibility reminded Davies that the pilot was still blaming himself for the death of Teddy Young and five other crewmen. Although everyone who knew the circumstances believed Moore's guilt was unjustified, Davies was fair enough to admit it was probably a contributory factor in his present stand. As a result Davies contented himself with a grunt of disgust.

"All right. If that's how you feel, go ahead and kill yourself while I've still time to put someone in your place."

Both Henderson and Adams relaxed as Moore smiled. "I thought you said it wasn't dangerous, sir."

"It isn't dangerous," Davies snapped. "Only things have a way of going wrong if you use men you can't afford to lose. As a leader yourself you should know that."

Moore was thinking of that last comment of Davies' with some wryness as he circled the airfield in A-Apple that afternoon. At the southern end of the field, two additional transporters, about 200 yards apart, were standing parallel to the row of poplars. Over a thousand feet above, two barrage balloons, festooned in ropes, were straining on yellow-painted cables. With their clumsy stabilizers holding them steady, both balloons were pointing into the stiff northeasterly wind. Two crash wagons and an ambulance were parked in strategic positions on either side of the transporters.

Moore's eyes moved to groups of men standing on the tarmac apron and in front of the hangars. He knew the mood of his crews from the short briefing he had given them after lunch. Although every man had known the exercises were a prelude to sterner action, once the screens and crossbars had proved innocuous, the resilience of youth had allowed the crews to treat them as a joke. But today, the sight of the barrage balloons and their cruel steel cables had changed all that. Even the most unimaginative pilot or navigator could now put two and two together. The only jokes quipped that morning had been the grim ones men use to hide their apprehension.

Accordingly, even though only four of his pilots were flying that afternoon, Moore had decided to give a short talk to all his crews. In truth, they were no wiser about the forthcoming operation when he had finished than when he started, but Moore had a leader's gift for raising his men's spirits and there was no doubt they were in a better frame of mind when they all filed out to watch the exercise.

The pilots Moore had selected to follow him were Machin, West, King and Smith. Paddy Machin, Baldwin's pilot, was a hard-drinking, hard-swearing volunteer from Eire. Jim West was a pink-cheeked, post office worker from Kent. Bill King was a tough salesman from Manchester. Jock Smith was a bank clerk from Scotland. All four men and their navigators were well into their second tour of operations.

The seat alongside Moore was empty. Hopkinson had put up a fight but Moore had been adamant. Until otherwise ordered, navigators would not take part in the cable cutting exercise.

Moore had already made two runs. Both had been at pilot balloons bobbing at the end of long coloured ropes. Even so he had not made them without misgivings. To deliberately fly a wing against any obstacle went against a pilot's every instinct and Moore was not convinced the rope would not foul a propeller if his judgment or the cutters proved faulty. So far, all had gone relatively well. On his first attempt, the rope had struck too near his starboard wingtip and instead of sliding towards the cutters it had slid the opposite way and dropped past him. On his second attempt he had struck the rope nearer the cutters but it had snapped before sliding into them. Although this had not proven the effectiveness of the cutters, the discovery the ropes were frail enough to snap under impact had done no harm to the waiting pilots' confidence.

During the exercises Moore was in touch with both Davies and Henderson in the control tower and with the two balloon transporters. As a help to Machin and the rest, his voice could also be heard on loudspeakers Marsden had set up that morning. Davies, too, was linked into the same circuit and his somewhat high-pitched voice emerged from the loudspeakers as Moore circled the field.

"How does that Mossie handle with those reinforced wings, Ian?"

"She's a little sluggish, sir, but not as much as you'd expect."

A third metallic voice sounded a few seconds later. "We're ready for you, sir. We're flying at 1,200 feet."

"Thank you, lieutenant. I'm coming around now."

Moore's reply to the balloon crew had a calmness he did not feel. In spite of their bright colour, the cables were an extremely difficult target for fast-moving aircraft and Moore was only too aware how easy it would be for a man to make a misjudgment when confronted with the real thing. If this happened, or equally, if the cutters did not work, no aircraft could be expected to survive, especially one constructed of wood. With the Mosquito a notoriously difficult aircraft to escape from, there could be only one fate for its crew.

The slate roof of The Black Swan slid beneath A-Apple's starboard wing as the Mosquito levelled out over the road. Through the roar of its engines Adams, who was in the control tower with Henderson and Davies, could hear the echo of Moore's amplified voice coming from below. "Levelling off now. Height one thousand . . . nine fifty . . . nine hundred. Holding at nine hundred. Speed 320 knots. Can't see balloon cable yet." A long pause. "Yes . . . there it is. Steady . . . steady . . ."

Without realizing it, Adams was gripping the balcony rail tightly with one hand while he shaded his eyes with the other. Unable to stand the bright sky, his myopic eyes turned the Mosquito into a blur as it swept towards the balloon.

When blinking only made matters worse, he turned to Henderson for help. "What's happening? Has he cleared it yet?"

Both Henderson and Davies were too tense to answer. Neither could see the cable at that distance but they could see A-Apple heading directly for the column of sky between the transporter and its balloon and knew the point of impact could be only seconds away.

For Moore the cable looked as thin as the edge of a razor as it sliced towards him. He made no effort to jink as the young test pilot down in Herefordshire had done. Deciding his task was to prove to the pilots below that the cutters worked, he was flying as true a course as possible with the intent of striking the cable with his starboard wingtip.

As the vectors closed rapidly, he could feel sweat in the palms of his hands. With the cable less than fifty yards away it took him all his will power to hold A-Apple on course. A moment later the cable struck like a whiplash.

Although the moment of impact was over in a second, Moore's highly-strung senses broke it into four separate events. First, there was the impact, a brutal clang and jerk that swung A-Apple violently off course. Second, accompanied by a bright shower of sparks, there was a spine-cringing, rasping of metal as the cable dragged along the leading edge towards the claw of the cutters. Third, there was a sharp explosion. Finally, he heard a twang like an enormous bowstring snapping as the two halves of cable writhed away.

Below, the breathless onlookers saw a puff of smoke break from A-Apple's wing as the cutters fired. Three hundred feet above the Mosquito the barrage balloon reared skyward, then began drifting west. Relieved cheers broke out among the crews who had been as silent as Davies and his officers during the last couple of minutes. Millburn released his own tension by grinning at Hopkinson. "You know all we have to do now, boyo? Chase those balloons and pull 'em down with our bare hands. Then we're a cinch for Barnum and Bailey's circus."

The call on the radio telephone in the Control Tower came just as King's Mosquito was sweeping towards the transporters. The duty officer glanced at Davies. "It's the officer in charge of the balloon crew, sir."

While Davies answered the call, Moore was watching King's progress through a pair of binoculars. As a puff of smoke broke from the Mosquito's wing and the aircraft began climbing away, Davies turned to Henderson. "We shall have to call it off for today, Jock. They've run out of cables and need time to graft the severed ones together."

Henderson, who had found the last two hours a distinct trial, could not have heard better news. "Anyway, they've had a couple of runs apiece." He glanced at Moore. "That's enough, isn't it?"

Moore shrugged. "Don't forget we've been using coloured cables. Ordinary ones will be more difficult to see."

Henderson had had enough of balloons. "As I see it, it's going to be no more difficult picking up Jerry's cables on the day than picking them up here. The boys have had some practice. Let's leave it there and not push our luck."

Davies, his bird-like eyes moving from man to man, broke in before Moore could reply. "I agree with that, Jock. The boys seem to have got the hang of it and they've proven to themselves that the cutters work. Anyway, we've no option because tomorrow everyone's going up to Turnberry to begin their training with the bombs."

"Turnberry?" Henderson asked in surprise.

"Yes. That's where 618 have been doing their training. The BIVs are there, the practice bombs are there, and so are the armourers used to handling them. Moreover, they've got the security angle screwed down."

"Then we won't need to take any ground staff?"

"No. Just aircrews, yourself and Adams. On second thought, you'd better take your armament officer too. He'll need to know how the thing works."

"Will you be there, sir?"

"Oh, yes. And so will Dr. Wallis." Leaving Henderson to digest the news, Davies turned to Moore. "Your boys only have three days, so they'll have to work hard. As you and our Flight Commanders have already had the course, you'll only stay there until Thursday. Get the training schedules worked out, put your deputy commanders in charge, and be back here on Thursday afternoon." Davies' eyes returned to Henderson and Adams. "I want you two to come back with them.

We're all going to High Elms on Friday morning to meet the Brigadier, General Staines and Major Dent."

"Do you want our navigators as well, sir?" Moore asked.

Davies paused, then shook his head. "Not at High Elms. They'll get their briefing with the rest of the crews on the same day as the operation."

Henderson could feel the hard rapping of his heart. "Does that mean we're going to find out what our target is on Friday?"

The grin Davies gave him was meant to hide his excitement but in reality it accentuated it. "That's right, Jock. I hope you'll agree it's been worth waiting for."

19

The Mosquito was flying at no more than sixty feet as it crossed the wide estuary. Two others were circling above it. Ahead lay a three-quarter mile stretch of flat sand that the incoming tide had thinly covered. Rising from it were two wide columns of sandbags seventy feet apart with their bases reinforced by stout timbers. Behind them, where the beach began shelving into grass-covered dunes, a long steel net lay in a protective crescent.

A bulldozer with a mechanical shovel and three wide-tyred trucks were positioned on either side of the steel fence. A fourth truck was trundling away along a wire-mesh track that had been laid down on the beach. On a dry spit of land a quarter-mile to the south Davies, Henderson, Adams and Moore were watching the flight of the Mosquito through binoculars. An Army sergeant with an R/T set strapped to his back stood behind them. They were all wearing greatcoats. The day was grey with a hint of drizzle in the wind.

The Mosquito was heading for the right-hand pylon. At a

range of approximately 900 yards, a *Highball* dropped from
it. Spinning like a huge tennis ball with backspin, it touched
the water with a splash of foam and then skimmed forward.
Above it, the Mosquito swung a few degrees to port and flew
cleanly through the gap between the pylons. A second later
the bomb struck the right-hand pylon and, clinging to it,
disappeared from sight. Davies gave a grunt of approval.
"That's his second bullseye, isn't it? Who is he?"

"Paddy Machin," Moore told him.

"He seems to have got it sewn up. Let's see what the
others can do."

The second Mosquito was slightly less fortunate. The
bomb it released missed the pylon by ten feet and went
skimming over the shallow water to the shelving beach. There
it struck the steel fence with a shower of sparks and dropped
back. A plume of sand rose and then, as its rotation ceased, it
lay inert and half-buried in the shingle.

Before the third Mosquito was called down, the bulldozer trundled forward and heaved the bomb out with its
massive shovel. Dumping it into one of the waiting trucks, it
turned and backed into position again. At the same time the
slight figure of a man in fisherman's thigh boots had waded
out to the right-hand pylon where he could be seen fumbling
beneath the water. The delay made Davies frown. "We ought
to have had these trials in Lock Striven. It might have been
too deep there to let Wallis paddle about looking for his
bombs."

"Why didn't we?" Henderson asked.

"We're too short on practise bombs. The earlier ones
tended to break up on impact so they had to be given
hardened steel casings. But they're still in short supply, as
you see. It's a bloody nuisance because there's the tide to
consider."

"Must we have water to practise on? Couldn't we just
use the wet beach?"

Thinking he knew what was behind the question, Davies'
frown turned into a scowl. "You're going to find out tomorrow
what the target is, Jock. Surely you can wait just one more
day."

With the enthusiastic Wallis now back again behind the
steel fence, the third Mosquito was called down. Piloted by

Matthews, it flew a few feet lower than the aircraft that had preceded it and its bomb struck the centre of the sandbagged pylon. The sight restored Davies' good humour. "All they need now is to shorten their bombing run and release time. That'll be critically important on the day. All right. Let's see what Harvey's boys can do."

With Harvey and Millburn not required back at Sutton Craddock until that evening, the two Flight Commanders had decided to supervise their crews' training in person and at the same time have more practice themselves. With the tide factor to consider, half of the Yorkshireman's flight was at the moment orbiting the estuary at six-thousand feet. The rest of his men were scheduled to arrive in thirty minutes' time.

D-Danny was the first aircraft to dive down and could be seen banking over the far side of the estuary. No one paid any attention to the large fishing boat that was beating out to sea in the deep channel just north of the testing range. All eyes were on the Mosquito as she headed toward the pylons, and the displacement waves that the fishing boat was pushing out went unnoticed.

On orders from Wallis, Harvey had set his bomb's rotation at 700 revs instead of the earlier 500 revs. Travelling at 340 mph at a height of 50 feet, he pressed his bomb release at 650 yards range. By sheer bad luck it was the moment when the first and largest of the waves was passing beneath D-Danny. As the spinning bomb struck the wave, a column of water was hurled up into the Mosquito's starboard propeller. Instantly the steady beat of the Merlin turned into a high-pitched scream as the metal tips of the propeller were bent outward. Momentarily out of control, D-Danny yawed and a line of foam appeared as her starboard wingtip actually touched the water. Somehow Harvey righted her and with a screech that made the onlookers wince she began clawing herself from the sea.

Moore grabbed the microphone from the sergeant. "Frank! Can you hold her?"

The Yorkshireman's voice sounded gruffer than usual. "I hope so. What happened?"

"Your Highball hit a wave. Jettison your second bomb,

Frank! Quickly! Then get straight back to base. Don't forget to alert the rescue services before you land."

D-Danny turned unsteadily out to sea before her second bomb dropped away. Although the beach was deserted, Harvey was taking no risks with the men below. The Mosquito banked gingerly again and the screech of its engine began to fade. Seeing the tightness of Moore's expression as he handed the mike back, Davies turned to Henderson. "I'm drawing Harvey and Millburn out now. I can't take any more chances with them at this point in time. Let their deputy commanders take over the rest of the training. We'll go and get our things packed now and then start back for the station."

She heard him cry out and awoke instantly. "What is it, Liebling?"

He did not answer and as she leaned over him she realised he was still asleep. In the dim light of the room she saw his lips move again and he muttered something she could not interpret. A moment later a moan broke from him and he jerked violently. Hesitating, she laid a hand on his shoulder. "Liebling; what is the matter?"

His sleep was too deep. As he moaned again, she shook his arm. "Wake up, darling. Please wake up."

His eyes opened and stared up at her. They were wide, the eyes of a man still in the grip of a nightmare. Then he recognized her and he closed them with a sigh of relief. She pressed against him. "Was it a bad dream, darling?"

He nodded without speaking.

"What was it about?"

His eyes opened again and his head rose from the pillow as if reassuring himself of her presence. When he still did not answer her, she bent over him again. "Tell me about your dream, Liebling, please."

Harvey shook his head. "I don't remember it," he lied.

20

It was exactly 1100 hours on Friday morning when Davies ushered his small party into the library at High Elms. Staines and Alan Dent were already present and in conversation with the Brigadier. A large object covered in white sheeting was resting on the polished table with an unrolled map alongside it. It drew the newcomers' eyes as they exchanged salutes with the Americans.

The Brigadier's welcome was as courteous as ever. "Thank you for being so punctual, gentlemen. I think I am right in believing you have all met at one time or another?"

Staines gave the British party his huge grin. "That's for sure. And the last meeting beat 'em all." His bushy eyebrows tilted towards Moore. "How's that crazy little navigator of yours? Have they given him a wooden leg yet?"

The corner of Moore's mouth twitched as he saw Davies scowl. "He doesn't seem to want one, sir. I understand he's making good progress."

"He sure picked a hell of a ship to fall out of. Maybe he thought he was jumping from a Mosquito."

Moore laughed. "After that dinner you gave us, sir, it's quite possible."

The rest of Davies' party was hardly aware of the conversation. All were trying to make sense of the tucks and folds of the sheet-covered object, and it came as a relief to them when the courtesies were over and the Brigadier called everyone to the table.

"I believe you all know the reason for this conference, gentlemen, although I understand that most of you still do not know what your target is. Firstly then I will call on Air

Commodore Davies to explain. After that we will go into the more technical details."

As Davies gave the soldier a nod of acknowledgment and rose to his feet, the tension in the library tightened like a bowstring. Davies' eyes were bright with excitement as they travelled over the curious faces. They halted on the square features of Henderson.

"Well, here it is at last—the reason you've been cursing me up hill and down dale for weeks and why you've had your men flying through hoops, cutting balloon cables, and generally acting like circus performers. I know how irritating the secrecy has been to you, but we've had no option. It isn't just your boys' lives that are at risk or even the lives of thousands of Allied soldiers. The greatest risk of all is to the invasion itself and all it means to the world. That's why, with every German spy in the business trying to find out when, where, and how, we've been forced to do the training piecemeal and to behave like actors in a third-rate thriller. Needless to say, the security situation is as urgent as ever, so you won't breathe a word outside this room of anything you're about to hear."

Davies paused like the master presenter he was. In the brief silence that followed Adams could hear the ticking of his wristwatch. As he coughed to relieve his tension, Davies' gaze moved around the table. "The invasion will take place in either Normandy or Brittany, gentlemen. The exact location you need not know at this time."

Loud murmurs ran around the table. For once the phlegmatic Henderson looked as excited as anyone. "Can I ask when, sir?"

"Very shortly, Jock. Within a few days, in fact. That's why we can't withhold from you the nature of your target any longer." Davies reached forward and jerked away the sheeting. "So here it is!"

A plaster of paris model was revealed. As men jumped to their feet to gain a better view, Millburn's voice was heard through the startled comments. "You see that? It's a god-damned bridge!"

Davies glanced at the American. "That's right. Probably the most important bridge in the history of warfare." Noticing Henderson's expression, Davies could not hold back the quip.

"You're looking surprised, Jock. Didn't I give you enough clues?"

The Scot was too fascinated by the model to answer. Expertly made, it depicted a wide road bridge spanning a river. Twin towers on either side provided anchor points. Three square piers supported the structure, two abutting the banks and a third rising from the river. A small town was built around the bridge and the major road it served. The river itself had steep banks lined with trees. The impression the model conveyed was a structure of massive proportions.

Motioning his audience to join him, Davies picked up the map and moved to the end of the table where he unrolled it. With Adams and Millburn anchoring down the ends, he picked up a pointer.

"I don't need to stress to any of you here the difficulty of destroying bridges from the air. From heavy bombers flying at altitude, they look no thicker than matchsticks and are as hard to hit. If medium bombers are used at low level, the bombs they carry aren't heavy enough and can't achieve a sufficiently high terminal velocity to do any real harm. Even a specialized heavy bomber unit like 617 Squadron, carrying the latest 12,000 lb block-busters, has made three attacks on the bridge at Anthéor without success and it's doubtful if it's any stronger than this one. However, although God knows how many sorties it has taken us, we and the Americans have managed to destroy all the important bridges in this sector of the Loire except this one. Here's its position on the map."

Davies' pointer came to rest on a spot between Angers and Tours. "You're probably wondering why we've been concentrating so hard on the Loire. The reason's simple. Jerry has considerable forces down in the south of France because we've given him cause to believe we might launch a simultaneous invasion down there. However, when we strike through Brittany or Normandy, he'll quickly rush these forces north and his only major obstacle is the Loire river which, as you probably know, varies between 500 and 1000 metres in width. His main route," and here Davies' pointer moved up and down the arterial road north and south of the bridge, "is here at Langeais, taking him up through Le Mans and then west or north according to where our landing sites are."

About to ask a question, Adams paused as the small Air

Commodore continued: "Of course Jerry could use the few bridges we've left, mostly on the extreme eastern and western reaches of the Loire, but these don't worry us. Our interdiction raids have done such damage and the approach roads are so narrow that we're confident our fighter-bombers can take care of any reinforcements that filter through this way. But this bridge and the main route it feeds are another matter. If Jerry moved fast—and he usually does—he could have his men and armour across that bridge in less than twelve hours and after that there'd be no stopping them until they reached our bridgehead. If that were to happen, our Chiefs of Staff believe it would have a significant, if not disastrous, effect on our invasion strategy."

On this portentous note, Davies' voice turned grim. "You'll understand why when I tell you that among other panzer units the enemy has at least one SS Armoured Division stationed at Limoges equipped with the latest King Tiger tanks. These brutes weigh over 68 tons and have armour as thick as a battleship. The average road bridge simply won't carry their weight but we happen to know this bridge will. Because just one of these monsters can wipe out a squadron of the light tanks we'll be putting ashore during the first few days, I hardly need stress the importance of holding them at bay until our beachhead is solidly established."

Men were looking puzzled as Davies paused. Three arms were raised, only to be drawn back when Henderson put the question, "It might be difficult to knock bridges down, sir, but I notice we still managed to do it to all the others that could have threatened our invasion beaches. So why have we left the most important one of all?"

Davies seemed to welcome the question. He glanced at Staines who was standing beside the Brigadier at the opposite side of the table. "As your B-17s have been involved in this action, sir, perhaps you'd care to answer that."

Staines' voice, which had been likened to ball bearings rolling inside a tin can, was in marked contrast to Davies' somewhat high-pitched delivery. "OK; I'll do my best. As your guys know, our interdiction raids aren't only to make it tough for the Krauts to rush up reserves when we invade. The other purpose is to fool him where the invasion is going to be. As we can't flatten everything, we've tried to spread out the damage so that no one sector will give the game away. That's why we had to stop at this bridge. If we'd clobbered it too, the Krauts might have been certain Brittany or Normandy was the place."

Raising an arm Adams was forestalled again, this time by Moore. "I'm still wondering why you left this key bridge. Wouldn't a nearby one have done as well?"

"Not really. We've had to destroy so many of the god-damned things that we felt we had to leave one big one to balance things out."

"But as it lies on a main route to the north, isn't its survival a giveaway in itself?"

Staines acknowledged the question with an appreciative wry grin. "You've got the problem, Moore. Fool the Krauts but don't fool 'em too much in case you don't fool 'em at all. We got around that by sending out two high-level missions *after* we'd decided to let the bridge stand. Only we didn't tell my B-17 boys that they were carrying low-yield bombs. That way they made it look real; in fact, they scored two or three direct hits. Now we're hoping the Krauts think we don't feel it important enough to go on trying."

Shaking his head at this example of think and double-think, Henderson aimed his question at Davies as much as Staines. "In other words this bridge mustn't be destroyed before the invasion, but must go down less than twelve hours after it?" As both men nodded, the Scot went on: "That's clear enough but why have we been chosen for the job? Surely the answer is to send out a large force of B-17s or Lancasters as soon as our troops land on the beaches. You said yourselves that only heavy bombers flying at altitude can clobber large bridges."

Staines answered him. "That was the original plan. In fact, it was the only plan until Barnes Wallis and your men proved *Highball* would work."

"But *Highball* only carries 600 lb of high explosive. How can that bring a bridge down?"

"You'll learn that in a few minutes. The reason you've been chosen in preference to B-17s or Lancasters is because neither force can guarantee to destroy the bridge inside that time limit. One of us would get it, sure we would, but it'd be a pure gamble we got it in time."

"But isn't our attack a gamble too?"

Staines shrugged his massive shoulders. "Less of a gamble than a high-level attack. And with the stakes so high, we have to grab the best odds we can get."

"But if it's the last bridge in that sector, won't it be heavily defended? At low level, we'll run into everything from LMGs upward."

At this point Davies took over. "Give us time, Jock, and you'll find we've thought about all that. But first you need to know the strengths and weaknesses of the bridge and for that we're fortunate enough to have with us a prominent member of the Loire River Board that one of our agents recently brought over from France."

With all eyes on Davies, no one noticed the start Harvey gave. As Davies nodded at the Brigadier, the elderly soldier picked up a telephone. "Hello, Taylor. You can bring Monsieur Boniface into the library now."

It was noon before Davies completed his briefing. His glance at Henderson was challenging. "Well, now that you've heard how we intend to clobber the bridge, do you feel any better?"

The Scot was looking shaken rather than reassured. "It's a hell of a chancey operation, sir." He looked at Moore. "Don't you think so, Ian?"

Moore's shrug was noncommittal. "It's difficult to say. I don't know if the bombs will work. That's Dr. Wallis's department. The rest depends on the defences. If they aren't strengthened any more and if Major Dent's boys give us cover, then I'd say we have a reasonable chance."

"But will the defences stay the same?" Henderson asked. He turned back to Davies. "When was the last surveillance, sir?"

"We sent a Spitfire over, three days ago." As Henderson opened his mouth to protest, Davies frowned. "We can't send kites over every day, Jock, or we'll make 'em suspicious."

"All the same, sir, three days is a long time. I think we ought to have another check."

Moore broke in before Davies had time to answer. "As this is a complicated operation, sir, I'd like to study the entire area before I lead the boys in. If I went out in the PR Mosquito we could take photographs at the same time."

This time Davies was adamant. "Right out of the question. You're going to be the Master of Ceremonies on the day and I can't take any chances with you beforehand. Nor can I provide you with an escort in case we let the cat out of the bag. You'll have to manage with photographs and models but what I will do is ask Benson to send another Spittie over." He glanced at the Brigadier. "Could you get the latest weather forecast for me?"

Nodding, the elderly soldier left the library, to return three minutes later. "There's a wide band of clouds across central France at the moment but it's expected to drift north this afternoon or this evening. The forecast for tomorrow is good visibility."

Thanking him, Davies turned back to Moore. "All right, I'll ask Benson to do another surveillance for us at their first opportunity. I'll have another chat with you when we get the photographs."

21

Moore's office telephone rang at 1030 the following morning. "Hello, sir. There's a Flight Officer Walton wants to speak to you. Shall I put her through?"

Moore knew nobody of that name. "Does she say what she wants, Tess?"

"No, sir. Just that she wants to speak to you." The Waaf was curious. "She has a foreign accent of some kind. Shall I ask what she wants?"

Moore was aware of the sudden hard rapping of his heart. "No, it's all right, Tess. Put her through."

There was no mistaking the voice that followed—Moore

had heard it a hundred times in his memory. "Am I speaking to Wing Commander Moore?"

"Yes. Moore speaking."

"I would very much like to see you, Wing Commander. Can it be arranged?"

In spite of the need for security, Moore was not finding it easy to act as if they were strangers. "When have you in mind?"

"As soon as possible, please. It is very important."

"It's very difficult this morning. But I might be able to manage an hour this afternoon."

"That will be wonderful. Where shall we meet?"

Knowing where the girl was staying, Moore paused. "As I'm pressed for time, could you meet me at Coninsby? Or is that difficult for you? It's a village fifteen miles from the airfield."

"I'm sure that will be all right. Where shall I see you?"

"There's a small café on High Street called The Tea Room. I'll try to be there by three o'clock, although if I'm a few minutes late you'll have to excuse me."

"I understand and I shall wait there. Thank you, Wing Commander. Good-bye for now."

Relieved the artificial conversation was over, Moore replaced the receiver and stood staring down at it. Five minutes later, when he walked out through the anteroom into the corridor outside, his pretty Waaf lifted her head from her typewriter and gazed after him. In the months she had served as his secretary, it was the first time the courteous young Squadron Commander had walked through her office without acknowledging her.

The tea room was old-fashioned and cosy, with copper ornaments, white tablecloths, and lace curtains. Anna, wearing an RAF uniform, was seated at a far table with her back to the door when Moore entered. She did not turn until he reached her table. "Hello, Ian. How good of you to come."

He paused by her chair. At close quarters her Glengarry cap enhanced her abundant dark hair. Her oval face, more beautiful than he remembered it, was slightly pale. For once in his life the self-possessed Moore felt restrained and tongue-tied.

"Hello, Anna. It's been a long time."

Her expression, usually so composed, told him that she too was in doubt how to handle their meeting. "Yes, it has. A very long time."

He made no attempt to kiss her as he dropped into a chair opposite. "I didn't think I was going to get the chance to see you. I'm sorry I couldn't come straight away but there's a bit of a flap on at the station at the moment."

"It doesn't matter. I told you that."

Her grey eyes were moving over his face. For him memories were flooding back: their first meeting in The Black Swan when she had looked as regal as a queen, the dance when she had defended Harvey against his criticisms, her warmth in his car later that same evening, her courage when he had seen her off at Tempsford to fly back into Gestapo-infested Europe. At that time Moore had believed she was the girl he had been looking for all his life. Back with her now, he knew his feelings had not changed.

"How are you, Ian?"

"I'm all right. I've been living on the fat of the land. It's you who've been having the hard time. I heard you'd been ill."

"It was nothing. I am quite better now. But you—I think like Frank you are looking thinner and a little older."

He gave a wry smile. "We are older, Anna. A year of war older."

"Frank says you received a wound in the leg shortly after I went back. Does it bother you very much?"

"No. It just stings a little in cold weather. Mind you, that could be old age."

Their laughter was self-conscious. "Old age," she said. "Sometimes I feel a hundred."

He smiled. "That makes you the prettiest old lady I've ever seen. For that matter the prettiest Waaf too."

She coloured slightly. "Thank you, sir."

Both felt relief when a skinny girl wearing an apron approached them. For the first time Moore noticed an empty coffee cup on the table. "More coffee? Or tea and scones?"

Taking their order, the young waitress moved away. Anna gave a laugh of delight. "English tea and scones! Sometimes I have to pinch myself to prove I'm back again. It all seems so cosy and sane." Her tone changed. "How did you know I was back, Ian? Did Frank tell you?"

"No. I understand he was ordered to keep quiet. It was Davies who told me."

"Davies?"

When he explained the reason, she nodded. "Yes; they made me promise not to contact anybody. I can't blame them, they have their reasons."

"But you have permission to see me?"

Her answer surprised him. "No. I'm doing this against orders."

"Isn't that dangerous for you?"

"I don't think so. But in any case I had to see you."

Deep in his mind a sunlit door opened. He offered her a cigarette and then noticed she seemed to be avoiding his eyes. It was so uncharacteristic of her that he found it difficult to frame his question. "We're not just making conversation, are we, Anna? You haven't another reason for wanting to see me?"

For a moment she showed resentment. "Why should I have another reason? Didn't you save Frank's life on the way back from Bavaria? Aren't we old friends?"

His smile was rueful. "I like to think so. But you give me the feeling you've something to ask me. Has it anything to do with Frank?"

The way her eyes met his again was a reminder of her courage. "You're very perceptive, aren't you, Ian?"

The sunlit door closed. "Not really. What's your problem?"

She visibly braced herself. "You're quite right. It is about Frank. I think his nerve is going."

Moore gave a start. "Frank?"

Her eyes and voice challenged him. "Why not? He's done far more combat flying than most men, hasn't he?"

"Yes. Far more."

"Very well. Then he deserves a rest. I'm asking you to take him off combat flying."

It was a plea that astonished Moore. "How can I do that? What reason can I give?"

"I've just given you one. If he continues flying he will kill himself and perhaps others too."

About to protest, Moore fell silent as the waitress arrived

with their order. Opposite him, Anna's face was pale from the step she was taking. Moore waited until the girl had disappeared into the kitchen before leaning forward. "Anna, that applies to any one of my men. They're all battle-fatigued."

She inhaled smoke. "I'm not talking about any other men. I'm talking about Frank."

"But how can I give Frank privileges I don't give the others?"

Guilt turned her bitter. "I thought you were his friend."

In spite of himself, Moore stiffened. "You want me to give him special privileges because of that? Do you think he would want them? If you do, you don't know Frank."

She winced. "I'm sorry. I shouldn't have said that. But who else can I go to for help?"

Moore relaxed. "Why are you so certain he needs help? I've seen no change in his combat efficiency." Before she could answer he went on. "This isn't like you, Anna. You're the girl who wants the Nazis overthrown more than any person I know. You've been risking your life to that end for years. And yet you're asking me to ground a first-class pilot. Thousands of other women must feel the same way about the men they love but they don't ask for them to be withdrawn from combat."

Her dark head bowed. "I know how it must sound. But he isn't well. He's finding it hard to sleep and has terrible dreams when he does."

"It's still a big step for you to take. I'm assuming he knows nothing about it?"

"Of course he doesn't. He'd probably never speak to me again if he did."

"Then why are you doing it?" A suspicion that had been in Moore's mind for days came to the surface. "Has it anything to do with this operation that's coming up shortly?"

Habit turned her expression blank. "What operation?"

"Something Davies said the other day made me wonder if you were involved. Am I right?"

She gazed at him for a long moment, then glanced around. There were only two other tables occupied and they were near the door. "Yes. It was I who brought the French engineer over."

"Then you know the operation will be dangerous. Is that why you want Frank grounded?"

She was nothing if not honest. "I suppose it is one reason. But it isn't only that. The war goes on and on . . . when will it end? Frank won't live through it the way he is going and I will be responsible."

Moore stared at her. "You? Responsible? How do you work that out? He's been happier than I've ever known him since you came back."

"One part of him is. But another part is feeling the strain. Until we met again this time, I don't think he was truly convinced that I loved him. Now that he knows I do, his attitudes are changing."

"In other words you're saying he doesn't want to get himself killed and lose the things he values. At a rough guess I'd say every second man in my squadron feels the same way."

She shook her head at his inability to understand. "No. It's not like that. Frank never thinks about himself. He is only thinking about what it might do to me. It comes from his background. He was taught responsibility from the day he was born. Even today he sends half his pay home to his invalid father. He's a rare man, one who knows there is not much love in the world and he protects those who give love to him. And protection has many faces. Do you know what he once told me?"

Moore dropped back in his chair. "Go on."

"He said that if his mother had lived he would have found the dangers of combat flying far harder to bear. Does that sound like a man who is thinking of himself? Sometimes I think he has only been free in the time between his mother's death and his meeting me. Frank is different from most men in that he accepts the penalties love brings and tries to honour them."

Moore was sitting motionless. He was remembering a 24-year-old pilot, Peter Marsh, who had been in his squadron the previous year. With a young neurotic wife who suffered hell every time he flew into combat, the strain had eventually proven too much for Marsh and his combat efficiency had suffered. Harvey had fought to have him grounded and in the end had substituted himself for the young man in the Rhine

Maiden mission, an act that had nearly cost the Yorkshireman his life.

The girl's pale face held Moore's eyes as he listened. "Not all men are natural warriors thirsting to kill their enemies. Some feel a need to live for those they love rather than a desire to die for those they hate. Although Frank has always done his duty as he sees it, he is not a warrior by nature."

Moved by her words, Moore took a moment to answer her. "I'm sure you're right. I think I've always known it. But have you thought he could ask exactly the same of you? If you were captured over there, he'd go out of his mind."

She was too intelligent not to have had the same thought. "Yes, I realize that. But what can I do? I've built up a large network over there and people have come to rely on me. If I didn't go back, some might even die."

As he met her eyes she suddenly understood. "You're saying he has the same responsibility towards his own men, aren't you?"

"Yes," he said gently. "And remember Frank hoards his men's lives like a miser hoards gold. He'd go crazy if they went out on this mission under another Flight Commander."

The despair in her voice made him wince. "You're right. We're trapped, aren't we, Ian? There's no escape for either of us."

He felt he had to offer her some hope. "I can't do anything about this operation. I need Frank for it and no one knows better than you how important it is. But I will promise you this. When I get back today I'll put in a personal recommendation to Davies that Frank is put on rest after it. He's near the end of his third tour and although I can't promise anything, since Davies views this operation as the big one, I think he will agree. After all, he has a soft spot for you."

Her grey eyes filled with tears. Impulsively she reached out and laid a hand over his own. "I couldn't hope for more than that, could I? Thank you, Ian. You're a wonderful person."

He felt as if an electric current were flowing from her hand to every nerve in his body. As his eyes lifted, her hand tightened. "Do one more thing for me."

He smiled. "What?"

"Apply for a rest yourself. You've been flying even longer

than Frank." When he continued to smile, her voice rose. "Please, Ian. It's very important to me."

Moore knew he was never going to forget that old-world tea room. For both their sakes he kept his reply light. "Then I'll have to, won't I? All right. After the operation."

She searched his face for his sincerity. When he nodded, she slowly withdrew her hand and glanced at her watch. "My bus goes in fifteen minutes. I had better catch it or Frank will wonder what has happened to me."

He felt like two people at that moment. The real man who could barely face the parting and the actor who was showing no emotion. "Can I drop you off?"

"No. The bus stop is in the marketplace. It's only just round the corner."

He knew that once she had gone he would remember a hundred things to say to her but he could think of only one in the silence that followed. "Before I forget, I had a memo from Davies this morning. All leave passes throughout the Command will be stopped after midnight tomorrow. You'd better know in case Frank hasn't heard yet."

Although both knew what the order signified, neither made a comment. For Moore the minutes were now slipping through his fingers like precious stones. As she gazed at her watch again, he rose. "I'll see you to the bus stop."

"No. Please. Let us say good-bye here. I hate saying good-byes in the street." As he sank back, she reached out for his hand again. "You will take great care, won't you?"

His mind was only on her and how beautiful she looked. "Care?"

"Yes. During the operation. It could be very dangerous."

He stirred. "Yes. We'll be careful. Both of us. Now you had better go or Frank will be in Scarborough before you."

Her hand tightened and she suddenly leaned forward and kissed him. Before he could respond, she turned and hurried toward the door.

Sitting in his chair, he watched her. She paused outside the window and gazed inside but the lace curtain hid her expression. Then she turned and disappeared.

The cosiness of the tea room had vanished but he sat another five minutes before calling over the waitress. When he finally rose and went outside, a steady drizzle was falling.

22

Moore had not been back at Sutton Craddock more than twenty minutes before Henderson phoned him. The Scot sounded disturbed. "Come to Adams's office, will you, Ian? Air Commodore Davies is here with the photographs."

Adams's large desk was littered with prints when Moore arrived. Henderson barely gave him the time to salute Davies before thrusting three photographs at him. "They have strengthened their defences, Ian. Take a look at these."

One print was an enlargement of the bridge. Adams, a specialist in photo interpretation, reached over Moore's arm and pointed at the twin towers at either side of the bridge. "Both have flak posts on them, Ian. We think they're quadruple-mounted 2cm Flakvierling 38s."

The second photograph was an oblique one of the river banks. Dark gaps in the woods that ran along them were emphasized on the print by arrows. "We're fairly certain these are gun sites," Adams said. "They'll probably be a mixed bag, from 88s down to LMGs. You'll have to keep below the trajectories of the heavier stuff."

"Look at the number," Henderson muttered. "There seems to be one every hundred yards."

Without comment Moore glanced at the third photograph. An almost vertical shot of the western reaches of the river, it showed a torpedo boom lying across the water like a knotted string. Another mile or so to the west were eight dark shapes zigzagging from bank to bank. Adams nodded at Moore's question. "Yes, they're the river barges we expected. When they're flying their balloons, they'll stretch a tight net on either side of the bridge."

"Then the defences are the same on both sides?"

Henderson passed over more photographs. "Exactly the same as far as we can see." He threw an accusing glance at Davies. "Can you really believe after all this that Jerry hasn't guessed our game, sir?"

Davies frowned. "How could he? He's just playing safe, that's all. We expected it; that's why your boys have had all this training. Their *Highballs* should skip over those torpedo nets as if they weren't there."

"Perhaps, sir. But *Highballs* can't knock out flak posts. And I never expected half this number."

Davies' frown deepened. "All right, Jock, I know the defences are heavy. But our job isn't to bellyache, just to find a way round them because that bridge must be destroyed. I promise to get you all the Typhoons I can to attack those flak posts. Happier now?"

Henderson's sigh said it all. "I haven't much choice, have I, sir?"

"No, you haven't. I came to give you your orders for the day and I'm short on time. We've decided to use Holmsley down on the south coast as your advance base."

The three officers exchanged glances. Feeling it was time to take pressure off Henderson, Adams put the question himself. "Why Holmsley, sir?"

"Why not Holmsley? You used it during the Crucible operation and found it satisfactory enough. And we're setting it up with a full range of communications. It gives us one big advantage. You'll save over four hundred miles at this end, so you'll have that extra fuel to stay longer over the target if it proves necessary." Fishing into a pocket, Davies pulled out an envelope and handed it to Henderson. "Here are your billeting orders. We weren't able to get you the same hotel as last time—the Yanks have taken it over. But we've managed a large house in Brockenhurst that used to be an old ladies' rest home."

As Davies hoped, the Scot's sense of humour came to his rescue. "It sounds just the place for us."

Davies grinned. "I'll promise you something a bit stronger than tea and scones." He turned to Moore. "I don't want the boys briefed until we get there. I'll be coming myself and you'll get plenty of warning."

Moore nodded. "What about our maintenance crews and spares?"

"I'll be sending Dakotas to ferry them down. There's no chance of using the roads. Transports are bumper to bumper all the way from London to the south coast. So the bombs might also have to be flown down."

"When do we leave, sir?" Adams asked.

In spite of the security guards outside, Davies lowered his voice. "You fly down the day after tomorrow. The divisions who're to spearhead the attack are already in their embarkation areas."

Adams's stomach seemed to contract. "Does that mean D-day has been chosen?"

Davies cast a glance of dislike at the rain that was beginning to beat against the window as the wind rose. "It has, but let's hope this weather improves. A delay now could foul up everything."

If anything, Davies was guilty of an understatement. The extensive mine laying of the enemy, plus the great mass of mined obstacles on the beaches and out beyond the low water mark, made a landing on a rising tide essential. The moon was also desirable at night. These factors fixed the possible invasion dates as the 5th, 6th, or 7th of June in that order of preference. After that, no opportunity would occur until the 19th of June and that date would exclude the moon.

Although the possibility of a delay had been taken into account, the very thought of it made strong men blanch. As Davies was expressing his anxiety, thousands of men were already aboard their transports and many thousands more were preparing to embark. Even if D-Day stood, they would be locked on board their ships for nearly a week, with all the boredom and discomforts that entailed.

But their situation paled beside the logistics behind them. Like some enormous glacier moving implacably down a mountainside, a million more men with all their weapons, artillery, armour and transports were converging on the embarkation ports. Another 1,000,000 tons of supplies were moving with them. And that was not all. Right across Britain and across the Atlantic to America, millions more men and millions more tons of supplies were clogging the pipelines. It

was small wonder men's minds were reeling even as they
revised their contingency plans.

Yet the dangers of launching the attack in adverse conditions were even greater. Combat troops would be seasick and
have the greatest difficulty in transferring into their assault
craft. On the beaches heavy waves and surf would make them
even more vulnerable to enemy fire. Perhaps most serious of
all were the risks involved in towing the Mulberry harbour
components across the Channel. The Phoenix units alone
stood taller than six-story buildings and no one was absolutely
certain how they would behave on such a long journey even
in calm weather. If they were to sink or capsize before they
reached the beaches, the chance of German reserves arriving
there first was almost ensured.

Meanwhile battle training continued wherever possible
with its attendant accidents. A hint of the horrors ahead was
given only two days after the assault troops were sealed in
their embarkation areas. Infantrymen of American Force U
were exercising in the Channel in a final assault rehearsal
when two flotillas of German E boats sighted them and
engaged. Two tank landing craft were sunk and another damaged. In all 749 men, mostly military engineers, lost their
lives.

Across the Channel, as capable as the Allies in working
out favourable tides and moon tables, the Germans had decided
the most likely time for the assault was the period between
the middle of May and the 7th of June. Enemy opinion was
also hardening that the massive buildup of shipping in the
south and southwest of England pointed to Normandy as the
Allies' objective. Field Marshall Rommel, appointed Inspec-
tor of the Western Defences in November 1943, had always
held this belief and had repeatedly made requests that all
available heavy armour should be kept in the Cotentin peninsula so that an immediate and massive counterstroke could be
made when the Allies landed.

His superior, Field Marshall von Rundstedt, did not
share Rommel's conviction, however, arguing that if panzer
reserves were tied up in this way and the Allies were to
thrust at Pas de Calais, the bomb-damaged roads and railways
plus the inevitable air offensive would leave the northern
sector at the Allies' mercy. He insisted that Panzer reserves

should be held at strategic centres where they could be rushed north or south as the situation demanded.

At the end of May, then, the disposition of the enemy forces in the proximity of the Normandy beaches were as follows: Seven German infantry divisions of the VII army were stationed in Normandy itself. The XXI Panzer Division and the XII SS Panzer Division were poised at the base of the peninsula. A third armoured division was in reserve near Le Mans, while the two heavy panzer divisions that Allied planners particularly feared were south of the Loire, the SS unit near Limoges and the XI Panzer unit north of Bordeaux.

In accordance with his advisers and his own instincts, Rommel had ordered a red alert the second week in May. Since then bleary-eyed gunners had been peering through the visors of every enormous gun post along the coast, expecting each dawn to see the ghostly shapes of Allied assault craft emerging from the mist. Knowing they would be subjected to a massive bombardment from both the sea and the air, they had lived under heavy strain but now, as May drew to a close and the weather deteriorated, they began to hope their prayers had been answered and the invasion was postponed. At the same time their commanders allowed them no rest and the watch was continued day and night.

23

633 Squadron received its full complement of BIV Mosquitoes the following day. Although its crews had been trained on them up in Scotland, until now they had remained officially in the hands of 618 Squadron. Now the transfer was completed, 618's crews flying them into Sutton Craddock and returning to Scotland with 633's aircraft.

Although meant to be only a temporary exchange, it was

not a popular one. Specially adapted by de Haviland for the squadron's many roles, 633's versatile Mosquitoes were a source of pride to their crews and men watched them depart with the feelings of a man being compelled to part with his favourite sports car.

In spite of the weather, which had not improved, Davies insisted on one last rehearsal with the BIVs before the squadron left for Holmsley. "I want the crossbar lowered to thirty-six feet, Jock." When the Scot gave a start, Davies held up his hand. "Hold on before you start complaining. I've got a good reason."

Henderson held himself in check well. "That's only twenty feet of clearance, sir. I thought you said we had more than that."

"We probably have but the Loire is an unpredictable river. In summer it's usually very shallow but in the winter it can rise by ten or even twenty feet. We expected it to be getting low by this time but the Brigadier's agents say the rains have swollen it again."

The overcast sky did nothing to quell Henderson's apprehension. "Are you saying the longer it rains the less clearance there's going to be?"

"It's possible but highly unlikely," Davies soothed.

"So this is just a precaution?"

"That's right. We can't afford to leave anything to chance. We'r ninety-nine-percent certain that thirty-six feet is the absolu.e minimum your boys are likely to meet."

The worried Henderson turned towards his telephone. "I hope so, sir, because we're getting perilously near the tolerance limit."

Adams was walking from the Operations Room where he had just pinned up two new posters when the last two Mosquitoes of Harvey's flight began circling overhead. Although he had everything packed and ready for the move down to Holmsley, Adams had a hypersensitive conscience and found he was happier working when his young colleagues were on duty.

Although the two barrage balloons were still on the airfield, they were not part of the exercise. To make the rehearsal as realistic as possible, Davies had originally intended

using them until Moore had drawn him quietly aside and
pointed out that the light was poor enough to make the
crossbar exercise dangerous in itself. To include the balloons
could do little more than add to the risks, for the cable-
cutting crews would hardly gain much benefit from one more
pass at them.

Tending to listen to Moore rather than Henderson when
flying matters were involved, Davies had reluctantly given
way and the balloons were now stationed on either side of the
airfield. Like great bloated weathercocks they had veered
northward during the morning and were now pointing directly
upfield. To avoid the dangers of a cross wind, the two transporters had been moved nearer the centre of the southern
perimeter fence. Lowered even more, the crossbar was now
halfway down the perpendicular sides of the screens. From
Adams's distant viewpoint the clearance between the crossbar and the ground looked perilously compressed.

Yet, so far, the majority of the squadron's nineteen Mosquitoes had flown through without serious mishap. West had
caught the right-hand screen with his wingtip—probably
because he was more intent on his height than his lateral
clearance—but his Mosquito had suffered no damage and the
screen had been quickly repaired. Now only two aircraft,
both from Harvey's flight, were left to complete the exercise,
with O-Orange flown by Austin making its approach. Austin
was a cheerful Cornishman, a stocky young man who had
once tried out for his county rugby team. Like all the Mosquitoes that day he was carrying no navigator. Moore could
see no point in taking any chances with the navigators' safety
when they could contribute nothing to the exercise.

O-Orange's flight path was taking it right over Adams
and he paused to watch it with the same fascination he had
watched all the Mosquitoes that morning. Even in those
desperate war years when men were being asked to risk their
lives almost daily, Adams still found it astonishing that his
young colleagues would accept such risks in training without
noticeable complaint.

With the Mosquito under full power as it swooped over
him, Adams had to stand his ground against the roar of its
engines and the blast of its slipstream. The trail of gasses
from its manifolds could be seen clearly against the uniformly

grey sky. Turning to follow it, Adams watched the grass of
the airfield shivering as O-Orange headed at zero height for
the transporters.

By the time it reached them its camouflaged shape had
shrunk to the size of a toy. Still watching it, Adams heard one
engine cough and falter. Before the fact fully registered on
his mind, the Mosquito swung sharply to the right and its
wing sliced right across the starboard screen. Immediately it
began spinning vertiginously like a toy struck by a petulant
hand. Rising for a few seconds as if its rotation were giving it
lift, it cleared the row of poplars and then dropped down. A
cloud of dust and smoke rose, followed by a thud more felt
than heard.

Adams gave a horrified cry. For a second the airfield
seemed stunned. Then men began shouting, sirens began
wailing and crash wagons roared into life. In the general
bedlam Adams found himself running across the tarmac apron
towards the field. Gasping for breath by the time he reached
it, he tried to flag down a speeding truck. When it ignored
him, his breathlessness brought him down to a walk.

Crash wagons and an ambulance were now converging
on the distant trees. Scores of running men and women were
streaming after them. Although the black cloud was still
visible, there appeared to be no fire and Adams blessed
Moore's instructions that the Mosquitoes should carry only
enough fuel to complete the exercise.

By this time men were hacking down the perimeter
fence to allow their vehicles through. In spite of his burning
lungs, Adams forced himself to run again but he still had
three hundred yards to cover when medical orderlies appeared
carrying a stretcher which they deposited in the waiting
ambulance. As it turned and began speeding along the perimeter track, Adams halted, wiped his glasses, and began walking heavily back.

He was halfway towards No. 1 hangar when a 25 cwt
transport caught up with him. As he turned and waved, it
slowed down and a sergeant from the armoury hauled him
over the tailgate. Dropping on a seat, Adams had to wipe his
glasses again before he could recognize the other three occupants. One was a corporal from the photographic section, the
other two were Harvey and Larkin. The blackness of the

Yorkshireman's expression made him almost afraid to ask about Austin. "How is he? Do you know?"

The look Harvey gave him was like a blow in the face. Larkin's reply was hardly more friendly. "He's alive, but that's about all."

For a moment Adams brightened. "He is? I didn't think . . . That's wonderful news."

Harvey's curse made him realize his mistake. Larkin's laugh was bitter. "I wonder if he's going to think so. I reckon he's going to have a problem runnin' up and down that rugger field without his legs, don't you? And a smashed-in face ain't going to help him either."

Unable to look at either man, Adams turned hot and cold. Not for the first time, his hatred of war and its mutilation of the young rose into his throat and choked him.

24

The crunch of Harvey's shoes on the wet sand made a harsh, punitive sound. The girl beside him stole a look at his face. His mood, as black as the darkness around them, had a physical quality that inhibited her and made it an effort for her to speak. "Frank, you must tell me why you're acting this way. It's our last night before you leave for Holmsley. You can't leave me in doubt like this."

She sensed a battle within him as he walked on. Ahead a pier loomed out of the darkness. As they turned and made for the promenade she heard his reluctant voice. "It's nothing to do with you, for God's sake. I lost a man today."

She turned sharply. "I didn't know you'd been on operations."

"It wasn't on operations. That fool Davies insisted we carry out one more rehearsal with the crossbar only thirty-six feet above the deck. Young Austin lost an engine on his approach and swung into one of the cranes."

"Was he killed?"

"No. But it would have been better if he had been." Sparing her the details, he went on. "That bastard Davies never knows when to stop. Although it was barely daylight, he would have used the balloons as well if Moore hadn't stepped in."

If proof were needed of his devotion to his men, it was being given to her now. "I'm sorry. Did you know Austin well?"

"Of course I knew him. He was one of my lads." For a moment, Harvey was not talking to her; he was confronting Davies. "You know what I believe? This whole operation is his idea. He could see the invasion coming off without his getting a slice of the glory. So when he heard about Wallis's bomb, he talked them out of using B-17s and cooked up this crazy scheme instead."

"Aren't you being unfair?" she protested. "Ideas have to come from someone. Otherwise how could we ever win this war?"

"There are ideas and ideas. And this one smells like Davies all the way. Aren't I right?"

When she did not answer he glanced along the darkened promenade. Only two people could be seen, a man walking on the opposite side of the road and an elderly woman walking her dog. "You know because you're involved in it, aren't you? Right up to the neck."

She could not hide a faint start. He noticed it and nodded grimly. "I guessed as much. Did you bring this French engineer over?"

She could see no point in lying to him now. "Yes. I wanted to tell you everything but they made me promise not to."

"They would. The bloody war makes liars and cheats of us all."

"I had no choice, Frank. Otherwise they wouldn't have let me see you."

"I believe you. In their way they're as bad as the bloody Nazis."

She tried to smile. "Not quite as bad."

His voice rose harshly. "Of course they are. We've plenty of those bastards over here too. Sometimes I think you see this country through rose-tinted glasses."

Aware his pent-up emotions were seeking relief by quarrelling, she did not answer. Ahead was a pillbox, with two soldiers standing outside it. Both stared at them curiously as they walked past. As they followed the bend in the promenade, yellow lights appeared on the quayside. Working with storm lanterns, half a dozen fishermen were preparing to offload a catch into a waiting lorry.

Above the clouds were turning threadbare, giving occasional glimpses of a watery moon. On their left the castle was a dark sentinel on its steep promontory. As they reached the second of the two jetties she paused. "Shall we walk to the end before we go back?"

Sullen, he followed her. Halfway down she caught his arm. "I know how you are feeling. But it wasn't your fault and you can't carry everyone's burden. We've only a few hours left before you leave for Holmsley. Until then let's see if we can forget the war."

He made no comment. As they reached the end of the jetty she motioned to a flight of steps cut into the sea wall. "Shall we sit here for a while? I like to listen to the sea."

They sat together without speaking. The tang of seaweed brought back long-forgotten memories of seaside holidays and the joys of childhood innocence. Distant voices and the clank of a crane floated across the water as the fishermen swung a net into the waiting lorry. Silver flashes in the water died and flashed again as tattered remnants of cloud were dragged across the moon.

Although Harvey had still not spoken, the girl could feel the night changing his mood. Suddenly he turned to her and motioned toward the beach.

"This used to be the popular side of town with fun-fair arcades and stalls—where kids brought their buckets and spades and Mums and Dads ate fish and chips. It's not a bit like the posh side where you're staying."

Relief made it easy for her to smile. "Did you come here often?"

His voice still contained a residue of bitterness. "Us? It

was forty miles from home. No, we used to manage a couple of day trips a year."

"Then they must have been red-letter days for you."

"Red-letter days!" Harvey turned to gaze across the harbour at the unloading fishing boat. "Aye, we used to enjoy them all right."

She knew enough of his past to measure the understatement: newly-washed sands instead of mean streets, an infinite blue sea in place of claustrophobic slums. She pressed against him. "Tell me about them."

He stared at her. "Why? They were only daft little kids' outings."

"They're not daft to me. Tell me what you did."

He shrugged. "We used to come by train. Mum, Dad, Jack and me, all loaded up with sandwiches and buckets and spades. I remember when Jack and I saw the sea, we used to go crazy and rush in and out like puppies."

She snuggled up against him. "Go on. What else did you do?"

This time a grin cracked his face. "We were allowed one icecream, one packet of crisps, and one ride on a donkey."

"A donkey?"

"Yes. They used to take kids for rides up and down the beach for a penny a time. There was a grey one with black ears and every year I'd wait until I could ride on him. I used to believe he recognized me because he would turn his head and nuzzle me with his nose."

"Then he must have recognized you."

"That's what I liked to think." He laughed. "You know something? If I'd had the money I'd have bought that donkey. I used to wake up at nights thinking about him slogging up and down that beach and I'd cry my eyes out. The ideas you get when you're a kid."

She found herself gripping his arm tightly. He turned and stared at her. "What is it, love?"

She hid her expression in his shoulder. "It's nothing. Shall we make our way back now? It's getting rather late."

She awoke in the early hours of the morning. He was moaning in his sleep and his body was bathed in sweat. "Liebling, what is it?"

Although her voice did not awaken him, it seemed to reach deep into his mind and bring him fresh torment. Twice he cried out and stiffened as if in physical pain. Then, as she stroked his wet forehead, he began to relax and his breathing steadied.

A ray of moonlight slipped through the window as she dropped back on her pillow. For a moment it enabled her to see the time on the alarm clock at her bedside. Two and a half hours more and he must leave to face the ordeal ahead.

She wondered if the invasion would take place. From a report given her that morning, she knew the weather was far worse in the south, with gales lashing the Channel. What she could not determine was whether the depression was stationary or moving south. A southern drift might just ensure an improvement before the deadline of the 7th was reached.

She knew she ought to be praying that the ships sailed. In a thousand death camps from Norway to the Spanish border, emaciated men and women saw an invasion as their only hope of survival. At a thousand clandestine radios her friends in the Resistance would be listening and praying. During her own endless months in Europe it had been her shining beacon, the hope that made all the suffering and danger bearable.

Yet tonight she did not want the ships to sail. Or if they did, like a million other women in Britain and America, she did not want her man to go with them. The truth brought her shame, but shame could not kill the wish as she gazed at Harvey's sleeping face.

The temptation to waken him was great. To suppress her fears of tomorrow, she wanted to spend the rest of the night in his arms. Then, as he stirred again and gave a restless murmur, her mind changed. Leaning over him, she pressed her lips gently against his cheek. "Get all the sleep you can, Liebling," she whispered. "Ich hoffe Gott bringt dich sicher zuruck zu mir. Ich liebe dich."

Lying back on her pillow, she lay watching the fickle moon. From the harbour there came the sad, evocative cry of a ship's siren. A shudder ran through her as she listened.

25

Down at Holmsley in the heart of Hampshire's New Forest, the news that 633 Squadron was paying them a second visit had been greeted with horror by those residents who remembered the first. By 10 o'clock the following morning their worst fears were justified.

The first aircraft to land was a Dakota containing executive officers, among them Henderson and Adams. Their arrival, however, was completely overshadowed by the presence of Warrant Officer Bertram, 633 Squadron's Disciplinary Officer. Known to one and all as Bert the Bastard, he was an object of terror to officers and enlisted men alike. To the innocents of Holmsley, it must have seemed as if Genghis Khan himself had arrived.

His stentorian orders could be heard almost before his brightly-polished, size-twelve boots hit the ground. A massive figure, contemptuous of the driving rain, he made an immediate beeline for the guardroom, while four of his underlings struggled to keep pace with him. Sweeping aside the resident Special Police like chaff, he sank majestically behind the only desk in the Nissen hut and began issuing orders. Telephones began ringing, boots thudded on the concrete floor, the very hut seemed to reel under the outburst of energy.

The results were miraculous. SPs ran out into the forest to draw a tight security ring around the airfield. NCOs requisitioned offices for Henderson and his staff. Ground gunners ran to the gunposts, ousted their protesting crews, and went on immediate alert. Cooks took over the messes, pulled contemptuous faces at the fare being served, and contacted local victuallers for new rations. Like an old hive being taken over by a new strain of bees, Holmsley began to hum with efficiency.

The takeover went on throughout the day. Dakotas flew back and forth, bringing in spares, equipment, and maintenance crews for the Mosquitoes. *Highballs* were brought in and stored away under strict security. As fast as men loaded up transports, more materiel came rolling towards them, giving them no chance to lower their weary bodies on the ammunition boxes that littered the ground.

With the airfield needing so much preparation, the Mosquitoes were not flown in until the late afternoon. As each pilot had been ordered to share responsibility for his aircraft's safety with his maintenance NCO, the crews spent the next hour finding their dispersal huts and ensuring the Mosquitoes were securely anchored down against the near gale-force winds. Only then did the Adjutant call the drenched men to his office and there were laughs and catcalls when they received their billeting orders. As they filed outside to climb into their transports, Larkin grinned at Hopkinson.

"Let's hope this doesn't get around, cobber. Or we'll be a bloody joke in the service."

"We're a bloody joke now," the Cockney grunted. "Haven't you heard what the erks are calling us? Davies' performing seals."

Baldwin's big laugh boomed out behind them. "Who cares what they call us, man, if we get the old ladies' comforts. I'll trade a laugh any time for tea and scones and a hot water bottle."

At first sight Kingsley House in Brockenhurst looked as if it might meet Baldwin's requirements. Large and late Victorian, it was set among lawns and prim hedges and surrounded by a high brick wall. Its interior belied its appearance however. Recently occupied by an Army Signals unit that had moved the previous week to its embarkation point in Portsmouth, its antimacassars and aspidistras had been replaced by wooden chairs, benches, and iron bedsteads. Scowling as he tried the last, Eric Miller turned to Paddy Machin. "For Christ's sake, it's like being back at Padgate doing basic training again."

No lover of Miller, the Irishman grinned sarcastically.

"You think so? The worst you could get at Padgate was the stockade. Here it could be a bullet up your arse."

Complaints could be heard all over the house as flyers and executive officers alike discovered the austerity of their quarters. Further depressing news, although not unexpected, came with the Adjutant's announcement that no evening passes would be granted and all men were to stay within the house grounds. A second announcement told them that Henderson, Moore, and two Flight Commanders would not be joining them until later in the evening.

Although few men would have admitted it, much of the crews' restlessness stemmed from their ignorance of the mission they were shortly to fly. Everyone knew by this time it must be connected with the invasion but, unable to hazard even a guess at its nature, men spent the early evening roaming over the large house in search of distractions. Others crouched over the radio in the hope of enlightenment, only to become more perplexed by the red herrings the BBC were giving out in their news bulletins.

The men's mood brightened considerably, however, when they discovered the Mess Officer had commandeered the large dining room and erected a bar from trestle tables in one corner. Another source of encouragement was the sight of beer crates which had been hastily obtained from a local brewery. A rumour also began circulating that Moore had purchased a crate of whisky before leaving Sutton Craddock and would be bringing it with him later in the evening. When the cook produced a dinner that surprised everyone by its quality, the resilience of youth took over and men began to relax. The icing on the cake came when the Adjutant allowed the bar to open at 2030 hours.

From then on 633 Squadron became its old self again. Armed with bottles of beer, Hopkinson, Larkin, and other inveterate gamblers found a quiet room for a cutthroat game of poker. Purcell and Wall, both cricket lovers, argued whether Sutcliffe or Hutton had been England's best opening batsman. Wainright and Dempsey found an empty game room with a Ping-Pong table and challenged a team from B Flight to a match. Half a dozen hardened drinkers, Machin and King among them, propped up the bar and became noisier as the evening progressed.

As always there were the quieter ones. Macdonald was lying on his bed reading an unabridged version of *Lady Chatterley's Lover*. Brought back from France in 1940 by some unknown NCO, tattered and thumb-marked, it looked as if it had been read by half the RAF. Allison had settled down to write to his widowed mother. Sugden and MacAllister, awed by the occasion, sat in one corner of the room, watching the antics of the old sweats and speculated in low, excited voices what the morrow would bring.

Back at Holmsley airfield, with Harvey and Millburn in conference with their maintenance crews, Henderson, Moore and Adams were awaiting Davies' arrival in the Scot's makeshift office. A temporary wooden hut, it leaked draughts at every joint and window and it was not long before Henderson turned to Moore. "Where's that crate of whisky you brought, Ian? In the car?" When Moore nodded, the Scot gave a chilled grin. "Don't you think we ought to check it out before you hand it over to the boys?"

Smiling, Moore went to the door. "I think that's an excellent idea."

Davies' Miles Master slid into the airfield twenty minutes later. Looking chilled in his blue raincoat, the small Air Commodore grimaced at the darkening, windswept sky as he jumped out of the Station jeep. "It's hardly encouraging, is it? How's everything going?"

Henderson led him towards a row of Nissen huts. "Very well, sir. We'll be operational tomorrow."

"What about the Operations Room?"

"We're going there now. I thought Dr. Wallis would be coming with you."

"He wanted to but he and Brigadier have to attend a special conference of the committee. He'll be here first thing in the morning. Wild horses won't keep him away."

The Nissen hut the four men entered was austere in the extreme. Wooden benches, littered with Signals equipment, sat against its bare walls. A single strip of threadbare carpet ran down the centre of a stained cement floor. A couple of filing cabinets, half a dozen wooden chairs, and an unlit coke stove completed the furniture.

Davies stared round in distaste. "Home away from home! Does all the equipment work?"

"Yes, sir. Marsden has checked everything."

"So if Staines is with us during the operation, he can keep in touch with his Mustang escort?"

"Yes. Either directly or through his own Operations Room. Do you expect him here, sir?"

"It depends how busy he is. But he's dropping in at 0830 hours tomorrow; he wants to attend the briefing. Major Dent will be coming with him."

Moore spoke for the first time. "What time do you want the briefing, sir?"

"As early as we can although God knows when we'll be needed," Davies grunted. "Make it 0930. That'll give Staines time to have a cup of coffee before we begin." He turned back to Henderson. "Did that consignment of beer get through?"

"Yes. I said the bar could open at 2030 hours."

"Then you'd better make reveille 0630 hours. That'll give 'em plenty of time to work off their hangovers—we can't afford to have them miss anything. What about the crate of whisky, Ian? They haven't got it yet, have they?"

"No, sir. It's still in the car."

"Then ration 'em to two shots tonight. They can do their celebrating when the job's over."

Outside a fierce gust of wind buffeted the hut and sent a metal object clattering across the tarmac. Henderson gazed around uneasily. "That wind's getting worse. Surely they'll have to wait for it to drop."

Davies stared with hatred at the rain-splattered window. "God knows what they'll do, Jock. It must be hell already for the troops who've embarked."

It was a remark not far from the truth. To make room for the ships queuing up at the crowded ports, many assault crafts packed with troops had been forced to move out into the storm-tossed sea lanes. Locked in their cavernous metal holds in artificial light, facing the terrors of beaches defended by murderous devices as well as shot and shell, troops were rapidly becoming exhausted from the cold, the stench of vomit, and their own retching stomachs.

Conditions above decks were hardly better. In tugs and lighters in a hundred estuaries, drenched and weary servicemen were struggling to drag out barrage balloons, Mulberry harbour sections, and all the other weird and ungainly objects that would be needed on the invasion beaches. In the Channel itself, flotillas of minesweepers, who for weeks had painfully swept the route to Normandy, would now have to beat all the way back to ensure the buoyed channels were not being swept away in the gales.

The story was much the same inland. On dozens of fields wooden gliders had to be held down bodily as the demon wind swept up from the coast. On Pathfinder airfields men were wondering how they would be able to find, much less illuminate, the night drop zones for the gliders and paratroops. Bomber and fighter-bomber crews, briefed on the imperative need to overwhelm the enemy defences before Allied troops landed on the exposed beaches, were debating how such accuracy would be possible in such weather conditions.

With only three days left before a postponement became inevitable, a decision had to be made soon. The pros and cons were almost equally agonizing. A cancellation at this stage would cause unimaginable chaos and many experts secretly believed it would end all chances of a repeat performance that year. Some believed it would mean an even lengthier postponement than that, for there were many men in Congress who urged that America's first priority should be the defeat of the Japanese. Certainly it would crush the morale of the Resistance groups in Europe and have an incalculable effect on the Russians who had been demanding a second front for three years.

Yet if the great armada were launched and then defeated, an even greater disaster might result. On a human scale, it would mean the futile deaths of thousands of young men. On a world scale, with the Japanese still undefeated, years might pass before the Allies were able to build up such forces again. In the meantime the European Resistance movement would wither away and the Germans would be able to turn their entire military might against the Russians.

Such were the world-shattering penalties of a wrong decision and the entire responsibility for launching the assault, code-named Overlord, or cancelling it, lay on the shoulders of one man who, at that very moment, was sitting at a desk in

Southwick House in Plymouth listening to the wind battering against the windows. During those last few fateful days it is difficult to believe the world could ever have known a lonelier man than Dwight David Eisenhower.

26

At a glance from Moore, Davies moved forward on the dining room table on which he and the Squadron Commander were standing. Here and there a nervous cough sounded from the rows of young men sitting on benches in front of him. In the style he always adopted at briefings, Davies sounded both relaxed and enthusiastic.

"So you've been told your target at last and the way you're going to clobber it! And you're a bit tight, aren't you? That's good, because a man without nerves can't raise his game when he needs to. In a minute you can let off steam by asking questions, but first I want to say this. This is the big one. Like ourselves, Jerry's been preparing for this invasion for a long time, so it's going to be a hell of a scrap. Thousands of ships and aircraft, heavy guns, divisions of tanks—it's something the world's never seen before and probably never will again. There's no wonder some of you might be feeling we're conning you when we say your contribution could be vital. But you'd be wrong."

As Davies paused, the only sound in the dining room was the wind outside. "Think of it as two Titans slogging it out with battle-axes. Sparks are flying off their shields and they're trampling down everything around them. No one can get near but you. To mix metaphors, you're Peter Pan with a small but very sharp knife in your hand. You buzz around the enemy giant's head and when he isn't looking you stick your tiny knife into his jugular vein. With all the blood flying about he doesn't even notice the prick but, in fact, from that moment on he starts bleeding to death."

Along with the other executive officers, Staines and Alan Dent were seated on a bench behind the long table. The grinning American general nudged Dent's arm. "You know something? After the war I'm going to be that guy's agent and take him to Hollywood. I reckon I'll make more bucks that way than staying in the army."

On the table Davies was rounding off his brief oration. "It's an opportunity few units get in wartime, so I know you'll all give your best to be worthy of it."

The low grunt that came from Harvey, who was sitting beside Millburn, could have meant anything. Frowning at him, Davies decided against a comment and exchanged places with Moore again. The young Squadron Commander's pleasant voice quelled the murmurs that had broken out. "You don't have to chatter like old ladies just because you're living in their home, you know. First, I'm going to run over our operational tactics once more so you'll know exactly what you have to do. Then, I'm going to throw the briefing open to questions.

"Our first attack will be made by our cable-cutting team who'll take out the three innermost balloons. Smith will act as reserve to cut any cable the others might miss. When this is done you'll then double back and tack on to the end of your respective flights."

Moore's eyes moved to his two attentive Flight Commanders. "Squadron Leader Harvey will now lead his Red Section through the gap in line astern. The interval between each aircraft will be five hundred yards. As you already know, your target is the pier in the centre of the bridge. You'll backspin your bombs at 800 rpm, keep right down on the water as you did in Scotland, and release the bombs in rapid succession—not simultaneously or they might collide. Then you'll retire out of range of the guns and go into orbit until further orders."

Moore switched his gaze to the American. "Squadron Leader Millburn will follow with his Blue Section and repeat the procedure. When you've all dropped your stores, a total of thirty-two bombs should be stacked. Any questions so far?"

A dozen hands rose. Moore picked the nearest. "Yes, Sugden."

Not expecting to be chosen, the young pilot sounded shy. "Why are we stacking the bombs, sir? Why can't they explode in the usual way?"

"Because they carry only 600 lb of Torpex and that's not enough explosive to destroy the bridge. By stacking thirty-two bombs we can build up a charge of 19,000 lbs, which is considerably more than the boffins estimate we need."

"But if they have percussion fuses instead of the ordinary kind, won't they explode on impact?"

"No, they won't, Sugden. It'll take the explosion of a nearby bomb to set them off."

Like others, Van Breedenkamp had been doing rapid calculations. "Why only 32 inert bombs, skipper?"

"As I'm acting as master of ceremonies, I'll be carrying two fused bombs. Your Flight Commanders will be carrying one fused bomb and one inert. As soon as the last man has dropped his load, you'll all stay out of blast range while we go in to explode the charge. With luck we might make it the first time. If we don't we've got three more chances."

The forest of hands was as thick as ever. "Yes, MacDonald."

"Why can't you use ordinary time-fused 500 lb bombs to blow up the charge, sir?"

Henderson saw Davies give a slight start. The use of bombs instead of *Highballs* for detonation had been one of the most hotly debated items in the earlier tactical discussions. Moore had preferred bombs but had eventually been overruled by Davies and the Committee. The young Squadron Commander gave no evidence of this in his reply.

"Three reasons, MacDonald. One, bombs would have to be dropped from at least 1,500 feet to get the right trajectory and one reason for flying low along the river is to avoid the heavier flak. Two, we need every *Highball* we can carry and the mechanism doesn't allow your Flight Commanders to carry both a *Highball* and a bomb. Three, that would only leave me to do the job and with all that flak flying about I couldn't guarantee to drop my stores within 120 feet of the pier."

"Is that how close the *Highballs* must be stacked, sir?"

"Yes. To get the minimum blast necessary to do the job, that's the distance. But don't look so worried. You've got a few spare bombs in case of accidents and you were all getting much closer than that to those sandbags in Scotland."

From the crews' faces, Moore could read their thoughts. There had been no lethal flak to distract them in Scotland. "I know what some of you are thinking. The central pier doesn't look much of a target. In fact it's eighteen feet wide, the same width as the sandbags. Moreover it's supported on a pile made of stones, as most of the Loire bridges are. As this pile is somewhat wider than the pier, it should catch most of your *Highballs* and stack them around its base."

"What if the bombs leap over it, skipper?" Matthews asked. "That pier has cambered edges. A bomb could ricochet off it and end up a couple of miles down river."

Moore nodded. "They would but for German thoroughness. If you take another look at your photographs you'll see a thin black line just above the water at the foot of each bridge arch. Those are nets to prevent saboteurs moving along the river in their boats. They were erected before the torpedo booms were laid down but they've been left as a second line of defence. They're made of heavy steel mesh to resist wire cutters and we're assured they'll withstand the impact of any bomb that strikes them. It'll simply claw its way down as it would against the pile itself. In other words Jerry is going to stack our bombs for us."

Although there were murmurs of admiration for the ingenuity of the plan, there was one question men were dying to ask. A sudden hush fell when Larkin asked it for them.

"There's one thing I don't get, skipper. For weeks you've had us flying through hoops and under crossbars and yet so far you haven't given us a single reason why. What's the catch?"

Knowing what the effect would be, Moore had been keeping his bombshell until the last. He released it now in his casual, laconic way. "There's no catch, Andy. You won't leapfrog the bridge after you've dropped your bombs. You'll fly through the arches."

There was a stunned silence, then an outcry such had seldom been heard at a 633 Squadron briefing. Smiling, Moore picked on a protestor he felt certain would inject humour into the revelation. "What did you think it was for, Stan? Flying through Jerry's aircraft hangars?"

Baldwin did not let him down. "Christ, no, skipper. I thought we were going through the St. Bernard tunnel. Man, this is the wildest thing I've ever heard."

Moore ignored Davies' frown. "Not when you think about it. By hugging the river right to the bridge you'll gain extra accuracy for that 120 foot stack and that's absolutely vital. A bonus is that hopefully you'll fly beneath the trajectory of the guns on the bridge." When Baldwin rolled his eyes, Moore smiled again. "You wouldn't want to waste all that training, would you, Stan?"

Baldwin grinned back. "I'm always ready to make a sacrifice, skipper. Just try me."

Moore waited for the nervous laughter to die away. "Any last questions?"

Purcell rose to his feet. "You said earlier the river's higher than usual because of the rain, skipper. As it's still raining, doesn't that mean it might cover the nets? And wouldn't that affect us when we try to fly through the arches?"

As a buzz of agreement came, Davies broke in testily. "You don't have to worry about that. Our agents tell us the nets are still three feet above the water. In the time left there's little or no chance of the river rising that much."

Although it was clear not every man was convinced, the murmurs died as Van Breedenkamp rose again. "There seems a high ratio of flak posts, skipper. Do you know how many Typhoons we're getting?"

Seeing Davies give a terse shake of his head, Moore turned back to the South African. "With such a heavy call on them we don't know the number yet. But I'm sure it'll be adequate. Major Dent has also promised to give a hand if necessary. All his Mustangs will be carrying rockets."

Eyes turned on the stocky American sitting next to Staines. There had been a time when the knowledge they were to be escorted by Americans would have brought chauvinistic rasp-berries from the Mosquito crews but recent combined opera-tions with Dent's men had given them full confidence in the Mustang escort. When no further questions came, Moore turned to Davies. "That seems to be all at the moment, sir. Would Major Dent like a few words with them?"

At Davies' invitation, the likeable Alan Dent took Moore's place on the table. "I won't take up too much of your time because I know your executive officers are waiting for their turn. But I'd just like to say we'll do our best to give you protection. We're not at full strength right now—those horse thieves from the invasion have been grabbing ships from all our squadrons—but we should have enough to give you top cover. And if your Typhoons need any assistance with the flak posts we'll be ready to help all we can. You'll get the coordinates of our rendezvous from your navigation officer. I guess that's all except to wish you guys good luck."

For the next hour tension eased while the crews were allowed to smoke, to study the model of the bridge, and to listen to the instructions of the specialist officers. Staines and Alan Dent also moved among them, the younger officer both accepting and giving advice. When all had been said and the men were back in their seats, Henderson had his customary last words with them. Unsure whether the table would take his weight, he contented himself by standing on the bench behind it.

"The operation will be called Titan. Your Squadron call sign will be Hornet, Major Dent's will be Sherman, the Typhoons' will be Battleaxe, and our station back here will be Achilles. I wish I could tell you when you'll be going out but as you can see from the weather, that's in the hands of the gods. After this briefing you'll go straight to Holmsley and air-test your aircraft. Then you'll stand by. In all probability you'll get plenty of warning because unless something unforeseen happens you won't be flying out until H hour plus five."

As a buzz of speculation broke out, Henderson went on to explain the need to keep the enemy uncertain of the main assault area as long as possible. "Needless to say we have agents and reconnaissance aircraft keeping an eye on those two heavy panzer divisions to make sure they don't pull a fast one on us and reach the river first. That's the reason we have to keep you on standby once this briefing is over."

A silence followed. Knowing the men were thinking about the flak posts alongside the river, Henderson felt he should add something more but felt oddly empty. "As Air Commodore Davies has told you, this is the big one. If our boys can establish a beachhead and then break out, the war could be over by Christmas and we could all start making plans for our old age again. So we've everything to play for and I know you'll all do your best."

Coughs sounded as he stepped down from the bench. Calling the men to attention, Henderson stood aside for Davies and Staines to leave the room. As he followed them, he suddenly had a feeling of unreality, as if the rows of erect young men were part of some unsubstantial dream. Not the most imaginative of men, Henderson decided the sensation must be due to the unlikely surroundings in which the briefing had been made.

27

While the crews were being briefed at Kingsley House, Holmsley was a hive of activity as the BIV Mosquitoes were made ready. Among the mechanics who were swarming over them, checking and re-checking every vital component, gun armourers were in evidence. Encouraged by Barnes Wallis's belief it was feasible, the manufacturers had managed to squeeze three Browning .303 machine guns into each BIV's nose. With the Mosquitoes carrying the complicated *Highball* mechanism, squeeze was the operational word but the modification had been made possible by setting the guns in a triangular pattern and extending their barrels well in front of the nose cone.

The problem of finding room for the ammunition tanks had proven more difficult and curses were heard all over the airfield as armourers edged the belts in at the expence of their chilled fingers. If anything, the weather had deteriorated. The drizzle had ceased but tattered shrouds of cloud were being pursued across a forbidding grey sky. The wind, gusting at force five, had now veered to west-northwest, and as pilots arrived and made their air tests they could see white-flecked waves even in The Solent's estuaries. The most optimistic of them could see no chance for the great armada of ships that hugged the coast all the way to Devon to begin its momentous voyage.

Nevertheless preparations went on as if the operation were imminent. By noon everything was ready but the installation of the *Highballs*. Because of the relatively untested mechanism that both secured and rotated them, Barnes Wallis had thought it advisable it should not carry the weight of the bombs longer than was necessary.

Accompanied by Brigadier Simms, the scientist had arrived just after 1030. His state of mind had shown itself immediately. He had exchanged barely a dozen words with Davies before asking to be taken to the *Highballs* where he had spent the next half hour examining the weapons and discussing their fusing with the specialist armourers who accompanied them. Yet his anxiety that the weapon should prove itself was fully matched by his fear the operation might be costly in lives. Time and again he questioned Davies and Moore about the tactics they were employing and when he was found talking to the crews, Davies began to fear Barnes' fretting might upset them. Accordingly, at the first opportunity that presented itself, he was politely but firmly whisked away to Kingsley House.

During this time the crews were under orders to stay fully kitted as if they were fighter pilots waiting to scramble. With the satellite airfield not equipped for a resident squadron, men could find little to do except wander from one dispersal hut to another or to listen to the radio. When Hall discovered an old dartboard in a storeroom, there was soon a queue of men waiting for a game.

When noon came and went and the weather did not improve, it became obvious the crews would not be needed that day, and when Davies refused to let them stand down, they became irritable and argumentative. Aircrews always hated delays. Excitement, even fear, could sustain a man for

a few hours and once he was airborne, the task itself and the
instinct of self-preservation took over. But a lengthy wait,
which gave him time to reflect on the dangers ahead, provided fear without its compensatory factors. Adrenalin drained
away, leaving men tired and apprehensive.

Knowing the novice crews would be the worst affected,
Harvey went in search of Sugden and MacAllister. Finding
them smoking in an empty dispersal hut, he dropped on a
bench opposite. "What are you two up to? Working out ways
of getting more beer coupons from the Adjutant?"

Uncertain of him, both gave dubious smiles. "Don't you
think we'll be going out today, sir?" Sugden asked.

"Not a chance. The Air Commodore will be standing us
down any time now."

"What about tomorrow, sir?"

"It depends on the weather. What's the matter? Don't
you like the waiting?"

MacAllister gave a self-conscious laugh. "Not very much,
sir."

"You'd be odd characters if you did. I didn't sleep a
bloody wink before my first op."

"When was that, sir?"

Harvey frowned. "When? Somewhere around January
'41, I think."

"That's over three and a half years!" MacAllister was
clearly finding it hard to believe. "It must be more than
anyone else on the squadron."

"No. Moore's head and shoulders in front. And Hoppy's
been going since the Boer War. You see, you can last a long
time in this game, if you don't try to be a hero."

Both men were visibly relaxing. Harvey chatted with
them another couple of minutes before rising. "Keep your
ears open for the stand-down. Davies can't keep us hanging
around much longer."

With that, the big Yorkshireman walked out. Had he
seen the hero worship on the faces of the two young men, he
would probably have turned back and dressed them down.
Although few men did their duty more conscientiously than
Harvey, few detested more the concepts of glory.

The stand-down came at 1600. Although it was a relief,
there was little enthusiasm among the crews to return to the

bleak and draughty Kingsley House. The strain that was causing heart attacks at SHAEF Headquarters was written on every young face as they climbed into their transports.

Staines had already gone, flying back to his headquarters as soon as it became obvious the operation could not be carried out that day. Davies waited a further hour before accepting the inevitable and driving back to Kingsley with Henderson and Moore.

"This bloody weather! Where the hell's it coming from? Only two more days and we've had it. Christ, it doesn't bear thinking about."

Henderson tried to lighten his mood. "I did see a patch of blue sky an hour ago. Maybe it'll clear during the night."

Davies gazed gloomily out at the grey evening and the windswept trees. "That's not what the met boys say. It's the wind that's the problem. It's not just the things the ships have to drag across. How can they send gliders and paratroopers over? They'd end up in Berlin."

Henderson cast a glance at Moore. "It's been a hard day on the boys. Don't you think we could double their beer ration tonight? Even if the green light came right away, they wouldn't be needed until noon tomorrow or thereabouts."

Davies shook his head. "I can't take any chances at this stage, Jock. I'll make things up to them once this operation is over."

The discovery they were still virtually on standby did nothing to aid the crews' spirits. Although the Mess Officer made certain the dinner that followed was a good one, it was a flat affair with men talking in subdued voices.

The incident that changed everything came just when dessert was being served. A mess waiter hurried to Davies and whispered something in his ear. Starting like an alerted terrier, Davies scampered to the door and exchanged words with a sergeant standing there. A moment later he spun around and shouted for Henderson and Moore to join him. As all three men disappeared down the corridor, a loud hum of speculation broke out. Millburn glanced at Harvey who was sharing the top table with him. "What do you think? Are they going for broke?"

Harvey was about to answer when both men heard the

heavy drone of aircraft. As the noise grew louder, men jumped up from the tables and poured into the courtyard outside. From every corner of the overcast sky the pulsating thunder of heavy bombers could be heard. Someone let out an excited yell. "It's started! The bloody thing's started!"

Nothing could be seen because of the thick clouds and the fading light but by this time the thunder of aircraft was an all-pervasive sound. As more men appeared in the courtyard their mood dramatically changed. Cheers, shouts and excited laughter came from all sides as Harvey gave Millburn a puzzled glance. "They're taking a hell of a chance, aren't they? How can they find their drop zones in this weather?"

The same doubts and fears had been debated all day at SHAEF Headquarters. But although conditions were still desperately poor for such a complex operation, meteorological forecasts had suggested a slight improvement in the day ahead. With conditions in the assault craft becoming well nigh unbearable, Eisenhower had made his fateful decision. D-Day would be June 6th.

Immediately 105 RAF aircraft and 34 small ships of the Royal Navy had begun weaving their intricate patterns of deception. Minesweepers had sailed out again through the buoyed channels and along with midget submarines were lying in sight of the Normandy coast. Behind them, as twilight came and went, the main armada of 5,000 ships was now on the move, an enormous wedge more than fifty miles wide plunging forward through the sea lanes. Scores of fighting ships ranged far and wide on the flanks to protect it from seaborne attacks.

For thousands of soldiers packed in the massive holds of the assault vessels there were no last farewell glances at the fair English coast. Their only sense of movement came from the deep hum of engines, the groaning of steel plates, and the sickening rise and fall of the deck beneath them. The first fresh air they had breathed for days would come when they were released to scramble down the nets into their landing craft. And that would be only to face their rendezvous with a murderous, shell-torn beach. Weary, seasick, frightened men wondered how they could ever have believed that war was glamorous.

28

At Kingsley House, after a long talk with Davies, Moore went to the small room on the third story where his two Flight Commanders were quartered. The heavy drone of aircraft was still blanketing the house as wave after wave passed overhead. He found Harvey, with a bottle of whisky at his elbow, hunched over a small cabinet. The Yorkshireman pushed the letter he was writing into a drawer before turning towards him. "Hello, Ian. What's the news?"

Moore offered him a cigarette, then dropped into a chair. "We take off at 1030 hours."

Harvey raised a surprised eyebrow. "That doesn't mean they're doing a night landing on the beaches, does it?"

"No. H Hour is around 0630. They've advanced our time by an hour in case those panzer divisions get their fingers out."

"So what time do you want reveille?"

"0500 hours. See your boys are tucked in by ten, will you? Where's Millburn?"

"He's having a talk with his lads in one of the rooms downstairs. I'm seeing mine at 2130." As Moore nodded, Harvey sucked in smoke. "What's your opinion of this job, Ian? Do you think it'll work?"

Moore hesitated. "In theory it sounds feasible."

Harvey's scowl expressed his opinion of theories. "It's got too many 'ifs' for my liking. If we can get below the trajectory of the guns, if we can get enough *Highballs* near the pier, if we get enough Typhoons. . . . Christ, it's nothing but a bloody guessing game."

"At least Davies is hoping to get us enough Typhoons."

"How many?"

159

"He's not sure yet but he's trying for fifteen."

"Fifteen? We need more than that."

"We're lucky to get any, Frank. Every unit commander in the fleet has been petitioning for more air support. Fifteen should be enough if Dent lends them a hand."

Harvey poured a glass of whisky and handed it to Moore. "Let's hope so. Because if they've got many LMGs and pom-poms along those banks it'll be like the Swartfjord all over again. And Jerry's sure to throw in fighters if the bridge is that important to him." The Yorkshireman's deep-set eyes searched Moore's face. "Do you really believe he'd have set up all those gunposts if he wasn't expecting a raid?"

Moore shrugged. "It depends what you mean by 'expecting'. As it's the only major bridge in the area, it's only prudent to defend it. But that's different from being certain of an attack."

"You think so? I can't see the bloody difference if the defences are strong enough." Harvey's tone changed. "Was Barnes Wallis with Davies?"

"Yes. He kept on asking me how dangerous the job is. Since 617's raid on the Ruhr dams he's been terrified of heavy losses."

Harvey's grunt suggested little sympathy for scientists or anyone else whose schemes sent young men into danger. "I suppose Davies is over the moon now that the green light has come on."

Knowing the Yorkshireman's basic dislike of the ambitious Air Commodore, Moore smiled. "I'd say he's nervous as well as excited. As it's his idea, he has a lot to lose."

Harvey's laugh was harsh. "*He's* got a lot to lose. That's bloody funny. In fact it's the best joke today."

Draining his glass, Moore rose. The Yorkshireman's tone changed. "Hang on a minute. We don't get the chance to talk very often. Have another drink."

"It'll have to be a quick one, Frank. I still have to talk to Millburn."

Harvey filled both glasses. "It's not that late. And he'll still be busy with his lads. Tell me something? Why didn't you try to see Anna?"

It was the one question Moore had not wanted. "Aren't you forgetting I wasn't supposed to see her?"

"That's just Davies' bullshit. You only had to ask me for her address. Why didn't you?"

"I'm not sure. Perhaps it didn't seem the right thing to do."

"What do you mean—the right thing?"

"It didn't seem right to use up your time. The two of you haven't had that much time together since you met."

For a moment Harvey's jealousy betrayed itself. "So you were being noble. Is that it?"

Moore realized for the first time that the Yorkshireman was half-drunk. "Let's leave it, Frank. It doesn't matter now."

"But it does matter. She likes you. That gave you a right to see her."

"I'm glad she does. I like her too and I think you're a lucky man."

A vein was standing out on Harvey's temple. "Don't give me that, Ian. You're in love with her. Why in hell won't you admit it?"

Moore's cheeks went pale. As he moved to rise, Harvey made a gesture of contrition. "I'm sorry. It's just that. . . . well, I ought to have suggested it back at Sutton Craddock."

Moore suddenly understood and sank back. "I never gave it a second thought, Frank."

"You wouldn't. But I did. And I'm not very proud of my bloody self."

Moore took a deep breath. "You're a fool for not trusting that girl. She'd do anything for you. Can't you ever get that into your thick head?"

The Yorkshireman's expression was full of self-dislike. "Aye, I know I should. But we are what we are." He reached for his glass, then glanced again at Moore. "You know something? In all the time I've known you, you've never mentioned a girl friend. Have you got one?"

"No. Not now."

"Why? What happened?"

Moore smiled. "Nothing dramatic. She wanted to get married and I didn't want any hostages to fortune. So she went off and married a merchant banker."

"A what?"

"A merchant banker. He works in London."

"Jesus Christ," Harvey muttered. "She must have been in a hurry to get spliced. Did you really tell her that—that you didn't want any hostages to fortune?" When Moore nodded, Harvey's face darkened again. "That's what I should have had the guts to tell Anna, isn't it? Right at the beginning."

Moore shook his head. "No. Anna's a different girl altogether."

"What the hell's that got to do with it?" The Yorkshireman's challenge was hurled against his own sense of guilt. "The principle is the same. You and I aren't going to live through this war, Ian. Christ, we should have been killed ten times already. So why piss about letting them hope otherwise?"

Moore leaned forward. "Why are you telling me this, Frank?"

Half-drunk though Harvey was, his native caution warned him he had gone too far. His grin was suddenly shamefaced. "Don't ask me. Maybe it helps a man to let off steam once in a while."

Moore did not press the point. "You do know that Davies has promised you a rest after this operation?"

If Moore had not been certain what lay behind the Yorkshireman's outburst, his aggressive reply would have confirmed it. "What's that to do with it? Do you think I need a rest?"

"We all need a rest, Frank. I'm taking one myself very soon. Has Henderson told you?"

Harvey's belligerence died. "Aye, he told me this afternoon. What about my lads?"

"Your lads will be all right. You've taught them to take care of themselves. So you're taking the rest. Is that understood?"

The void into which Harvey's bleak eyes were staring held little rest or comfort. "Aye, all right. But let's get this job over first."

Satisfied, Moore drained his glass and rose. "You go on leave tomorrow night. With the invasion on, the Top Brass don't like it but Davies has insisted. So you can make your plans accordingly." Moving to the door, Moore turned. "Just one last thing, Frank. No fancy stuff tomorrow. We fly in, do the job as quickly as we can, and then make for home. All right?"

The smile that transformed the Yorkshireman's face was astonishingly gentle. "As I said once before, Ian, I couldn't be fancy if I tried. You watch yourself tomorrow too. OK?"

The two men's eyes met for a moment, then Moore closed the door. Left alone, Harvey dropped on his bed and lay back. Sensing his mood Sam scrambled to his feet and nuzzled his arm. When he encountered no resistance the dog, daring greatly, jumped up on the bed. Still expecting a reprimand, he felt the man's hand reach out instead and stroke his shoulder. In a seventh heaven, Sam sank down alongside his master and gazed at him with worshipping eyes.

Few men in Kingsley House slept soundly that night. The roar of troop-carrying aircraft overhead was too much of a reminder of what was facing them tomorrow. The incessant noise had another effect. In spite of the importance Davies laid on their mission, men found it difficult to believe their small unit could have such an important effect on an operation so earthshaking.

Their feelings were shared by the thousands of Allied troops now waiting off the Normandy coast for dawn. For every landing craft already in position, dozens more were weaving intricate patterns as they sought their own assembly points. The huge silhouettes of assault craft and warships heaved and tossed against the night sky. Wave after wave of aircraft thundered overhead. Evidence was there for every man to see that he was one among thousands and that he was backed by the greatest concentration of firepower the world had ever seen. Yet men still felt desperately alone and impotent.

Many were retching miserably. Many were bitterly cold; with the heavy sea still running, the climb down the scramble nets had been a wet and perilous operation. Many had run out of words and were huddled like foetuses on the wet decks. A few talked in whispers. Others, unlucky enough to be stationed near their NCOs or officers, made half-hearted

pretence of drying and cleaning their weapons. One act,
however, was common to all. Every man kept glancing at the
sinister shore ahead.

Flashes were illuminating the clouds behind it. Far inland,
Pathfinder aircraft were dropping their flares and German
gunners were firing up at the descending gliders and paratroopers. Men were already dying, by fire, by bullet, by
bayonet as they swung down to earth. But to the men crouched
in the landing craft, with cold spray blowing over them, it
was all too distant to be real. To them it was little more than
summer lightning playing over the land.

They were watching for the first signs of dawn. As the
flashes momentarily ceased, men noticed a grey streak on the
horizon. Instantly a brutal hand gripped their stomachs and
squeezed. Suddenly a man had no friends and no colleagues.
Suddenly he was naked, his loneliness total, and he wanted
to cry out from the sheer agony of it.

Like an enormous creature sensing the dawn, the armada
could be felt stirring throughout its length and breadth.
Through the hum of engines and the splash of waves, shouts
and the clang of metal could be heard. As ashen men waited,
a hundred spears of flame stabbed the darkness behind them.
Seconds later, as if the Angel of Death were flying overhead,
there was an eerie rustling sound, followed by a rolling crack
of thunder. As the great shells rained down on the coastal
defences, crimson flashes ripped the night apart as if satanic
giants were lifting and slamming down the manholes of hell.

The juddering flashes ran along the coast to each horizon
as heavy bombers joined in the attack. Then came the rocket
launchers, ear-splitting phalanxes of white-hot spears that
could wipe out an entire village in one salvo. Flamethrowers
joined in, their dragon's fire licking across the beaches towards
the gun emplacements. To the stunned Allied troops it seemed
nothing born of woman could survive the awesome attack
and yet within thirty seconds German batteries began their
counter barrage. Great waterspouts climbed into the crimson
sky. Landing craft were flung aside like toys, hurling hundreds of struggling ants into the tossing sea.

The noise was the greatest terror. It screamed and thundered, howled and ripped until men believed their eyes
would burst from their sockets and their brains would spill

from their riven skulls. It made their mouths gape open so that they looked like death heads in the juddering light. Its monstrous, metallic power rendered their flesh into jelly and as their landing craft began moving forward they knew neither will nor discipline would be able to urge them into action.

Yet when the landing ramps dropped into the surf, they discovered the same terrible machinery had taken control of them, even though mines and other devices of death were adding to their terror. Holding their weapons aloft, they leapt into the icy sea while around them comrades screamed, clutched their entrails, and collapsed in bloody froth. With mines exploding, shells falling, with bullets searching for them, the assault troops began running, stumbling, and crawling across the fearsome beaches. D-Day had begun.

29

By 10 a.m. that morning it was still overcast but the cloud base had risen to 4,000 feet. On Holmsley airfield the Mosquitoes were ready for action. They had undergone a second maintenance check, had been air-tested again, and their form 700s had been signed. Now they were waiting at their dispersal points like sprinters at their blocks.

Not that they looked that way to everyone. The last act in their preparation had been carried out by the specialist armourers, and to crews used to the Mosquito's graceful lines, the twin crescents of the *Highballs* that protruded from their bomb bays was a disfiguration. Baldwin's big laugh sounded as he emerged with half a dozen men from their temporary flight office. "Hell, man, they look like pregnant old sows. Jerry'll be laughing so much he'll forget to fire at us."

Although the comment was an exaggeration, it gave men
the chance to laugh and ease their tension. Awakened early,
they had been brought to the airfield at 0800 hours where
they had been given a second briefing by their respective
Flight Commanders. Now they were ready to go and nerves
were tight. With the wind still gusting and chilly, most of
them had brought their leather flying jackets and they were
grateful for them as they stood in small groups, talking in low
tones and smoking incessantly.

In the makeshift Operations Room, Davies was having a
last word with Moore and his two Flight Commanders. Barnes
Wallis, nervous and fidgety, was present, as were Henderson, Brigadier Simms, and Adams. Staines, massively committed now that all his squadrons of B-17s were engaged over
the beaches, had phoned a message through earlier. He
doubted if he would be able to come but asked for all rele-
vant news of the operation to be sent to his headquarters.

There was one final occupant in the draughty Nissen
hut. With experience telling Sam he was to be left behind,
the dog was lying despondently beside Adams's chair, his
eyes on the big, leather-jacketed Yorkshireman.

The red spots on Davies' cheekbones were evidence of
his excitement. "It's early days yet, but the latest reports say
our beachhead troops are holding their own. The glider and
parachute drops were botched up—men got dropped all over
the place and so got picked off in twos and threes—but oddly
enough it helped rather than hindered because it made Jerry
think it must be a spoof operation. However, he appears to
have made up his mind now. Our reconnaissance patrols say
he's moving up reinforcements as fast as he can. So your
orders stand: you take off at 1030 hours and rendezvous as
arranged with your Mustang escort over the Isle of Wight.
The Typhoons will arrive at the bridge ten minutes before
your ETA and will attack the gunposts right away."

"Why only ten minutes, sir?" Millburn asked.

"We don't want to give away the game too soon. Otherwise Jerry might be able to rush up mobile guns."

Harvey's north-country voice broke in. "How many Tiffies
are we getting?"

"Two flights. Sixteen in all." Certain that Harvey would

protest, Davies anticipated him. "Thank your lucky stars you've got any. It's more than I expected."

"What are the latest reports on the two panzer divisions, sir?" Moore asked.

"There's report of activity around the base near Bordeaux but they don't appear to have moved out yet. Until we get local reports we're not certain about the SS Division at Limoges because the recce aircraft we sent out at dawn was shot down. But although they'll probably be pushing on now, we've no reason to believe they broke camp earlier than expected. Any more questions?"

When men shook their heads, Davies glanced at Barnes Wallis. The white-haired scientist said a few diffident words and then shook hands with each pilot in turn, a measure of his anxiety. A moment later Davies led the way out to the airfield where transports were waiting to carry the crews to their aircraft.

A loudspeaker blared over the sound of muted voices. Stamping out their cigarettes, men tossed their parachutes into the transports and climbed in after them. As the 25 cwts moved off, Davies and the remainder of his party made their way to the balcony of the control tower.

Below, Merlins were firing and hurling moisture and grit into the faces of the mechanics. Three minutes later an NCO came out on the balcony and fired a green Very light. As it dropped sizzling into a pool of water, Moore nodded at Hoppy and advanced his throttles. Followed by other Mosquitoes, A-Apple taxied to the end of the east-west runway. There it swung round and paused like an animal scenting the wind.

Thirty seconds later a metallic voice in his earphones gave Moore clearance. Instantly the Merlins broke into thunder and A-Apple began moving forward. Faster and faster, hurling spray from its wheels, it bounced and bounced again as the two huge bombs hugged in its belly held it down. Then it broke free and with a triumphant roar soared over the perimeter fence and the pine trees beyond.

In quick succession the rest of the Mosquitoes followed. Faces upturned, Davies and his party watched them as they orbited the airfield. When the last Mosquito was airborne, they slid expertly into battle formation and turned south.

As Adams stood listening to the beat of their engines dying away, a mournful sound below made him start. Turning, he saw Davies was staring at him. "What's that?"

Adams cleared his throat. "It must be Sam, sir. Harvey's dog."

Henderson was frowning. "He doesn't usually do that, does he?"

Adams shook his head. "No. At least I've never heard him do it before."

The howling came again, eerie in the silence that followed the thunder of engines. Seeing Barnes Wallis's expression, Davies turned irritably towards Adams. "You look after him when Harvey's flying, don't you?"

"Yes, sir."

"Then for God's sake go and shut him up."

Hopkinson was not the most impressionable of men but there was awe in his voice as the double phalanx of Mosquitoes swept past the Isle of Wight. "Just look at those ships, skipper! They're throwing everything they've got at Jerry."

Although the cutting edge of the armada was now across the Channel, which was over a hundred miles wide at this point, there were more than enough ships below to justify the Cockney's comment. Every haven and estuary in The Solent was discharging them, many towing weird objects in their wake. Through the haze of smoke, white-flecked waves could be seen. The weather had moderated somewhat overnight, but it was still a grey and blustery day.

Moore was leading the squadron out at two thousand feet. With wave after wave of Allied aircraft backing up the beach assaults, a few more blips on the German radar screens would make little difference. The need to duck beneath them would come when the Mosquitoes left the beaches behind and headed for the Loire.

Ahead, the horizon was barely visible for the smoke of ships. As the Isle of Wight began sliding back, Moore heard a familiar voice. "Hello, Hornet Leader. Sherman Leader here. Do you read me?"

Above, the ghostly shapes of Alan Dent's Mustangs were sliding out of the cloud base. "Hello, Sherman Leader. You're in good time this morning."

"Yeah, some noises in the night kept us awake. You have any idea what's going on?"

Moore smiled. "I think it's a flap of some kind. Perhaps we'll find out more in a few minutes."

With their Mustang escort now in position, navigators were able to relax and pay more attention to the scene below. Although for safety they were flying above the left flank of the armada, the sea below was alive with naval vessels probing for enemy U-boats. To their right a great tangled skein of drifting smoke half hid the great armada. Although the Mosquitoes were still sixty miles from the enemy coast, black clouds on the horizon betrayed the ferocity of the battle raging there.

A sharp flash and a puff of smoke alongside a Mosquito brought a yell from Larkin. "You see that, skipper? The bloody matelots are firing at us!"

As always, Moore's reprimand was delivered quietly. "Keep the channel free of chatter, all of you." As two more shells burst to starboard, he turned to Hoppy. "Give them our recognition signal."

Hoppy fired two Very lights through the flare chute. The firing ceased, only to begin again two minutes later. Warned that the Luftwaffe might come out in strength, the naval gunners were taking no chances. As the Mosquitoes reeled under the fire, Moore led them three degrees to port before resuming on a parallel track. Above, the Mustangs followed suit.

Fifteen minutes later, the great arc of invasion beaches lay on their starboard side. Even at the height they were flying, crews winced at the spectacle. Seen through binoculars, the sight was awesome. Out at sea, the guns of battleships were still hurling their huge shells into the pulsating smoke. Above, countless aircraft were wheeling and diving. Amphibious tanks were breasting the waves like strange sea monsters. As the gusting wind gave glimpses of the beaches through the smoke, hundreds of tiny black shapes could be seen, some lying motionless, others running forward. Other strange objects shared the beaches and dunes with them:

flame guns to burn out stubborn defenders, armoured cranes
to surmount walls or bridge gaps, tanks equipped with flails
to blow up minefields. Enemy shells were bursting on or
around them and the white, lethal threads of tracers were
cutting men down as they ran. Lowering his binoculars,
Hoppy turned his pinched face to Moore.

"Thank God we're up here, skipper."

Moore hoped the Cockney's gratitude to his Maker would
be as fervent in forty minutes' time. Below, the high hedgerows of Normandy were now sweeping past. As the Mosquitoes penetrated deeper, men could see that the approach
roads were choked with transports. Certain now of the Allied
intentions, the Germans were rushing up reinforcements
without further delay. At ten o'clock half a dozen Allied
fighter-bombers could be seen strafing a long column of
trucks.

With the Mosquitoes now detached from the invasion
aircraft, Moore led them down to zero height. Behind them
Dent's Mustangs did likewise. As crenellated buildings rose
ahead, Hoppy tapped Moore's arm. "Vire, skipper."

Remembering there were heavy flak defences around
the town, Moore led the Mosquitoes westward. On the horizon the great granite peak that was Mont-Saint-Michel could
be seen rising from the Saint-Malo estuary. Forty seconds
later, on Hoppy's instructions, he swung back on course. As
green and golden fields unrolled beneath the aircraft, flocks
of birds exploded into flight and grazing cattle stampeded.
Ahead, a single shaft of sunlight made a rainbow on the dark
horizon. Knowing that by this time the German Observer
Corps would have plotted their course and notified Luftwaffe
Fighter Control, pilots and navigators shared their observa-
tion between the countryside below and the grey sky above.

A dark smudge appeared at one o'clock. Glancing down
at the map strapped to his knee, Hoppy pointed at it. "Angers,
skipper. On the Loire."

There was not a man among the British and American
crews who did not feel a snap of tension as the broad river
swung into view. A one-time playground for the kings of
France and their mistresses, its magnificent châteaux had
been a mecca for tourists before the war. Now, if Davies and

his superiors were right, it might decide the fate of Europe if
it could be turned into a barrier against the fanatical Nazi
armour that was streaming northward towards it. Moore lifted
his face mask. "Hornet Leader to squadron. Fall into line
astern and follow me to port. Now."

Like a knot unfurling, the Mosquitoes became a long
taut rope. Behind them the Mustangs rose to give them air
space, then settled down again. Banking steeply to port,
Moore flew over a shattered bridge, then lowered A-Apple
until its swollen belly was no more than sixty feet above the
water. "What's our ETA to Langeais, Hoppy?"

The Cockney glanced down at his knee again. "Six more
minutes, skipper."

30

Dieter Sommer was sitting at the entrance of his tent, a
copy of Jagerblatt on his knee. Ahead of him was the one-
time cornfield his squadron, Number 2 of No. 1 Fighter
Wing, was using as a makeshift airfield. Busily attended by
mechanics, the latest Focke-Wulf A3s were dispersed over it.
Here and there, pilots could be seen examining their aircraft
or chatting with their mechanics. Fully kitted out to fly, they
were finding it difficult to stay in one place for any length of
time, although a number of them were crowded around a
radio outside a flight office tent.

No one understood their state of mind better than
Sommer. For months, he and his colleagues in the Luftwaffe
had been undergoing intensive training, both theoretical and
practical, on the part they must play in Operation Doctor
Gustav Wilhelm, the code name for the Allied invasion. To
men of Sommer's aggressive mentality, too much emphasis
had been placed on the future during this training and not

enough on the present. To be withdrawn from combat and
forced to sit on one's backside, while every day Allied bombers flew overhead to blast communications and factories, not
only in France but in the Fatherland itself, had seemed the
height of folly. If things went on this way, what would be left
to defend when the invasion did come?

Even so, when the momentous news of the invasion had
broken that morning, Sommer and his men had expected an
immediate call to battle. Instead they had been told to go on
standby and to await orders.

It was always the same, Sommer thought. All orders
from High Command these days seemed to be too early or
too late. No wonder that on every front the Allies appeared to
be winning.

Then his telephone rang. It was Radener, the airfield
commandant. "Sommer, we've got urgent reports from our
Observer Corps. A unit of Mosquitoes with a Mustang escort
is heading south at low level. The last report put them just
west of Mortain. See if you can intercept. You'll get coordinates from Fighter Control after takeoff."

Tossing his copy of Jagerblatt away, Sommer was out of
his tent in two strides. His shouts brought his three Ketten-
führers running towards him. "It's a scramble! Get your men
airborne!"

Loudspeakers were already blaring out across the field.
Signal rockets and Very lights began arching up from flight
dispersal points. As mechanics frantically worked on engines,
pilots raced towards their aircraft. One engine fired, then
another and another. Like sharks kept hungry and now thirsting for blood, Focke-Wulf after Focke-Wulf tore into the grey
sky. As the Flights closed up into a tight line, Sommer
switched on his radio. His Flight Controller came on almost
immediately. "Head for sector Siegfreid-Quelle. Hanni
zero."

Sommer's acknowledgment was brief but exultant. "Victor, Victor. We're on our way."

A moment later, like a great scythe sweeping across the
sky, the formation swung southwest and headed towards the
Loire.

*   *   *

The scene in the Nissen hut at Holmsley was one Adams had seen many times in the Operations Room at Sutton Craddock. With radio silence enforced on the Mosquitoes' outer leg, men could only guess what was happening and with no physical action to act as a safety valve, they betrayed their stress in different ways.

Davies' practice was to talk at great length during the first half hour and then begin to pace up and down, pausing every minute or two to stare at a map of the operational area. This time, however, he was frustrated by Barnes Wallis who kept plying him with anxious questions about the crews' safety, questions which Davies answered in shorter and shorter sentences. In contrast to both men, the Brigadier kept all his anxieties within himself and tended not to venture a word unless addressed directly. Henderson, torn between the desire to catch the first scrap of news and the need to occupy his mind, would every now and then go outside to seek such an escape. The imaginative Adams needed no such diversions, for in his mind's eye he was with the Mosquitoes, leaping the hedgerows and following the straight, poplar-lined roads down to the Loire.

The first telephone call came just after 1130 hours. Marsden, who was sharing the watch with one of his Signals sergeants, held out the receiver to Davies. "It's General Staines, sir."

Davies grabbed the phone. "Yes, sir. Davies here. Have you any news from your boys?"

"That's what I phoned to ask you," Staines said wryly. "I guess we're both too impatient; they can't be there yet. You'll be in touch as soon as you hear something?"

"Yes, sir. Right away."

Another ten long minutes passed, then the telephone linked to High Elms rang. The start the Brigadier gave when answering it made all eyes turn on him. He spoke in low tones for thirty seconds before replacing the receiver. The impatient Davies was the first to speak. "Well? What's happening?"

The elderly soldier turned. "We've just received reports from agents who've been trying to keep an eye on the two armoured divisions. It seems both of them moved out during the night."

A stir ran around the hut. Davies looked shocked. "I thought you said they wouldn't move until Jerry was sure of our intentions?"

The Brigadier sighed. "That is what everybody believed. But it looks now as if Rommel might have ordered them north before our troops landed. The Bordeaux division left by rail, the SS by road."

Everyone hurried to the map of France that was pinned to a makeshift blackboard. "If they were ordered to move that soon, isn't it possible they might have been sent up to the Calais area?" Henderson asked.

The Brigadier shook his greying head. "Even if they had been, they would certainly be rerouted towards Normandy by this time. I think we must assume they are both making for that bridge, gentlemen."

Henderson's frown deepened. "If the Bordeaux division is coming up by rail, it could be there before Moore, couldn't it?"

"It's possible but I doubt it. Our air raids and French saboteurs have damaged the track in too many places. And, of course, they must leave the railway to cross the bridge. I'm more worried about the SS panzers. They could well reach the bridge first."

Davies turned away, allowing only Adams to see his expression. In advancing his plan instead of a high level raid, the Air Commodore had risked far more than his own reputation. His attack on the Brigadier betrayed his state of mind. "What I can't understand is how they've fooled your agents. An armoured division can't be moved without a hell of a lot of fuss and commotion. The preparations must have begun yesterday at the very latest."

"It seems they left dummy tanks at dispersal points," the Brigadier told him. "It has been very cleverly done because it deceived our reconnaissance aircraft also."

The gentle reminder that it was not only the SOE who had been deceived moderated Davies' tone. "So what can we do now?"

Barnes Wallis, who had been listening anxiously, spoke for the first time. "I suppose it's not possible to warn Moore?"

Henderson gave Davies no chance to reply. "No, sir. If we open up communication, Jerry will pick up the transmission and vector fighters towards him."

Davies swung around. "Not necessarily. There's no certainty Jerry will guess our objective if we word our message carefully."

Henderson stood his ground. "They're not fools, sir. With two armoured divisions moving towards that bridge, they'll know its importance to us. Anyway, what's the point in taking the risk? Moore's not going to waste any time getting there as things stand now."

To Davies' credit, he saw the sense in the Scot's argument. Turning to gaze at the map again, he nodded his head and sighed. "You're quite right, Jock. There's nothing we can do but sit tight and hope for the best."

31

The Mosquitoes were hugging the river like a line of cormorants. Although at that height the pilots were forced to keep their eyes fixed on the shivering water, navigators were free to take stock of their surroundings before they entered the zone of flak that would concentrate their minds on survival.

At this point, the Loire was some five hundred yards wide. Sandy beaches were visible on both sides, some relatively wide, others narrowed by the recent heavy rain. Both banks were well wooded. A sandy island with half a dozen trees flashed past.

The river widened and a small town appeared on the left bank. A large island and two shattered bridges linked it to the opposite shore. Hoppy, who prided himself on his French pronunciation, glanced up from his map. "The Isle du Loisirs and Les Rosiers, skipper."

Smiling, Moore lifted A-Apple over the island and settled her down again. Glimpses of a road could be seen through the trees on the left bank. A few neat houses, then a magnificent church with two impressive pillars flashed into sight a couple of minutes later. "Saint Clemens des Levees, skipper."

Ahead the superb chateau of Saumur was rising on a hill that overlooked the river. Below it, streets and traffic could be seen. With only minutes to go, the Mosquito crews were making the jokes men make to one another before battle. Millburn in T-Tommy, feeling he should encourage his shy young navigator, jerked a thumb at the chateau as it flashed past. "Those old kings and dukes sure looked after their mistresses, didn't they, kid?"

The New Zealander glanced back. "Was that built for a mistress, sir?"

"They say most of 'em were. Who said diamonds are a girl's best friend?"

Back along the line Baldwin was making a similar comment to Machin. "Imagine giving all that to a dame for a piece of nookie. Isn't it something, man?"

Machin grinned cynically. "And you think you're generous when you buy yours a glass of shandy."

Another wrecked bridge flashed past. Half a minute later Moore's calm voice broke radio silence. "Hornet Leader to squadron. Your target's coming into sight. Take a good look at it."

Ahead, beyond a bend in the river, two lines of bloated shapes had appeared in the grey sky. On either side of the balloons, aircraft could be seen rising and diving like gnats. "Hornet Leader to Battleaxe Leader. Do you read me?"

Moore's earphones crackled with static. "We read you, Hornet Leader." The accent was English. "Welcome to the bun fight."

"How is it going?"

"We think we've knocked out three posts so far. But the trees are giving us trouble. Jerry's sited his guns among them and they're deflecting our rockets."

"How long can you stay with us?"

"Not much longer." There was a loud rush of static and then: "We're getting short of rockets and ammo. But we'll do the best we can."

Moore next called in Alan Dent. "We're starting our attack, Sherman Leader. Give us cover, will you?"

Back along the river the Mustangs rose like a flock of birds and made for the cloud base. The line of Mosquitoes, flying nose to tail now, remained at zero height. As they swung around the last river bend, their target appeared ahead. Shielded on either side by its screens of balloons and torpedo nets, straddling the broad river on its three huge piers, the bridge looked massive even at a range of four miles and men felt their hearts sink at the sight. Its flak defences added to the impression of impregnability. In spite of the Typhoons' ferocious attacks, tracer was still squirting up from both river banks and the sky was pockmarked with bursting shells. Moore's calm instructions came as a relief. "Climb to 2,000 feet. Now!"

A-Apple, followed by the line of Mosquitoes, went into a steep climbing turn. Gazing down at the fires burning in the woods, Moore could see the problems the Typhoons were having. Aware of the excellent camouflage the trees gave them, the Germans had cleared only limited arcs for their guns to traverse. Half a mile away a Typhoon was diving like a goshawk on a double line of tracer. Although the rockets it fired were well aimed, the high trees deflected them and the hidden pom-pom followed the Typhoon vengefully as it climbed away.

The guns were concentrating on the fighters attacking them but black bursts among the Mosquitoes indicated there was firepower to spare. Circling away from the shells, Moore lifted his face mask. "Take over, Cable Cutting Section. The rest of you orbit out of range."

It was the signal for the four cable cutting Mosquitoes to break away and dive down to four hundred feet. Forming into an arrowhead they made straight for the three balloons in the centre of the river.

Occupied as they were by the Typhoons, the apparently suicidal manoeuvre caught the flak gunners by surprise and the four Mosquitoes took full advantage of it. Machin struck his cable first and Moore, who followed the Mosquitoes up

river, saw sparks as the braided cable slid along the reinforced wing into the cutter. There was a puff of smoke and
the cable whip-lashed away, allowing the balloon above to
break free.

West was equally successful with his strike. King was
less fortunate. He appeared to hit his cable cleanly but it slid
away from his wingtip. Smith, lying well back in anticipation
of a failure, headed straight for the offending cable. This time
it severed cleanly and the balloon joined the others that were
drifting away in the westerly wind.

By this time the flak crews had recovered from their
surprise. A line of shells arched from the southern bank as
the four Mosquitoes dived down to the water. From A-Apple
circling above, they looked frail beside the huge bridge and
Hoppy held his breath as Machin headed straight for it. For a
moment the Mosquito vanished from sight, only to shoot out
from beneath the bridge like a swallow and begin climbing
towards A-Apple. Shouts of relief sounded from the Mustangs' crews who were watching the perilous manoeuvre from
their station beneath the cloud base.

Hoppy had barely drawn breath before West flashed
through the opposite arch. Smith also went through safely
but luck deserted King. When his Mosquito was only forty
yards from the northern arch a burst of LMG fire sliced
through his elevator and rudder controls. Slewing sideways,
the Mosquito hit the bridge above the central pier. For a
second the pieces seemed to hang there like a fly crushed
on a wall. Then the flaming wreckage dropped into the
water.

Dent's voice came before Moore could make his request.
"We've got that post spotted, Hornet Leader. I'm sending
men down to help the Typhoons. We'll try to keep them busy
while you make your attack."

Knowing fighters would already be vectored towards
them, Moore wasted no time. "You can go in now, Red
Leader. Good luck."

In D-Danny Harvey was sweating freely. Like Moore,
he was too old a campaigner not to read the signs. Whether
or not the Germans had suspected the bridge might face a
specialist attack, they had obviously given it the flak defences

its importance deserved. Knowing full advantage must be taken before the Typhoons ran out of rockets, the Yorkshireman called his section into line astern and dived down. Levelling out at 300 feet over the river bend, he led them towards the centre of the river. There he banked steeply, lowered D-Danny's belly down on the water, and headed towards the balloons.

D-Danny began to tremble beneath the rotation of its inert bomb. Behind D-Danny the rest of Red Section was curving in pursuit. "Red Section, your interval is five hundred yards. Get your switches on as soon as you level out. Your setting is 800 revs."

The bridge was looming larger by the second. On either bank of the broad river Mustangs were now sharing the Typhoon attacks on the gun posts and their rockets could be seen shooting out like fiery spears. Recognizing the new threat from the Mosquitoes, enemy gunners were reacting according to their dedication. Some had decided to defend themselves until the strafing fighters were forced to withdraw. Others, accepting their first duty was the defence of the bridge, were turning their guns on the approaching Mosquitoes. Among these were the deadly 37s whose shells could blow an aircraft in half.

In D-Danny the crack of steel seemed to be coming from all sides. Peering through the smoke that was drifting over the water, Harvey made for the gap in the balloons. As he shot through it a sudden whiplash of tracer from one of the anchored badges made him swing violently to port. Cursing, he pulled D-Danny back on track and yelled at his navigator. "You got all the switches on?"

Hanson's freckles were dark against his pale cheeks. "Yes, skipper. Everything's ready."

Ahead the bobbing torpedo boom reached from bank to bank. Beyond it the bridge was looming higher like some medieval castle. Aiming the Mosquito's nose at the central pier, Harvey waited until the last possible moment, then gave a yell and felt the aircraft kick as the bomb fell away. Touching his rudder to prevent the bomb bouncing back on him, he headed for the left hand arch.

Above, the bridge looked enormous but the arch looked

impossibly low. Gritting his teeth, Harvey aimed D-Danny's nose at an invisible point between the curving sides and the shadowy roof. Beside him, Hanson pressed back in his seat.

Time slowed down for the two men. The stained grey walls and the roof closed around them as if they had entered a catacomb. The reverberations of the engines sounded like the voice of doom. Then, miraculously, they were back in daylight and climbing away from the bridge whose gunposts were spitting shells after them.

Moore's voice came, this time tight with relief. "Good work, Frank. Your bomb hit the button."

Harvey was too concerned about his men to answer. Red 1, Larkin, had already released both his bombs which were bounding over the water. The first struck the torpedo boom on its second bounce and spun away like a mad thing to sink near the northern bank. The second bomb leapt the boom and struck the left side of the pier. From there it ricocheted into the steel net where it spun for a moment, then sank.

The sight was a relief to Moore who, like Davies, had feared the net might not hold the heavy impact of the bombs. Below, Red 2 was making his attack. Shell bursts seemed to be clinging to the Mosquito like a dozen rabid bats as Wainright fought his way towards the bridge. One bomb dropped away, then the second. Both cleared the boom and struck the pier. One ricocheted away into the net, the other sank down the pile. A second later a shell burst right in the aircraft cockpit, fusing the contents into mangled metal, flesh and bone. The stricken Mosquito struck the water, whipped over in a cloud of steam, and broke its back. Wainright and Dempsey would not play table tennis again.

On the river banks the Typhoon pilots and the Americans were also paying a heavy price for their courage. The heavily protected gun posts on the bridge were proving resistant to attack and a Mustang was ripped open from end to end as it levelled off after releasing its rockets. A Typhoon was also hit as it swept inside the balloons to attack a 37mm post on the opposite side of the river. Rolling over slowly, it struck one of the sandbanks and burst into flames.

Meanwhile Red 3 had released its bombs and dived safely beneath the bridge. Red 4 was equally successful, but not before an LMG had drilled a line of holes along its rear fuselage. Puzzled why the fire was not lessening after the efforts of the fighter-bombers, Moore found the answer when he caught sight of vehicles speeding along the roads that flanked both banks. Many of the lighter flak guns were mounted on trucks and half-tracks and these were being rushed up from the eastern side of the bridge. Whether the Germans had guessed what the Mosquitoes were doing was open to question, but it was clear they believed the aircraft were now committed to attacking from the west and they were resiting their defences accordingly.

Moore wondered if he could counter the move by throwing in his Blue Section from the east. Then, catching sight of the second line of balloons, he remembered his four reinforced Mosquitoes carried no spare high-powered cable cutters. With no gap in the screen to fly through, Millburn and his men would find it impossible to fly low enough to launch their bombs. In spite of the buildup of defences, the attack would have to continue as before.

Red 5 had just released its *Highballs*. One struck some object in the water and bounded almost to the southern bank before sinking. The other struck the steel net at the south side of the pier.

Red 6 released one bomb that struck the pier but the second one hung up in the bomb bay. Seeing glycol streaming from the Mosquito's starboard engine as it emerged from the bridge, Moore ordered Pulford to make for home.

Red 7, the last aircraft in Harvey's section, was flown by Sugden and MacAllister and neither young man had dreamed of an ordeal as brutal as this as great thuds buffeted them in their seats. Trying to draw a sight on the bridge that was only a blur through the smoke, Sugden was late in releasing his bombs. A second later he was fighting for his life as his Mosquito, relieved of its burden, leapt towards the upper structure of the bridge. Panicking, Sugden pulled hard back on the column. Missing the bridge handrail by only a few feet, the Mosquito shot up like an uncontrolled rocket. Surprised by the manoeuvre, the gunners were slow in reacting and the two trembling youngsters managed to climb away to safety.

A distant metallic voice sounded in Harvey's earphones

as the Yorkshireman sank back in relief at the Mosquito's escape. "I'm afraid that's it, Hornet Leader. We've no more rockets and we're getting low on fuel."

Moore could be heard answering the message, "Thanks, Battleaxe Leader. Your boys have done a fine job. Good luck."

The Americans were facing the same problem as the Typhoons as the British aircraft rose into the grey sky and disappeared. Rockets could be expended but ammunition had to be conserved in case the Luftwaffe arrived. With his lower section out of rockets, Dent called down his upper section to take their place.

The respite was only brief but it gave the gunners below time to prepare for the next action. Trucks rushed into new positions, shells were hurried up, empty magazines replaced, full ammunition belts fed into LMGs. In the unnatural silence that had fallen, men paused as they heard birds singing.

The respite was short-lived for friend and foe. Four miles down river, to protect his men, Millburn had been orbiting his Blue Section over the river bend. Now, as Moore and Dent came to a decision, an order reached the American and the tight circle of Mosquitoes began to unfold. Nudging one another, the German gunners crouched behind their sights again and waited.

In the Nissen hut at Holmsley, tension was growing. Five minutes earlier Staines had telephoned to say the operation had commenced and his Mustangs were in action. Knowing that Moore would be in touch the moment he had news worth telling, Davies had so far refrained from contacting him but it was clear his patience was wearing thin.

With emotions at this pitch, there was little wonder every man swung around when the Brigadier's red telephone rang again. Once more they wished the elderly soldier had a more powerful voice as they tried without success to overhear him. His expression when he replaced the receiver made Davies frown. "More bad news?"

Simms gave a sigh. "I'm afraid it is. We've received a radio message that German tanks have been seen in the outskirts of Azay-le-Rideau."

There was a rush towards the map. Scowling as Henderson blocked his way, Davies used his elbows without ceremony. "Where's Azay?"

Henderson laid a finger on the map. Davies gave a start. "That's only a few miles from the bridge, isn't it?"

"Six miles to be exact, sir," Adams answered.

Davies peered down. "Isn't that a bridge at Azay?"

"Yes, sir. It crosses the Indre, a tributary of the Loire."

Davies swung round on the Brigadier. "Don't tell me it hasn't been bombed!"

The soldier sighed again. "How could it be, Davies? It lies on the road from the south. If we'd destroyed it but left the Loire bridge standing, we would have given the entire game away."

"What tank division is it?" Davies demanded. "Did they tell you?"

"Yes. It is the SS panzer division."

"Oh, Christ. That's the one with those bloody King Tigers, isn't it?" When the Brigadier nodded, Davies pulled himself together and hurried over to the radio operator. "Send this message. *Achilles calling Hornet Leader. Tiger tanks reported six miles from bridge. Imperative they do not cross. Repeat imperative. End of message.*"

Adams met Henderson's glance as Davies stood back and the operator's key began tapping. Shaking his head, the big Scot walked to the end door and disappeared.

32

Larkin's twangy voice sounded urgent in Moore's earphones. "Davies is right, skipper. The town's full of armour. And there's more still crossing the far bridge."

Moore glanced back along the river. Three miles away Millburn's section could be seen nearing the screen of balloons. "Close up your stations, Blue Section Leader. We're pushed for time."

In T-Tommy, Millburn relayed the order. "You hear that, you guys? Three hundred yard intervals. Move it!"

Although the Mosquitoes were still out of range, one of the impatient 37s had already gone into action, laying a transverse barrage through which the aircraft would have to fly. Millburn pulled a wry face at his navigator. "We're going to miss those Tiffies, kid. Hold on to your seat."

With most of the stricken guns replaced and the Typhoons forced to leave, it had been clear for some time that Millburn's Blue Section would have to run a heavy gauntlet of fire. In an effort to compensate, Moore and Dent had decided that the Mustangs would harass the guns on the south bank while Harvey's Red Section and every other Mosquito that had dropped its bombs would concentrate on the north bank. Not for the first time that day Mosquito crews were grateful that their leader had demanded their BIVs should be armed.

Except for the one 37, the rest of the shore gun crews were waiting until the Mosquitoes cleared the screen of balloons. As T-Tommy leapt towards the gap, tracer squirted out from one of the nearby barges. On an impulse the American swung the Mosquito to the right and thumbed his gun button. A man crouched behind the LMG leapt to his feet and then collapsed. A second man jumped into the water to escape the fire. With the counterblow bringing him relief, Millburn swung back on course.

Behind the trees, the gun crews were waiting. The line of Mosquitoes looked like giant dragonflies as they darted up river. As T-Tommy came within range, four guns opened up. With luminous shells swirling towards him, Millburn sank lower until his spinning propellers were only feet above the water. Thud-thud-thud-thud—the four heavy explosions burst before the windshield and splintered it. The men flinched and the stench of cordite bit their throats as the smoke swept past.

More guns opened up as Millburn flew deeper into the battle zone. With the rest of his section entering it, the stretch of water turned into a giant pyrotechnic display.

But the bridge was now coming into range. Lifting T-Tommy up to fifty feet, Millburn took aim and began counting. Feeling the Mosquito kick twice as he released his

bombs, he swung towards the right-hand arch, only for
T-Tommy to stagger as a shell burst just above the starboard
wing. With only seconds left before collision, Millburn fought
for control. As the arch tilted drunkenly towards him it
seemed his efforts had failed. But with a wingtip almost
scraping the far wall, T-Tommy emerged at the far side.
Feeling the Mosquito's sluggishness as he put it into a climb,
Millburn turned to examine the wing, and saw Dalton slumped
forward in his harness.

"What is it, kid? Are you hit?"

When there was no reply, Millburn reached out and
tried to haul the navigator back. As Dalton lolled towards
him, the American recoiled. The right side of the young New
Zealander's head was split open like a ripe melon and was
discharging its contents down his tunic.

Two-thirds of Millburn's section were already under heavy
fire. Van Breedenkamp managed to land both his bombs near
the pier and shot out from under the bridge relatively
unscathed. Blue 2 also had two hits although Wall and
Tomlinson were half-blinded by smoke. Blue 3 had no chance
to release its bombs. Receiving a full broadside from a chain
of shells, it reeled sideways and its port wingtip struck the
water. Cartwheeling in a great cloud of spray, it broke into
pieces. Petrol from its tanks ignited and flames ran in all
directions.

Blue 4, leaping over the flames, had a long gash torn in
its starboard wing but managed to release both bombs on
target and to escape under the bridge. Blue 5 was entering the
worst of the blizzard when a sharp call on the R/T disturbed
the pilot's concentration and forced him to break away. "Hawks,
Sherman Leader! Coming in from the east!"

Dieter Sommer had found his Mosquitoes at last. Twice
he had been wrongly routed but since the enemy force had
risen into the scanner beams, Fighter Control had been able
to give him an accurate fix. Now, as his gruppe swarmed in
just below the cloud base, his prey lay exposed below.

There was one obstacle in his way: the section of Mustangs that Dent had sent to give high cover. Although heavily
outnumbered, they were already sweeping in to do battle.
Ordering his rearmost staffel to engage them, Sommer led his
other two sections into a steep dive.

Below, Moore and Dent were issuing urgent orders. Every aircraft except the remainder of Blue Section was to engage the Focke-Wulfs. It meant lifting the harassment from the guns but if the enemy fighters were to be checked there was no alternative. With engines screaming under full throttle, Mustangs and Mosquitoes alike climbed to form a defensive screen while the last four Mosquitoes resumed their attack.

Miraculously Blue 5, 6 and 7 passed through the gauntlet unscathed. Blue 8, flown by Hall and Keegan, was hit by a shell in the bomb bay before it was halfway down the death run. With both *Highball* percussion fuses exploding, two brilliant flashes lit up the drifting smoke. From the shore the pieces that came fluttering down looked no bigger than dead leaves.

Moore had broken off engagement with the Focke-Wulfs to take a quick look at the situation across the river. He discovered a long column of Tiger tanks was making its way along the main road that led to the bridge. They were led by the Divisional Commandant flying a death's-head pennant. As the Commandant halted the column for a moment to assess the situation ahead, Moore flew low over the road. Beside him Hoppy gave a whistle of dismay. With their 88mm guns jutting aggressively forward, their twin machine guns, and their immensely thick armour, the Tigers looked like pocket battleships on wheels. Neither man now could doubt the Brigadier's claim that if such monsters were allowed to break loose among the Allies' thin-skinned amphibians, the slaughter would be worse than wolves savaging a flock of sheep.

Moore turned to the Cockney. "Send this message: *26 bombs around pier. Will now attempt to detonate. Hornet Leader.*"

Back at Holmsley news of the Focke-Wulf attack had already reached the Nissen hut via Staines's telephone link. Barnes Wallis, who had been waxing hot and cold since the Mosquitoes had reached the bridge, was now finding his concern for the crews outweighing his desire for his weapon to succeed. "How can they detonate the bombs now? If the guns aren't under attack, they'll be slaughtered when they go in."

Stiff-lipped now that the pressure was on, Davies refused to admit his own fears. "Moore'll find a way and they've got a good fighter escort. Don't forget it should need only one bomb to send the rest sky high."

At the opposite side of the hut Adams was feeling sick. To be sitting safely there while his friends were being cut to pieces seemed an obscenity to the sensitive Intelligence Officer.

Over Langeais, aircraft were milling about and snapping at one another like gnats on a summer evening. One went spinning down in flames, its pilot trapped in the cockpit. A second lost a wing but its pilot baled out, his parachute dropped into the river. A Focke-Wulf fired a burst at Moore's Mosquito, missed and climbed back into the melée. As Moore was about to contact his flight commanders, Harvey's D-Danny swung in alongside him. The Yorkshireman sounded breathless with the effort and strain.

"You'll be wanting me in a minute, won't you?"

"I might," Moore told him. "Stay close by. Millburn, hurry it up."

The earphones crackled with static. "It's OK, skipper. I'm on my way."

The American, detailed in battle orders as the first pilot to attempt the detonation of the bombs, had been keeping a close watch on the progress of his Blue Section. Now, in spite of structural damage and a corpse in his cockpit, the American was already making for the river bend. The sharp-eyed Hoppy gave a start. "He'll never make it, skipper. Look at his starboard wing!"

Moore responded immediately. "Blue Leader. You've got aileron damage. Break off."

"It's OK, skipper. I can make it."

"You'll never control her at low level. I said break off. That's an order."

With great reluctance T-Tommy levelled out. Watching it climb away Harvey felt no surprise. Death had spared him many times but he had felt in his heart it would claim him today. And this was the moment. With the guns freed from attack, it would need a miracle for a single aircraft to run their gauntlet unscathed. A vision of Anna came to the Yorkshireman and he thrust it desperately away before it could unman him.

"All right, Ian. I'll go down and see what I can do."

A mile back, the first two tanks had already crossed the bridge and two more were rumbling towards it. Moore glanced at the battle-scarred Mosquito rising and falling on his port beam. His quiet reply made Hopkinson stare at him. "No, Frank. We'll take this one. Stand by in case we don't make it."

In D-Danny Hanson's frightened eyes closed in thanksgiving. Harvey, after giving a wild start of hope, was immediately filled with self-loathing. "To hell with that! The battle order says I go next."

Moore had already put A-Apple into a dive. "Never mind the battle order. We have to destroy that bridge quickly and I've got two fused bombs to your one. That doubles our chances."

Harvey followed him down. His shout of protest was aimed as much at the Judas within him as at Moore. "Don't do it, Ian! For Christ's sake, don't do it. It's my turn down there."

Moore's voice changed tone. "Stop arguing and obey orders, Red Section Leader! On the double!"

To reach the river first, Harvey put D-Danny into an even steeper dive. Remembering a similar situation over Mindenburg less than two months ago, Moore struck hard at the Yorkshireman's weakness. "I thought you didn't know how to be fancy. While you're playing the hero, your men are under attack. Get back up there and help them, God damn you."

D-Danny quivered, dived another hundred feet, then banked slowly away and began to climb. Through the shouts of battle on the radio channel, Moore thought he heard a sob of torment. Moved, he glanced at his navigator. "All right with you, Hoppy? They have done one run already."

The small Cockney looked drawn and chilled. Although he had never questioned his pilot's decision in nearly a hundred missions, first with Grenville and then with Moore, he was close to it now. But the loyalty between men who share common danger, a bond that can transcend the love of women or even of life itself, won the day. Bracing himself, the Cockney gave a wry shrug. "If you say so, skipper."

Giving him a grateful glance, Moore put the Mosquito
into a steeper dive. Levelling off above the river bend, he
gave a nod. "Switches on, Hoppy."

A deep tremor ran through A-Apple as the two bombs
began rotating. There was no flak ahead at the moment; the
gunners were afraid of hitting their own fighters. Lowering
the Mosquito down on the water, Moore headed for the gap
in the balloons.

The river swept below like a giant waterfall. In the few
seconds before they entered the battle zone, both men found
their senses turning abnormally acute. Suddenly they could
feel the rapid beating of their hearts, the pulse of blood in
their wrists and temples. The roar of the engines broke down
into its component parts: the pounding of pistons, the hammering of tappets, the rush of hot gases. Sights previously
unnoticed were suddenly distinct . . . flat-bottomed boats
resting on sandbanks . . . a dead tree trunk rising from the
river . . . a small cottage half-hidden by trees. Images of
loved ones became lifelike. The senses are never so acute
nor the doors of memory so ready to open as when death
is near.

A-Apple swept through the screen of balloons and the
guns on both banks opened up. Luminous bridges of tracer
began to span the river, beautiful to see and death to touch.
Bursting shells made kaleidoscopic patterns and pounded the
weaving Mosquito like the fists of a crazed boxer. In the
cockpit every muscle in Moore's body was rigid, his toes
clenched up inside his flying boots, his hands white on the
control wheel. Alongside him, saliva was trickling unnoticed
from the side of Hopkinson's mouth as the navigator jerked
up and down in his harness.

Above them, Harvey was trying to track their progress.
The crossfire and the smoke were so dense the Mosquito was
flitting through them like a wraith. But it was still flying and
halfway down the death run Harvey saw splashes and two
black spheres bounding towards the bridge. As Moore swerved
towards the left-hand arch, Harvey's yell seemed to shake
D-Danny from nose to tail. "He's going to make it! You hear
me, lad? He's going to make it!"

A second later his exultation died in his throat. On the

bridge, the two Tiger tanks had joined in its defence. One fired at the Mosquito as it dived towards the arch, the other swivelled its turret and waited. As A-Apple swept clear and headed towards the eastern screen of balloons, the tank gunner put a long burst full into it.

It was like an arrow piercing the heart of a running deer. Faltering, the Mosquito flew on another two hundred yards as if on reflexes only. Then it staggered again, its nose dropped wearily, and it struck the water near one of the anchored barges. Somersaulting and cartwheeling, it hurled up a long cloud of spray before it smashed into a sandbank. Steam poured from its red-hot engines as it lay half-submerged in the water.

"Ian!" In D-Danny Harvey was hoarse with shock. "Ian, for Christ's sake! Can you hear me?"

In reply there was only the sounds of battle and the dismayed voices of the Mosquito crews who had seen the crash. With a curse, Harvey swung D-Danny around. Realizing his intention, Hanson gave a shout of warning. "The bombs, skipper! They'll go off any second!"

In his need to find out if Moore were alive, Harvey had forgotten all thought of personal survival and he was heading straight for the bridge when the first of Moore's bombs exploded. Like a depth charge erupting, it was followed by a series of underwater white flashes that radiated out almost across the river. A split second later the streaks seemed to contract, then to hurl themselves upwards in a massive explosion that dragged a huge column of water high into the air. Caught in the violent blast, D-Danny was tossed upwards like a leaf in a gale.

For a full ten seconds the entire bridge was hidden beneath a cloud of vapour. Then, as hundreds of tons of water showered down, its vague shape began to appear. Crews able to watch felt their hearts sink when the huge structure appeared undamaged.

The appearance was an illusion. The pile beneath the water had shifted, leaving the central pier without support. Like a slow motion film being speeded up, one granite slab slipped and fell, followed by another, and yet another. Seconds later, the entire pier collapsed on itself and dust rose and mingled with the vapour.

The great span above defied this defection of its main support for more endless seconds. Then a jagged crack appeared halfway along its northern section. As the section sagged, the crack widened. A moment later both sections, carrying the Tiger tanks with them, plunged with a roar into the foaming water.

A few shouts of triumph were heard from above, but most crews were too busy fighting for their lives to respond. For Harvey, the destruction of the bridge was only a hindrance to his need to find out if Moore was alive. With his Mosquito back under control again, he dived over the eastern sandbank but could see no sign of life in the crushed wreck below.

It took a shout of warning from Hanson to regain his attention. As he caught sight of a Focke-Wulf diving down on him, something broke in the Yorkshireman's mind. Turning his Mosquito on a wingtip, he headed straight at the Focke-Wulf. Avoiding collision by only a few feet, the startled German pilot went off in search of easier prey.

Such prey was provided by Sugden and MacAllister. In spite of their heroic efforts to defend the battle-damaged Mosquitoes, the American Mustang pilots could not be everywhere and three Focke-Wulfs had latched on to Sugden, whose controls had been damaged. Like a stembuck being slaughtered by jackals, he was flanked on two sides by fighters while a third closed up behind for the kill. Raging upwards, Harvey saw the danger and urged his Mosquito on.

He was too late. Sommer had used the tactic often and it seldom failed. Closing in behind the terrified youngsters he peered carefully down his reflector sight and fired a long controlled burst. Rolling over, the Mosquito went into a spin and exploded in a vineyard.

Harvey was seeing everything through a red mist. Brushing aside Sommer's wingmen as if they did not exist, he swung on the Squadron Commander's tail. Sommer, who was making the mistake of watching his kill spin into the ground, never knew what hit him as his main fuel tank exploded in a ball of fire.

Under Millburn's guidance the Mosquitoes had been trying to form a defensive circle. As his mind cleared, Harvey added his own orders. Painfully, with Focke-Wulfs snarling

in and Mustangs struggling to hold them back, the surviving
Mosquitoes vanished one by one into the thick cloud. Dent,
sweating and battle-stained, shouted his last battle order.
"OK, you guys. Break it off. We're going home."

One by one the Mustangs followed into the clouds. They
left behind them the debris of war: burning wreckage, dead
friends, and a drifting pall of smoke.

----------------- 33 -----------------

Adams came round the bend in the path and halted.
Ahead of him a young deer had stepped daintily out of the
wood. Ears cocked and velvet nose lifted, it was testing the
evening air. As Sam, delayed by the forest scents, made
towards Adams, it spun around and dived back into the
undergrowth.

Adams came out of the wood a few minutes later. Gorse
in full bloom reached forward to a shallow hill. Beyond it, the
horizon had a saffron afterglow. During the late afternoon,
the sky had cleared. Now it was luminous, with a rising
moon.

Adams leaned against a stile. He could hear activity on
the airfield as mechanics worked on the surviving Mosquitoes
but the noise was far enough away to accentuate the silence.
To the west, a black arrowhead of birds was winging for
home. As he watched them, Adams's eyes suddenly stung
with pain and he lowered his head on his arms.

Sam's bark and the sound of footsteps made him start
guiltily. The wood was full of shadows and he only recognized
Henderson when the Scot came out into the twilight. If he
had noticed Adams's distress, he made no comment. "Hello,
Frank. They said I'd find you out here somewhere."

"Did you want me? I'm sorry. Once I'd debriefed the crews I couldn't think what else to do . . ." Adams's voice trailed off lamely as Henderson shook his head.

"I'd have sent a messenger if I'd wanted you." Keeping his eyes averted, the Scot rested his elbows on the stile and grimaced at the heath beyond. "What—no tents or ammunition dumps? I didn't think there was a square acre down here they weren't using."

A hundred yards away Adams could see three New Forest ponies grazing among the gorse. Like the Scot, he knew he was only making conversation. "They could have moved out during the last few days."

"Aye, I suppose so." Pulling out his cigarettes, Henderson offered them to Adams, then remembered he was a pipe smoker. The smoke he exhaled hung in the still air. "Why couldn't it have been as calm as this last night?"

With no explanation to give, Adams offered none. "At least we seem to be hanging on to the beachhead."

"Aye. If you can believe anything you hear."

Adams could keep the conversation impersonal no longer. "What's the latest news of the wounded?"

His betrayal of their unspoken pact brought a reproachful glance from Henderson. "The MO has found Millburn cracked three ribs when he crash-landed. There's a chance Wall might lose a foot and Tomlinson's going to need a face graft. But they're the lucky ones, aren't they?"

"Yes, I suppose they are," Adams muttered.

"You suppose!" With the wraps pulled away, Henderson's grief was naked. "I lost nearly half my lads today. And the finest Squadron Commander and friend a man could have. All on a harebrained scheme of Davies' that I never believed in."

"You don't think it helped the beachhead?"

"How can we ever know that? Those tanks might never have got past our fighter-bombers."

Adams sighed. "Isn't that war?"

The Scot exhaled smoke. "I've had a bellyful of war, Frank. I'm up to here with it."

Knowing that Henderson, a professional airman, was confessing things he might regret later, Adams bent down to pat Sam who was gazing through the stile at the ponies. Henderson's eyes followed him. "Did you notice how that dog acted when Harvey got back? You'd have thought he'd known what had happened."

Adams winced. "What state was Harvey in when you left?"

"Not too good," Henderson confessed. "The hospital had to put him under sedation."

Adams could hold back the truth no longer. "You know what's wrong with him, don't you?"

Henderson stared at him. "That's an odd question, isn't it? He's certain Moore was killed. And weren't they close friends?"

"Yes, but there's more to it than that. Moore didn't attack the bridge first just to make certain of destroying it. He went first to save Harvey's life. And Harvey knows it."

The Scot frowned. "I agree it was a hell of a decision. Davies intends putting him up for a VC. But aren't you making it too personal? Moore was a first-class Squadron Commander and he'd been told the tanks mustn't cross that bridge."

Adams knew it was the protest of a professional soldier fighting to keep sentiment at arm's length. "No. Before Moore took off he asked me to give a letter to Davies if he didn't return. It was addressed to Anna Reinhardt."

Henderson's frown deepened. "Are you saying she was the reason?"

"Not altogether. I believe he did it for both of them. Moore told me in confidence that Anna had begged him to get Harvey grounded. She believed his nerves were going and that she was the reason. That was why Moore got the MO to examine him."

"Oh, my Christ," Henderson muttered. Giving Adams a look of dislike he cursed again and swung away. "Why the hell did you have to tell me this? Weren't things bad enough before?"

No one could have understood the Scot's outburst better than Adams. In his time with the squadron, Adams had known many brave men, so many that to his shame their

names sometimes blurred in his memory. But certain names
he could never forget: Grenville, Gillibrand, Barrett and
Young of the old squadron; Moore, Harvey, Millburn and
Hopkinson of the new. Of them all, Moore was the man who
stood the tallest in Adams's Pantheon. Closest to him in mind
and character, Moore was the man Adams would have chosen
to be had not fate burdened him with too many disadvantages
and too many years.

"I'm sorry," he muttered. "But it's not an easy thing for
a man to keep to himself. And it does explain Harvey's state
of mind. What will happen to him now?"

"Davies is resting him after tonight. I doubt if they'll let
him fly operationally again. He's done more than enough."

Adams knew it should have been good news but life was
never that simple. "Do you think that's a good idea? He's the
type who'll suffer hell if he's in a safe job while Anna's risking
her life back in Europe."

The Scot shook his head. "She's not going back. Before
the Brigadier left with Davies, he told us the Gestapo had
picked up one of his agents holding a passport photograph of
Anna. Since it's blown her cover, the SOE can't send her
back now."

This time Adams felt intense relief. "Have you told
Harvey?"

"Not yet. He was too heavily sedated. I'll tell him in the
morning."

The afterglow was fading. A distant intermittent drone
broke the silence. A thin flame was moving across the dark
eastern horizon. Henderson nodded at it bitterly. "There's
another poor bastard who's not going to make it. His fuel
tanks have caught fire."

They stood watching. One by one the heavy bomber's
engines faltered and died. The thin flame dipped and plunged
down. A brilliant flash lit the horizon, then died away. Henderson cursed again. "Four and a half bloody years, Frank.
Christ, it's an eternity."

Across the heath the ponies were now drifting towards
the hill. A muscle was working in Henderson's cheek as he
watched them. "What I find hard to take is that Moore might
have made it if he'd been allowed to carry bombs instead of
those damned *Highballs*."

Adams found the thought too painful for words. Catching
his expression, Henderson gave a grunt and pushed himself
away from the stile. "We're getting too broody, Frank. Let's
start back."

They paused outside Henderson's office. Lights were
appearing all over the airfield as mechanics worked on the
surviving Mosquitoes. "What do you want to do?" the Scot
asked. "I shan't need you again tonight. Shall I arrange
transport to take you back to Brockenhurst?"

Adams thought of the bleak house without his friends
and his mind recoiled. "I'd rather stay here if you don't
mind."

Taking another look at his grief-stricken face, Henderson
made his decision. Entering the office, he opened a drawer of
his desk and drew out a full bottle of whisky. "Moore gave
this to me just before he took off, so it couldn't be more
fitting." Handing it to Adams, he pointed at a side door.
"There's a small room in there with just a table and a few
chairs. Get inside, shut the door, and pour yourself a few
drams. It'll help to soften the edges. I'll join you after I've
had a word with Townsend and Powell."

The Scot returned forty minutes later. As he entered the
office the red telephone on the desk began ringing. Davies'
voice was impatient. "Where the hell have you been, Jock?
This is the third time I've called you."

Henderson's sarcasm was barely veiled. "I'm sorry, sir.
But we do have one or two problems at this end. What do
you want?"

Davies spoke for some time. When he finished, Henderson let the receiver fall on to the hook and dropped into a
chair. He sat staring at the wall for a full minute before rising
wearily and pushing his way into the side room.

To his surprise it was in darkness. "Frank! That was
Davies on the blower about those damned enemy rockets.
Now that the invasion's started, our people think the Ger-
mans might start launching them within the next two weeks.
As it's an urgent matter, Davies wants you to leave for
headquarters tonight to get the latest intelligence on them.
Sorry. There seems no end to it, does there?"

There was no reply. Puzzled, Henderson fumbled for

the switch. As light flooded the room, he saw Adams slumped forward with his head and arms on the table. The bottle of whisky and an empty glass stood near him. Beneath the table, Sam raised his head and made a questioning noise.

The Scot drew closer. "Frank! Did you hear what I said?"

A snore was his only reply. Walking over to waken Adams, Henderson changed his mind and gave his shoulder a defiant squeeze instead. Picking up the half-empty bottle, he sank into a nearby chair while the dog sighed and laid his head on his paws again.

The scream of a drill came through the thin walls of the hut. A Merlin engine fired, ran a few seconds, then died. In the adjacent hut someone began tuning a radio—a high-pitched wail died away and a woman could be heard singing "It's a Lovely Day Tomorrow." Sipping his second large whisky, with Adams still mercifully asleep, Henderson sat staring into his mind and at the young ghosts who were parading through it.

ABOUT THE AUTHOR

FREDERICK E. SMITH joined the R.A.F. in 1939 as a wireless operator/
air gunner and commenced service in early 1940, serving in Britain,
Africa and finally the Far East. At the end of the war he married
and worked for several years in South Africa before returning to
England to fulfill his life-long ambition to write. Two years later,
his first play was produced and his first novel published. Since then,
he has written twenty-four novels, about eighty short stories and two
plays. Two novels, *633 Squadron* and *The Devil Doll*, have been
made into films and one, *A Killing for the Hawks*, has won the
Mark Twain Literary Award. He is also the author of *The War God*
and *633 Squadron: Operation Cobra*.

A towering novel of friendship,
betrayal and love

THE LORDS OF DISCIPLINE

by Pat Conroy
author of <u>The Great Santini</u>

This powerful and passionate novel is the story of four cadets who become bloodbrothers. Together they will encounter the hell of hazing and the rabid, raunchy and dangerously secretive atmosphere of an arrogant and proud military institute. Together, they will brace themselves for the brutal transition to manhood . . . and one will not survive.

Pat Conroy sweeps you dramatically into the turbulent world of these four friends—and draws you deep into the heart of his rebellious hero, Will McLean, an outsider forging his personal code of honor, who falls in love with Annie Kate, a mysterious and whimsical beauty who first appears to him one midnight in sunglasses and raincoat.

(#14716-1 • $3.75)